Operation: Pleiades

Full Contact

Toby Heathcotte

Full Contact will thrill you with danger, make you live each moment and stir the imagination into frenzy. The first in the *Operation: Pleiades* series is breathtaking. *Full Contact* draws you into an intense world where you must suspect everything. I was captivated from the first sentence to the last. Each step Maya and Dylan took to finding to the truth kept me at the edge of my seat. Ms. Heathcotte has started off this series with a no holds barred bang. Each novel will be written by various authors and I look forward to more of the *Operation: Pleiades* series and other novels by the author Toby Heathcotte. *Operation: Pleiades* Book 1: *Full Contact* is a read I would recommend.

Reviewed by M. Jeffers **Road to Romance**

From start to finish **Full Contact** is fantastic! Definitely one of the best reads of the year! A fascinating premise using the Anasazi indian's legendary disappearance to explain an alien race determined to 'reclaim' the Earth is brilliant and believable. Reading this book is like a watching a movie, smart, exciting, suspenseful and colorful with characters and images coming to life upon the pages. The seven 'sisters of the Pleiades' each get there own book in this series and this first of the series is an indication that it will be the must- read series of the year!

Johnna Flores
Reviewer for Karen Find Out About New Books
Reviewer for Coffee Time Romance

**** *This is one intense sci-fi saga!* At times it reminded me of the old TV Mini Series called "V" (Visitors). In a nut shell, aliens want humans wiped out so they can claim our planet as home. Human fight for their survival. The author placed this scenario in our not too distant future and included enough tech info to make the story pretty realistic. Since there were seven baby girls and only Maya is in this novel, I can hope to see six more stories. If those stories are half as good as this one is, then Toby Heathcotte has a new fan in me! Riveting! ****

Detra Fitch, **Huntress Reviews**

Toby Heathcotte has done it again, written a winner! This time she has written a thrilling series about seven women abducted and altered by an alien race to help take over the earth. **FULL CONTACT** is the first in the **OPERATION PLEIADES** series, it grabbed my attention right from the beginning and never let go. Even now, I am on pins and needles waiting for the next book in this exhilarating series.

FULL CONTACT is a breathtaking, action packed, romantic thriller that will capture you as a fan for this exceptionally well written series by Toby Heathcotte. Don't miss your chance to read the first book in **OPERATION: PLEIADES: FULL CONTACT.**

Donna**, eCataromance Reviews**

Full Contact is utterly thrilling. Nothing is as it seems. Book One of the *Operation: Pleiades* series is amazing. After witnessing everything Maya is experiencing, the rest of the series promises to be just as intense. As Maya didn't know about her "sisters", they also don't know of their past, and of the purpose the Anaz-voohri has in store for them. Ms. Heathcotte grabbed this ball and ran the full hundred yards! Taking this concept of an alien race intent on destroying the human race, and taking over the planet while using innocent victims to do their dirty work, certainly gave readers a hint of Ms. Heathcotte's incredible imagination.

Robin Taylor, **In the Library Reviews**

Published by Triskelion Publishing www.triskelionpublishing.com
15508 W. Bell Rd. #101, PMB #502, Surprise, AZ 85374 U.S.A.

First e-published by Triskelion Publishing
First e-publishing July 2004
First print publishing September 2005

ISBN 1-933471-48-4
Copyright © Kristi Studts 2005
All rights reserved.

Cover art by Triskelion Publishing

Prologue

A Small Town in Pennsylvania, 2003

The Anaz-voohri commander climbed the ladder to the second story window of the small gabled house. A focused beam lit the interior and he saw a white crib painted with yellow daffodils where a two-year old girl stirred in her sleep. Light dappled the pink teddy bear lying on the floor.

Easy work for one with so much training and intelligence, the commander would have this worthless little human back at the spaceship in minutes with time left for a celebratory drink before departure.

As he thought, *I am ready*, a pulsing sound filled the room. The crickets ceased their chatter.

The commander floated through the closed window. Deftly, despite his long cloak, he turned off the baby monitor on the dresser and moved to the bed.

The little girl's eyes flew open, registering first confusion, then fear. The commander chuckled. Humans were so easy to terrorize.

When he laid his hand across her nose, she breathed in the potion, and her body went limp. He picked her up, wrapped the quilt around her, and carried her through the beam of light and out the window.

With the girl draped over his shoulder, the commander climbed down. Once on the grass he pulled the ladder away and retracted it, annoyed at the necessity of its use. He much preferred floating during the entire hunt. He had greater skill than any of his peers, yet he could not maintain the energy required for so many objects of prey in one night.

With long strides, the commander carried the ladder and the girl across the lawn. Within minutes, he strolled into a clump of pines then emerged on the other side, away from the town. Through the stubble of a bean field, he headed toward the disk-shaped spaceship, the size of a small house.

A slender semaphore on top of the golden dome directed a beam of light. The whole ship shimmered with a luminous glow. Pictographs of dancers in space helmets adorned the housing, fashioned of a material more like skin than metal. White lights blinked around the circular base and down a column through the center. The entry, etched with a teal blue and mauve zigzag pattern, resembled the Anasazi tombs of his noble ancestors.

Open, now, the commander mentally directed. The jagged edge of the menacing door pulled apart like claws.

A cry of anguish split through the still night air. "My baby's gone!"

The commander carried his tiny burden inside. The young Anaz-voohri at the controls bent his head. The machinery of his mind was visible through the thin creases of his bald pate. The pilot, in a dark blue cloak, passed his hand over the instrument panel, and the spaceship began to vibrate.

The commander strode into the adjoining room where Kokopelli decorated the interior dome. The whimsical figures played horns and guitars.

A tall female Anaz-voohri with a bald head and a mauve cloak stood watch over seven small beds. In six of them little human girls slept.

Gently, the man laid the youngest and smallest of the seven girls down in the last empty bed. She didn't awaken.

While the female attendant scanned the body of the tiniest girl with a cone-shaped instrument, the commander turned toward a glass cabinet and thought, *Martini, dry, two olives.* The martini slid into the cabinet, and he picked it up. The only thing about humans that impressed the commander was their alcoholic beverages. He took a sip. "Delicious."

He asked the attendant, "Is this girl going to be worth the effort?"

"She is healthy. Perfect readings."

"Good. Assuming they all survive the tests…not a given because they're such weaklings…im-plantation of new DNA should go easily."

"Most of them should, Commander. They will have the best of care."

The commander smiled as he glanced at the children. "The end of humanity has finally begun."

Chapter One

Upstate New York, 2022
Dylan Brady crouched behind an oak and touched his parka sleeve, assuring himself for the twentieth time that the Rocket Propelled Grenade still lay capped inside the launcher cradled beneath his arms. Cold night air kept his senses sharp as he waited. Muted light from the distant megalopolis filtered through the oaks.

Two men walked down the country road toward him. The tall one wore a long cloak, a rather dated fashion, but otherwise they both looked normal, the shorter in a hunting coat and hat. Dylan could hear them speaking in a conversational tone although he couldn't make out their words.

They didn't appear in any hurry. The tall one reached out with one hand and tapped a mailbox at the edge of the road. The mailbox quivered and disintegrated. The hunter laughed.

If Dylan had had any doubts about their identities, he didn't now. He set off behind them, keeping a steady gait near the berm. He stayed in the shadows careful not to bend twigs or create other noise.

The men passed a farmhouse and turned off the paved road into the woods behind. The ambient light increased enough that it glinted off the trigger of Dylan's RPG. The bright light couldn't have come from the city, which lay in the opposite direction. Excited, he slipped behind a tree.

There in a clearing for anyone to see hovered an Anaz-voohri spaceship.

As an operative in Mythos, Dylan had read reports about the spaceships' appearance, but seeing one was far more breathtaking than he had anticipated. What a stunning vehicle, sleek and trim. He would love to pilot one, probably the rush of a lifetime.

Why in hell wasn't the Global Security Sector here to see this? The GSS had the authority to seek out and destroy Anaz-voohri life, but they failed their mission more often than not. The Anaz-voohri had the ability to pass as human, but only for a short time. Because of this limitation, Dylan knew they hadn't directly infiltrated GSS, but many of their hybrids had. Who knew what unholy alliances had happened internationally? Whether the public had awareness of the fact or not, the future of mankind depended largely on the efforts of the secret society of Mythos.

The two men ambled toward the intricate door, which opened silently.

Dylan hoped he'd get his chance. It might come rapidly or not at all. God knew he was ready to die if he had to, but at twenty-six, he had a hell of a lot of living yet to do. Just in case, he opened his fallout dosimeter and attached it to his belt. With the trust in God that his mother had taught him as a child, he prayed for his safety and that of any innocent people in the area.

By tapping the standby code on the crystal-shaped medallion around his neck, Dylan let the folks at Mythos Headquarters know he'd close in momentarily. They needed to stand ready to trace fallout and evacuation. If they had to contact him, he would hear their voices through a chip embedded beneath his ear.

"Farewell, Commander." The hunter held out his hand to the tall man. "It was good to see you again. I'm happy to know your plans are moving apace."

The commander shivered. His head began to lose its hair and rounded human shape. His pate grew bald with rough creases of stretched Anaz-voohri skin, which hid internal machinery. "I am low on energy. I must get inside."

Dylan lifted his arm, pointed the RPG at the ship, and held firm, ready to pull the trigger. He knew his aim had to be precise to keep the blast as contained as possible. He didn't want to destroy farms for miles around, not to mention himself.

The hunter nodded. "I understand. I will say good night, then." He hesitated, perhaps to say one word more.

The commander ascended the ramp, the metallic interior of his head aglow.

"I've only got a minute," Dylan whispered and fingered the trigger. "Move, you son of a bitch."

As if he had heard, the hunter turned and ran directly toward Dylan so fast that his hunting cap fell off.

Dylan fired the RPG into the doorway of the spaceship just as its fingered edges meshed together. He dove behind a great oak tree. Dropping the spent launcher, he clapped his hands over his ears. Crouched against the tree, he yelled to release his breath to withstand the coming shock wave.

What the hell? Had it misfired?

The spaceship's warp drive must have kicked in because it shot into the sky. Then came a thunderous sound as the ship blew apart. The dark vault of sky exploded with gaseous fumes and flames.

Dylan read the dosimeter and shouted into his wrist phone. "Fallout will head due south of my location. We're good here, no measurable contamination." Mythos operatives would take care of the details of evacuating the surrounding farms and people in the path of the fallout.

The hunter, a hybrid confederate of Mythos, fell at Dylan's feet, gasping, hands over ears.

"It's all right, man." Dylan knelt and patted the hybrid's shoulder. "Look."

The hybrid rolled over and gazed up at the sky. The brilliance of the explosion illuminated his features, square face with close-set but kindly eyes. He looked as human as anybody. "We did it. Shit, we did it."

"There's one less Anaz-voohri crew to harass the human race." Dylan shuddered with relief. "And we have you to thank." He held out his hand.

Pulling to his feet, the hybrid shook Dylan's hand. "I'll say this, buddy. You've got guts." He shook his head. "But, this is it for me. It's my last time. Tell your boss I need a new identity and free passage to Tahiti, if he can manage it."

"I'll tell Archer." Dylan knew the fellow had been more helpful than any other hybrid in fighting the Anaz-voohri. "I know he'll honor your request, if he can, but I hate to see you leave. You're making such a difference."

"Get a grip, Dylan. We may have won this skirmish, but the Anaz-voohri will win the war. GSS can't stop them. They're always coming up with new weapons. As soon as they figure out how you and I destroyed this ship, they'll have new safeguards in place."

Dylan looked up with a sense of gratitude at the fire winking out in the sky. "This is a victory and you're a hero. Savor it."

"They'll win. They can clone those machine-men faster than we can procreate."

Though he'd not admit it to the hybrid, Dylan remembered the huge losses suffered in the terrorist wars and the massive electro-magnetic field that destroyed part of Europe. Undoubtedly, the Anaz-voohri culprits had orchestrated both. With no home planet of their own, they were ruthless and would do anything to subdue humankind. Because of their origin with the Anasazi Indians, Anaz-voohri truly believed Earth belonged to them. "No, we'll beat them. One spaceship at a time."

A look of incredulity spread across the hybrid's face. "How do you know that?"

"We don't have a choice."

New York City

In a yellow acetate jumpsuit, Maya Rembrandt sat inside the crystal chamber of the computer station with her forty-something boss, Frank, beside her, both in stocking feet.

"All you need to do," Maya said, "is think *fairy* and ease your palm across it. Now watch me." She cleared her mind and waved her hand lightly across the control board, thinking the word *fairy*.

After a moment, a faint image of fluttering wings appeared before her on the lower corner of the wall-sized computer monitor.

"Flying," Maya whispered, and the image fluttered up, crisscrossing the screen. She turned to her colleague. "Now, you do it." She released any thought of the fairy from her mind.

The winged creature faded into the amorphous grayness.

"Okay, one more time." A look of resignation spread across Frank's pudgy face. He intoned, "Fairy."

"You've got to mean it. I don't know why that's important. It just is." Maya smiled, hoping she looked encouraging.

Frank scrunched up his shoulders, closed his eyes, and whispered the word again. Maya tried not to think of the image. She wanted him to succeed on his own. When he opened his eyes, the screen had not changed.

Angrily, Frank shoved himself away from the terminal, and his chair slammed against the interactive light bank. "There must be a glitch in my programming."

"Or the computer's." Maya felt disappointed. Why couldn't she teach people to interface with the computer?

"I'll take a look tomorrow and see if I can figure out what's wrong."

"If anybody can do it, you can." Frank rose and straightened the lights then pulled his shirttail out and shined the lenses with it.

Maya thought Frank spoke with grudging admiration. It probably galled him to take instructions from her. After all, he had fifteen years seniority. He liked saying he'd been at NexTech when she was still riding a tricycle. Not too far from the truth. Actually, she'd been seven back in 2008, riding her first bicycle and starting fifth grade. Her intellectual development had always soared far ahead of her physical and emotional development, according to her psychologist father.

With a tentative look, Maya said, "I need to leave a little early this afternoon if you don't mind."

Frank raised a questioning eyebrow.

Maya thought him deliberately obtuse from time to time. "I've got a meeting at the art museum for the fundraiser."

"You gotta do what you gotta do."

"It's good for the company, Frank. Remember, we talked about it. When the company was still Microsoft, it funded a lot of charities. This will help us get back some of that good will."

"So the Prez says." Frank shrugged and walked toward his office cubicle, opening his waistband and unzipping the fly to tuck his shirt back in. The half dozen technicians at work in the room didn't even notice. They'd gotten used to their slob of a boss.

Maya closed the file called Fluttering Fairy and shut down the terminal. She noticed a new female technician hailing her. "Something I can help you with?"

In her small glass structure, the technician pointed toward the computer interface. "I keep getting a message with my name on it. Seems simple enough, but then I can't delete it."

"That's a hacker trying to destroy your station. Scoot over." Maya slid in beside the girl and showed her how to protect her work. "There are a lot of them out there, so you have to be vigilant."

"Thanks, Maya, how do you know so many tricks?"

"The key is respect. You have to respect the intelligence of the machine, and it will respect you."

Back at her station, Maya gazed into the mirror-paneled footlocker. She pulled the scrunchee out of her ponytail and fluffed up her wavy brown hair. Every time she tried to let it grow, she got impatient. Long hair was supposed to be sexy, but it caused too much trouble. Maybe she should add some red highlights. She applied lipstick, glad at least her lips suited her face well enough. Maybe soon she'd find a fellow who thought so.

Maya pulled running shoes out of the locker, stepped into them, and flipped the cross pieces down. With a fanny pack and windbreaker, she sprinted down five flights of stairs and out onto the sidewalk.

A blast of cool wind hit her face as Maya headed down Eighty-Sixth Street. The remains of rubble from a recent attack were still visible behind store fronts and low buildings that had sprouted on each side. Between the religious extremists and other terrorists of unknown origin, it was all the police could do to keep civilized society together.

Yet holly wreaths and smiling Santas adorned the shops, giving stark reassurance of the hopefulness of the human spirit. What could the citizens do? They just had to keep going. Everybody knew it.

Only a few people trod the street outside despite the fact that it was near five in the afternoon. Soon they'd come pouring out of the buildings and head toward the subways and buses. A New York City police officer in blue suit and black gas mask stood at the intersection and nodded to her as she crossed. It comforted Maya to have the local police present when she ran. She never knew when someone might try to harass her. A woman alone on the streets wasn't as safe as she should be.

The sky looked overcast, whether from the lack of sun or the presence of soot. Maya took her face mask out of her fanny pack, snapped the gear on, and jogged toward the art museum.

A month before, Maya had volunteered as the NexTech representative to the fundraiser committee, knowing Lola was a member. It gave them a chance to do something together. Even though they'd lived across the street from each other ever since Maya could remember, it became harder and harder for them to keep their friendship alive. Mother or Father seemed to need Maya every minute she had free from work responsibilities. If not, then Lola would be on a date and not have time.

Maya wished she could move out of her parents' home but had been unable to find a place of her own. The housing authority listed very few vacancies each month. At least she had a good salary and could afford to rent in the Manhattan area if an apartment ever came open.

I'm on my way, Lola, Maya thought into the Nanobot she had recently ingested.

On her last yearly checkup at the Center for Evolutionary Medicine, the doctor had prescribed a Nanobot programmed to monitor a slight fluctuation in Maya's blood sugar level. She'd agreed to ingest it and also asked for a prescription for a Nanobot to send and receive email. The goal had been to allow easy access so she could keep her hands free when on the move.

Lola didn't answer. *Can you hear me, Lola?* The email Nanobot only worked sporadically. Maya hoped the one for blood sugar had a higher success rate. She'd not find out until the next checkup.

When she arrived at the art museum, tarps covered the second floor. The floors above were destroyed by a terrorist bomb blast several months before. Thankfully, the first floor and basement survived with most of the valuable work stored there in the event of an attack.

Maya sprinted up the stairs, removing her mask and stashing it. Once inside, she slipped into a seat at the conference table where the seven other committee members chatted. Lola gave her a big smile of greeting. Lola was everything Maya was not – tall, voluptuous, blonde, outgoing, and charming. This evening Lola looked great in a floor-length tunic dress of royal blue, very tight and revealing. She had a waiting list for the job of being her boyfriend.

The chairwoman, an executive from Harkins Theatres, whisked through the remaining agenda. Only last minute details remained for this well-planned event. She dismissed the meeting with reminders to be on time tomorrow for the fundraiser, giving Maya a sideways look. Everybody laughed.

"Some of us work for a living, you know." Maya grinned. She loved this group of people with their devotion to art, their willingness to rebuild, and their positive attitudes. It wouldn't take long to refurbish the Kandinsky exhibit, and Maya's favorite, the Andy Warhol collection. "See you tomorrow."

After good-byes and well wishes all around, Maya and Lola left the museum and set out on foot for home. Dusk had settled, and the air felt chilly although the wind had died down. They stopped at a Mexican food vendor and bought tacos and drinks, eating as they walked along.

"So how's the tattoo doing?" Lola asked with a teasing grin. "Are you sorry you did it?"

"It still hurts. Why didn't you tell me how much it hurt?"

"Because you'd have changed your mind. You need to do more stuff like that. Make a statement about yourself, besides being hugely smart."

Maya laughed out loud. "Oh, yeah, what do flames over your breasts say about you?"

Lola pushed her torso out pridefully, even though the cut of the dress hid the tattoos from view. "Every guy who sees them gets an immediate erection, that's what. All I have to do is take my clothes off."

The fact that Lola bordered on lewdness endeared her to Maya, who would never dare to act so brashly. Lola never confirmed how many men Lola had actually slept with. She doubtless exaggerated on that topic as she did on everything.

After chewing a crunchy bite of taco, Maya swallowed. "The worst of it is that Mother knows about the tattoo."

"Damn. How'd she find out?"

"I let out a little moan while I applied moisturizer to it. Mother heard me and just walked right into the bathroom. I was naked, too." The memory of that moment made Maya blush. She didn't understand why she felt uncomfortable in intimate moments with her mother. After all, the woman had borne Maya. "Mother was not happy with me, to say the least."

Lola rolled her eyes. "I can just picture her now." She set her food down on the sidewalk. Then hands on her hips the way Mother always did, Lola whined, "Who put you up to this? I'll bet it was Lola. She's no good. You stay away from her."

When Lola bent to pick up her food, somebody down the street whistled. She and Maya ignored the whistler.

"That's pretty close." Maya remembered her mother had been less kind than that but didn't mention she'd called Lola a tramp.

"Well, there's no love lost on my side either." Lola looked triumphant. "There's no undoing the tattoo. So there."

"It still hurts." When Maya gingerly touched the spot on the small of her back, she glanced behind her and saw a man in a dark running suit duck inside the stairwell of a basement apartment. Half jokingly, she asked, "Is that guy following you or me?"

Lola nudged Maya's shoulder as they walked along the rutted sidewalk. "You're kidding, you nerdy little thing. There's nobody back there."

"Except for about a hundred pedestrians." Maya turned and searched for the police officer who ought to have been among the people. "Oh, well, guess I was mistaken."

"If there is somebody following us, he's after me, I'll bet." Lola took a drink of her soft drink.

Maya laughed. "I don't doubt that. How's it going with Jed?"

"Actually, I called that off about a month ago. Didn't I tell you? I've met a new guy who's a lot more interesting."

They turned into the last commercial district before home. Design pads and storage sheds lined the street, awaiting reconstruction after a bomb blast had leveled several stores.

While waiting for the stoplight to change, Maya said, "Maybe you should save one of your boyfriends for me."

"Oh, Maya, you could be so gorgeous. Any guy in his right mind would love to go out with you."

"You know what happens when we get past looks, huh? Like with Mark?" The memory of that brief affair haunted Maya. Her first real boyfriend. While she'd been at Yale and MIT, the male students considered her a freak, as a teenager in graduate school. She had never fit in with them, but with Mark, she'd thought things could be different. Such a good-looking and interesting guy, but he just quit calling.

"You scared him to death." Lola threw her taco wrapper in a circular receptacle. "You're just way too intelligent and accomplished. Nobody knows what to say to you."

"You don't have any trouble talking to me." Maya gave her friend's waist a squeeze. "Thank goodness."

They turned into a side street where a row of brownstones stood on each side. With a sizzling sound, the glass on the streetlight in front of them shattered.

Lola registered alarm. "What happened?"

"I don't know." Maya dreaded the only conclusion she could make. "It sounded like an electronic blast."

"A shot? It can't be."

They heard running feet behind them. When Maya looked in the direction of the sound, she saw people scattering. Why were they running away?

The street emptied except for Maya, Lola, and a tall man, who headed toward them.

The man held up a phase gun. Maya couldn't see his face. She didn't know whether it was the man she'd seen earlier or not. He pointed the gun at them.

Lola must have seen him, too. "What the hell is he doing?"

Trembling, Maya dropped her taco wrapping and soda can on the ground. "Let's get out of here!"

"Oh, dear God, he's going to shoot us!" Lola's face contorted with fear.

Horrified, Maya grabbed her left hand with her right and started to speak into the video phone. Its face went dark. "Not now!" she screamed. Damned things never seemed to work when she wore them. She slapped the phone, which came unclasped from her wrist and dropped to the sidewalk. She scrambled to pick it up and yelled into the phone even though she hadn't heard the service connect. "Help, nine-one-one, help us. Somebody's trying to kill us!"

A shot hit the window in the building beside them.

Lola turned toward the man as she gathered her skirt in her hands. "Leave us alone. Are you crazy?"

A shot rang out, but Maya didn't know where it went. "We've got to get out of here!"

Lola broke into a run down the now empty street. Her big steps twisted the dress, and she ran awkwardly.

Terrified, Maya followed her, footsteps pounding in her ears. Had she gone insane, having to run for her life? Was this some awful dream and she would awaken safe in her bed at home?

As Maya ran, she tried to stuff the phone into her fanny pack. The Velcro must have come undone because the pack fell to the sidewalk. Maya stumbled over it and scraped her knees on the concrete. Try as she would, she couldn't manage to pick up the fanny pack.

"Get up!" Lola screamed back at Maya. "We have to get out of here."

Heart thumping, Maya struggled up. Her hands and legs stung as she ran behind Lola. How in the world could this be happening? Someone was trying to kill her. Who would want her dead? It couldn't be true. She ran on, bumping a sidewalk railing as she passed.

Another electronic blast crackled over Maya's head. Then another. She screamed, "No, no, stop. Don't kill us." Maybe they should veer into the alley up ahead or hide in the stairwell. She couldn't think what would be best to do.

Lola moaned and dropped to the sidewalk with a thud. Her body lay in a hideous position.

Sickened, Maya dropped down beside Lola and tugged at her shoulder. "Get up, get up." Lola's head lolled to the side, and her wide-open eyes stared vacantly.

Maya heard another blast. She was about to die. She scrambled over her friend and sobbed as she raced on down the street, praying Lola would follow. Maya looked back, mindless of what lay ahead of her. The man knelt beside Lola and pointed the gun at Maya.

Bile rose in Maya's throat, the taste of fear so gross she almost choked. She hurtled toward home. If she could only get there, she would be safe.

Chapter Two

Maya turned the corner in terror. She could hear no sound except her own gasps and her footsteps pounding in her ears. The façade of her brownstone home looked like heaven. If she could just get inside, she would be safe.

A glance down the street revealed nothing. Maybe the man had not followed her.

She fumbled for her fanny pack then remembered she'd lost it and banged on the door. "Mother! Father! Help." Sobbing, she collapsed on the front steps.

Terrence Rembrandt opened the door almost immediately and knelt beside her. "Maya, dear, what's wrong?" His big, fleshy face bore dark stubble and a worried frown.

Words tore out of Maya's throat. "Call the police. Lola. Hurt. Help her." She clutched the lapels of her father's shirt.

Behind him her mother, Carolyn, appeared. Her red satin caftan swayed as she held the door open and spoke in a low pitch. "Gracious, get her inside. The whole neighborhood will hear."

Guided by her father, Maya staggered across the cobblestones of the narrow foyer into the living room. She dropped onto a chintz couch. "Someone shot Lola. Call the police. My cell phone is gone. I lost it. Call the police."

"What on earth?" Carolyn and Terrence looked at each other in a strange way.

Maya feared they didn't believe her and jumped to her feet, energized. "I'll call them myself."

"I'll do it, dear. Don't worry." Terrence spoke nine-one-one into his wrist phone.

While he gave the address and their names to verify the phone signature, Maya tried to regain control of her breath and her thoughts. She panted as she said, "On Walnut

Street, near Chase. That's where it happened, just down the block from our house."

"A shooting on Walnut Street, near Chase," her father said into the phone.

Carolyn dashed into the kitchen and returned with a glass of water and two pills. She held them out to Maya. "Here, take these serotonin tabs. You'll feel better."

"No, I don't want to. Lola's hurt. She might be dead."

"She might not be." Carolyn had a look of exasperation on her face. "In any case it won't help her for you to be all upset. You feel nervous, don't you?"

"Now, Mother," Terrence waved Carolyn away, "let her do what she wants. The police will be here soon."

Tears streaked down Maya's cheeks. She remembered the way Lola had looked, so bizarre, lying on the sidewalk. "I shouldn't have left her there alone."

Carolyn dropped the tabs into Maya's palm. "Wasn't the sniper shooting at both of you? You couldn't just stay there and wait to be killed."

"Why would someone shoot at us?" Maya clamped the tabs so tightly her nails cut into her skin. "We've never hurt anyone. It's insane."

Within minutes, an NYC officer arrived. Carolyn offered him a seat, but he refused and stood beside the door. He confirmed that Lola had died in the street. "The bulletin just came through. The deceased is one Lola Compson. Is that your friend?"

Maya blanched. "She's really dead?" A feeling of coldness settled over Maya. She felt hollow inside.

"I'm sorry to say that yes, she is." The officer took out an electronic recorder. "Please tell me what you know."

Holding back grief, Maya described the events and her whereabouts prior to the shooting. When asked, she did not know about Lola's activities before the meeting.

The officer tipped his hat back on his head. "Why do you think the sniper broke off? You say he didn't follow you home?"

"I don't think so." Terrified, Maya shook her head. "Do you mean he might try again?"

"You need to be careful. Drive instead of walking. Stay with others as much as possible." The officer seemed sincere and pleasant. "We don't have much to go on unless someone comes forward as a witness. That doesn't mean someone won't, but you've got to know these are tough cases. People don't like to expose themselves to possible retaliation."

Carolyn set her hands on her hips. "You might want to investigate Lola's boyfriends, Officer. She had a lot of them."

Terrence nodded at the police officer and obviously agreed that investigating the boyfriends would be a good idea. He ran a hand through his black hair, rumpling it.

Maya wondered when her parents became detectives. They didn't seem one bit concerned that Lola was dead or that Maya might meet the same fate. "Mother, would you please refrain from bad-mouthing Lola. She's dead, for goodness sake."

"Well, she was wild." Carolyn got that look of moral high ground that she wore so often. "Maybe one of her boyfriends shot her, and that's why he didn't hit you."

"Maybe that's possible." Maya thought this all very alarming. "Every effort should be made to find them. If you want her boyfriends' names, they'll be in her address book, I'm certain." Her hands shook uncontrollably. She clasped them together, uncertain why she felt such hostility toward her parents, particularly her mother. No doubt they felt as upset as she and didn't know quite how to show it. Maya had just gone through a bizarre experience. All of them might act a little strange under the circumstances.

The officer opened the foyer door. "Miss Rembrandt, we may want to talk with you again. Maybe you'll remember more of what the suspect looked like."

"I'll do whatever I can to help. I want him found." Maya had come close to dying herself. She had no framework for knowing how to deal with that. Her spirit would have undergone annihilation.

After Terrence closed the door on the officer, he squeezed Maya's waist. "You did well. I know how difficult that must have been for you, but don't put too much hope in the police. Snipers do their ugly work then fade into the night."

Carolyn nodded. "It's a sign of the times."

When Terrence hugged Maya, tears formed in her eyes. This was all just too much. She trembled all over and leaned against her father, whispering, "I was almost killed, too."

Terrence's support kept Maya from falling. "Maybe you'd better take the serotonin." His voice sounded kind.

"Here, dear." Carolyn held up the glass of water. "Take these while I get some antiseptic and bandages for your knees."

How could Maya have thought that her parents weren't concerned about her? She'd been wrong. They loved her and wanted to help her. They wanted her to take the pills, so she would despite their clouding effects. She needed her parents' support right now. Maya took the glass and swallowed the pills, dreading tomorrow but knowing she had to get through the day.

On a side street in the Bronx, Dylan Brady carried a heavy box upstairs to a second-floor office. The sign on the door read "Psychic and Spiritual Counselor." When he went inside, the psychic herself, Sybil, bent to pick up wrapping papers and stashed them in the trashcan with her well-rounded butt turned toward him.

"This is the last of the books." Dylan smiled. "Where do you want them?"

"Anywhere's fine." Sybil wiped sweat off her pretty brow. "Just open the flaps and I'll put them away now."

"How about you call it a day?" He set the books down, straddled a straight-back chair, and swiped dust off his jeans.

"Why, you tired?"

Tired, was she kidding? Helping Sybil move compared to taking a break from his workout at the gym. "No, but I'm hungry. Let's get a bite and have a little fun. You can finish tomorrow."

"I'd better do this instead." Sybil picked up books and stacked them in a bookcase. "I've got appointments starting in two days. I need to get the office shaped up."

Dylan felt his blood pressure begin to rise. "Level with me, Sybil. You've put me off a half a dozen times lately. What's up?"

"Well, you know." Sybil's voice cracked. She sat on the desk and took off the scarf, wiping her bald head, then started again. "I really appreciate all your help. Not just moving. You know what I mean. I'd never have been brave enough to start my own business without your belief in me. You've got such a terrific gift. It's meant a lot to me just to be around you. To learn about clairvoyance and how to do remote viewing from you."

"Well, you're welcome." Maybe Dylan was wrong to get angry. "You've got quite a bit of ability yourself. I guess I helped you develop it."

"You're such a handsome guy and so talented. But, well, lately I've been thinking we should call it off. I think there should only be one psychic per family."

"Family?"

"We'd get in each other's way."

Where in hell is she going with this? "I asked you out for supper, not to get married."

"You don't even tell me what you do for a living." Sybil nearly shouted. She'd obviously stored up a lot of shit. "You take off at odd times, come back dirty and unshaven, and never give an explanation. And all those guns you've got at your house? What's that about?"

"You've known all along I can't talk about my profession. If you're such a good psychic, why don't you just figure it out for yourself?" Dylan regretted that remark but didn't intend to apologize. He knew from his own experience that psychics had a low success rate with their own emotional involvements, so Sybil probably couldn't read him. It never worked when he was this pissed, so he didn't even try to find out her real reasons. He'd bet a lot she found another guy.

Sybil appeared to try to manufacture some tears. "I just don't feel comfortable with you. I think we should end it."

"You know something, woman. There's nothing to end." Dylan hit the door with his fist so hard that the glass panel shuddered.

When he got down to the street level, the cold air felt good on his face. What had gotten into him? He didn't love Sybil. Sometimes he didn't even like her. Why in hell didn't she let her hair grow?

Man, though, she'd hurt his pride. He'd felt just the same way when Cassie called it off. She'd leaned on him when her sister died, then she took off with some GSS officer. Probably a hybrid, if the truth be known.

Rumor had it that a lot of hybrids worked for the GSS. That was the way they obtained so many Anaz-voohri weapons. Somebody of mixed blood, a cross between a man and an Anaz-voohri, had to have mixed loyalties even though they looked like humans. At least his hunter friend had decided to work for the good guys.

Espionage was too dangerous a game for playing kissy face, anyway.

Climbing into the driver's seat, Dylan drove to the rental yard and turned in the truck. He donned his denim jacket and jogged the three blocks to Mythos Headquarters. A light snow fell, the kind that chills the air but doesn't stick.

No sign hung over the basement apartment to give any clue to a curious public as to what kind of work went on inside. A plastic holly wreath decorated the old-fashioned plank door. Dylan spoke his code name into the quaint speakerphone. "Apollo here."

The heavy door swung open, revealing its back side of reinforced concrete. A continuous strip of lighted baseboard edged the carpeting. Dylan strolled down the corridor, entered an elevator, and dropped two stories.

The main room of Headquarters contained wall-to-wall plasma screens, only one of which appeared active tonight. Two soldiers sat before it. They wore interface headsets and talons on their fingers to merge into the computer screen where they engaged in practice combat with computer-generated images of Anaz-voohri.

A map covered another wall. Lights pinpointed each of the GSS offices throughout the world, including their splinter black ops group, Operational Readiness / Intelligence on Nations. The world governments had originally created GSS to seek out and destroy Anaz-voohri. When it fell into corrupt practices and failed to inform the public of the extent of the Anaz-voohri threat, ORION became more powerful.

Points on the map glowed to indicate violent events or other activities by either organization that Mythos considered suspicious.

As usual, the founder and one of the world's wealthiest men, Lawson Archer lay in a chaise lounge, appearing to nap. Dylan wondered if the man even had an apartment. He'd made himself available to his men at any time or place, ever since he recruited Dylan into Mythos out of the Global Military four years before. Archer was shrewd, intelligent, and one of the true patriots in America. Dylan felt great loyalty to the man and his organization

Dylan glanced at a green light flickering on the map at New York. "Something happening here?"

"Could be." Archer rose and adjusted his lanky frame. "What are you doing back? It's your night off, isn't it?"

Dylan shrugged and gazed at the board. "What's up?"

"Hit and run sniper tonight on Walnut Street."

"Who was the target?"

"Just one so far. Female named Lola Compson."

"Is she anybody?" Dylan sat down at an empty terminal.

"Don't know yet."

Dylan clicked on the local police band, typed in his secret code, and read the report as the unsuspecting police officer on the other end typed it in. "Two women marked by a sniper. One killed. One got away and is cooperating with investigation. A Maya Rembrandt. No leads. Probably ex-boyfriend of one woman or the other."

"May be nothing." Archer leaned over Dylan's shoulder. "On the other hand, those hit and runs are a trademark of ORION. Let's stay on it for a while to see if we can find a link."

Glad to be thinking about something other than Sybil for a while, Dylan pulled up the deceased's file. He found nothing to distinguish the victim except a drunk driving arrest. Her father had evidently bribed somebody because the court had never held a hearing on the charge. "She doesn't seem like a security risk."

"I know but something about the situation troubles me."

"This investigation happened really fast. It's only been an hour since the woman died."

"Why don't you see what you can get by doing some remote viewing?"

"Right." Dylan left the screen up and went into a room reserved for his use. It contained all he needed for his sessions – a daybed, a fridge, and an epad, an electronic notebook. Pulling off his boots, he lay down on the daybed and covered himself with a quilt his mother had made when he was a child.

For a moment, he let himself remember the way she looked, sitting in a window seat, sewing the patches together. Such a sweet woman, full of love for him and his dad. Dylan missed his parents, but he didn't let himself dwell on their unsolved murders. Even after seven years, rage filled him at the thought of their untimely, unfair deaths. Always suspicious of collusion between the Center for Evolutionary Medicine and the Anaz-voohri, Dylan trusted that one of his jobs, or something another Mythos soldier discovered, would lead to resolution.

He didn't worry about that tonight. Dylan turned the imaginary switch in his brain, the switch that took him to a place of infinite clarity. He sighed deeply and opened himself, knowing images would come to him, helpful pictures that would show him Walnut Street an hour ago.

Consciousness of his body ebbed as Dylan waited. He rested in his awareness of the complete knowledge present in the cosmic mind and available to each who chose to take it.

Into the quiet space of Dylan's mind came a hazy image of a marksman crouched on an empty sidewalk.

Dylan couldn't seem to focus in on his appearance in any detail, but the weapon looked like ORION regulation issue, a replica of an Anaz-voohri phase gun. Ahead of the marksman, two women scrambled down the street. The marksman sighted down the barrel and took aim at the back of a woman in a running suit. She screamed and fell but got back up. He sighted the other woman in a long dress and squeezed the trigger. The woman fell. He took aim at the first woman and tipped the rifle up. Then he shot two rounds into the air. He rose and casually walked down the sidewalk and into a stairwell.

Dylan waited for more pictures to come. When he felt satisfied that he had witnessed the important components of the crime, he opened his eyes. He always felt very rested after a session. He swung his legs off the daybed and reached into the small fridge's freezer for an ice cream bar. He devoured it, savoring the chocolaty coating, and wished he had another. Scribbling a note on his epad, he clicked send, a requisition for more ice cream bars. One of the perks of being a Mythos operative was that he had access to real ice cream instead of the synthetic crap most people had to eat.

When Dylan opened the door, Archer rose and walked across the space between them with a questioning look.

"ORION definitely had an interest in Miss Compson," Dylan said, "but not the other woman, it seems. She was a clear mark, and the shooter didn't even take aim at her, so she may be a lucky bystander."

"Or he intended to scare her. Guess we need to find out more about this situation. You up to taking this on?"

"Sure."

Archer handed Dylan a disk. "Here's the info we've got so far. See if you can figure out why ORION killed

Compson and why the Rembrandt woman's alive for another day."

Chapter Three

Clad only in a robe, Maya leaned over the basin in her third-floor bathroom and applied cover-up to the circles under her eyes. Even though she usually worked Saturday mornings, she'd called in sick and rested throughout the day as much as possible so she could get through the evening.

Maya promised herself to try to find the courage to introduce herself to men after the auction or at least respond to any who spoke with her. She'd rarely had opportunity to meet men in such a safe environment. This was probably the right crowd in which to find someone to date, and Lola would want her to. She had to honor Lola. Maya needed a friend now.

A knock at the door accompanied her mother's voice. "Maya, may I come in?"

Surprised that Carolyn had not barged in like she usually did, Maya said, "Okay."

With hair done up in its customary elongated cone, Carolyn's heavy-cheeked face appeared in the mirror behind Maya. She bore a look of genuine concern. "Let me help you, dear."

"I'm fine." Maya didn't feel okay. She felt empty and raw.

Picking up the hairbrush, Carolyn pulled Maya's hair back with a practiced hand. "It's not necessary to go to the fundraiser, if you'd rather stay home. Everyone will understand. Why don't you let me call and make your apologies?"

"I really want to do this, for Lola's sake." Maya's voice sounded hollow in her own ears.

"That's what your father said you'd say. She was a good friend to you, and I know you're going to miss her." Carolyn brushed Maya's hair and pulled it back in a ponytail.

Maya didn't want to talk right now. She'd end up in tears again despite another dose of serotonin. She had to depend on the stupor effect to get her through the evening. She didn't want to let the committee down but especially owed an appearance as her personal honor to Lola's memory.

"The police haven't called, so I guess they haven't found any witnesses yet." Carolyn walked into the bedroom and picked up the dry cleaner's bag containing Maya's dress. "We were thinking we'd go with you. Would you like that?"

"That would help." For Maya, the thought of getting the car out and driving to the art museum by herself had seemed a daunting task. She followed her mother into the bedroom where she'd grown up. This year's décor involved yellow, one of Maya's favorite colors, but one her mother had chosen on a whim. Usually Maya didn't care what the room looked like, but she liked the pretty wallpaper flecked with daffodils. She pulled the turquoise silk dress out of the bag and hesitated, not wanting to disrobe. "I'll meet you downstairs, all right, Mother?"

When her mother left, looking miffed, Maya took off the robe and put on the dress. She looked terrific in it. Lola would be proud. In her honor, Maya added red lipstick, took down the ponytail, and shook her hair free. A curl here and there made her hairdo more flattering. Lola had been right. Maya could look decent with a little effort.

Carrying turquoise strapped pumps, Maya trekked downstairs to meet her parents. Art was the one interest they all had in common. Perhaps it went with the name. She felt grateful for her parents' kindness. Father had once tried to trace the family's genealogy back but hadn't been able to make the connection to the Dutch painter. That, of course, didn't keep Mother from claiming it.

When the three arrived at the art museum, her parents wanted to see the lithographs set up for the auction and began the walk around the perimeter of the display in the lobby. Hundreds of art patrons roamed about, carrying plastic glasses of champagne. Their dress ranged from chic to geek.

Maya sat with the rest of the committee. All acted relieved to see her and expressed sorrow about Lola. They'd heard the details of the shooting on TV. No one could possibly imagine the motive. Neither could Maya unless Mother had been right about a boyfriend. Maya would never denigrate her friend before the committee and dreaded having to talk about the experience. Finally, the time came for the auction.

The committee member from a Nitrogen-Pac manufacturer, a young man with a blond goatee, functioned as emcee. Maya stood beside him and held up the first lithograph to begin the bidding. The woman from Harkins sat nearby to take the money credits.

While they sold the first panel, Renoir and Goya lithographs, the man with the goatee made comments about the audience. Maya inferred that he intended to amuse her and take her mind off the tragedy. She thought that sweet but his jokes came across as crude and distracting.

Scanning the audience, she looked for interesting men. One in particular caught her eye, primarily because he seemed to watch her intently. She didn't know how she could come to that conclusion since practically every man in the room had to watch her, at least to some extent, if they paid any attention at all to the auction. She'd been so distraught and so doped up, she didn't trust her logic. When the goatee started on the sampling from the twentieth century, she held up a Kandinsky lithograph from the 1930s.

The man in the back appeared interested in the Kandinsky because his gaze left Maya and traveled to it. Maya got a chance to appraise him. He looked attractive in an unkempt way with black hair, black eyes, and a good strong jaw line. He leaned against the wall, arms folded.

Something about his posture read cocky. His jeans and t-shirt looked way too casual. Maya felt curious about him but doubted she'd want to be alone with him. He certainly stood out from the rest of the men in the room.

When the Kandinsky sold, Maya held up an Andy Warhol called Triple Elvis. It showed the twentieth-century actor Elvis Presley brandishing a pistol in a triple exposure look.

That's the one, Dylan thought. If he had to blow Mythos's money, he might as well have something he really liked. "One thousand dollars," he called from the back of the room.

Maya glanced up with an expression of surprise. She'd certainly been looking him over. Maybe she thought he caught her at it. Dylan chuckled and decided to give the pretty woman a pass. After all, she'd been through quite a lot in the last twenty-four hours.

Without any further bid, the emcee called out, "Sold."

Dylan went to pay the cashier, get some champagne, and hang out until he could collect his purchase. He intended to create a chance to talk to Maya later. Until then she was very easy to watch with her beautiful, chocolate brown hair and graceful manner. She seemed comfortable with the limelight, or at least used to it. She looked very shapely. Her skin intrigued him most. It glistened with pink highlights. Once he'd glanced up to see if some theatrical light caused the effect, but the lights, trained on the emcee as well, didn't pink his skin. Maya's had an uncommon texture, like strawberry ripple ice cream.

With the last lithograph finally auctioned off, Dylan tucked his Triple Elvis under one arm and found Maya shaking hands with a patron. He waited for her to finish and said, "Maya Rembrandt? I wanted to meet you. I'm Dylan Brady."

"Oh, hello." She gave him a public smile that looked marvelous nevertheless and shook his hand. "You bought the Warhol. He's one of my favorites. I love the Fifties painters. You must too."

Maya appeared smaller up close than she'd looked on the platform. Her head barely came up to his shoulder. That fact surprised Dylan, but he didn't know why. "Actually, I like Fifties music. That's why I bought the Warhol. Elvis was a singer, you know."

"Oh, no. Well, I guess I forgot." Maya obviously did not know that Elvis was a singer. Maybe she'd thought him a gunslinger. She smiled a bit. "Clearly, I need to do more research."

"That's all right. Actually, I'm surprised that you are out so soon after your close call."

A look of dismay crossed Maya's face.

Dylan didn't want her to feel afraid of him. "It's all right. Be careful while the investigation is ongoing."

Maya looked uncertain when she thanked Dylan. He hoped she assumed he was with the police, at least for now. As usual, he didn't want to tell an outright lie unless the situation turned life threatening.

Another patron claimed Maya's attention, and Dylan took the chance to leave. He'd not accomplished his goal. He still didn't know whether ORION had targeted Maya or not. Now that he'd actually seen her and touched her, it sickened him to think those double-dealing bastards might yet harm her. She was one sweet jewel, but what could ORION want with her? It must have something to do with her job at NexTech.

On Sunday Dylan slept in, luxuriating in a day off. When he finally crawled out of his warm bed, he stepped onto the hardwood floor and pulled his jeans over bare skin.

Outside the loft window, snow had left a light coating, enough to make the apartment roofs and trees across the street shimmer in morning sunshine. He pressed the button to pull the Murphy bed up against the wall, allowing his gun collection mounted on the under side of the bed to show. He phoned in his breakfast order to the deli down the street.

Besides the Compson murder assignment, he'd finished up some old business the night before, rather more poignant than he'd expected – a going away party for the hybrid hunter. He'd departed for Africa under an assumed name, Tahiti with its country club life style being too expensive a relocation for Mythos to manage. Hopefully a new hybrid with access to the Anaz-voohri would come forward. Without that help, it could get more and more difficult to isolate and eliminate them.

Dylan hung the Triple Elvis in its metal frame on the landing so that it would be the first thing anyone coming in the front door and up the steps would see. He thought Elvis looked very cool brandishing his revolver.

Meeting Maya at the art museum had been an unexpected treat. Her involvement would make this new assignment more interesting, not that he'd get to know her personally. He liked looking at her and imagining what it might be like to make love to her, but he'd had about all the relationship escapades he wanted lately. There was no chance that he'd become a three-time loser.

The huge, hot breakfast delivery arrived. On the table of the diner booth, Dylan set out coffee, pineapple juice, bacon, eggs, toast, potatoes, and pancakes. He pulled a dime out of a jar, dropped it into the tabletop jukebox, then stashed the jar beneath the table. Elvis Presley's voice entertained him with *Blue Suede Shoes* while he read the newspaper and ate.

No local news he hadn't known the night before, but internationally the disease authority seemed to have averted a new viral hemorrhagic fever scare. Dylan thought it treacherous and cowardly to use disease as a weapon. An enemy should be visible with a firearm and a modicum of courage, to kill or be killed.

Turning to the sports section out of habit, he checked the basketball scores. The Knicks had won, but he didn't really care. Nothing important ever happened until baseball season began, several months away yet.

The obituary page listed the Compson funeral as the next day, Monday. He noted the time and place. It could be enlightening to see who attended. Murderers did show up from time to time, often enough to make funerals worth the effort.

When he finished eating, he felt full and satisfied, the way only a good meal or a good woman could make him feel. At least he had one of the former; the latter he may have to do without, if they all went weird like Sybil and Cassie. Actually, he liked it better that way. He was a loner by nature. He downed the last of the coffee, plopped on the leather couch, and turned on the Jets game.

The next afternoon, Dylan intentionally arrived early for the funeral and took a seat in the back row far to one side so he could watch people come in and notice how they acted. Because he believed it important to give respect to the dead, he wore a white shirt and corduroy blazer with his jeans. The church, Presbyterian, had seats made of natural wood, brown carpet, and a plain cross over a dais.

Since there was no coffin present and the body had not been presented for viewing, it probably had been cremated, or would be when the police finished with the autopsy.

On an easel flanked by baskets of poinsettias stood a large glamour shot of Lola Compson. She bore a broad model's smile and long blonde hair that swirled in such a fashion as to follow the swell of her breasts. Then the image faded to black background, giving the illusion that her boobs arose from an unplumbed depth. She'd been one hot chick. Who would want her dead? Perhaps a deranged man or a jealous woman.

A funeral just before Christmas seemed somehow sadder, especially for someone who hadn't lived much of her life. Lola had been the same age as Dylan.

Dylan watched the mourners file into the church, several white-haired people and an assortment in their twenties. He figured Lola must have had a lot of friends. Her father and two young men sat on the front row. They all seemed stricken, as did the older mourners near them, probably grandparents. The obituary had said the mother had passed on several years ago.

Maya came in, flanked by two middle-aged people, no doubt her parents. They attended her closely. Maya gazed at the photo and talked in an animated way to her mother and father. She didn't seem particularly sad. Two local police officers standing at the back chatted, arms folded.

Once the minister began to speak, Dylan turned toward the front of the room and noticed a thin man sitting across the aisle. He appeared to watch Maya, not anything unusual, except for the round patch on his sleeve that displayed the Orion Constellation, the insignia of ORION.

Even operatives of the black ops, despite their mission to seek out and destroy Anaz-voohri and hybrids, had friends and relatives. So perhaps this man had attended for honest reasons. On the other hand, Dylan took a good look at the ORION officer – thin, wiry, early forties, graying hair with sideburns longer than folks usually wear them. Yes, Dylan could ID the guy if necessary later on.

Dylan remembered the night of the murder when he'd done a remote viewing session to try to find the sniper. The image of the man had been too hazy for identification. Dylan regretted the imprecise nature of his clairvoyance.

At the end of the ceremony, the family and friends left first. As Maya went up the aisle, Dylan watched her. Again, he noticed her lack of emotion. In fact, she looked somewhat expressionless. When she glanced toward him, he nodded, but she didn't appear to recognize him. Perhaps he'd not made such a memorable impression at the art museum, after all. Considering the nature of funerals, he'd wait and try to catch her at her workplace later in the week.

Maya awakened the morning after Lola's funeral filled with resolve. Relieved to be alive, she wanted to express gratitude and kindness. For the moment, she wished there was a God to pray to. In any case, she could resume her duties and carry on her life with serious purpose. She'd stop worrying about whether or not she looked good enough and devote herself to her work, her parents, and the art museum. She felt very lucky to have people in her life, at work and at home, supporting her.

Glad to have a job to go to, she had missed her computer during this forced absence. She wanted to get back inside and meld with it. Then she would feel ever so much better. Nothing like being on task to wipe away cares.

On rising from bed, Maya noticed her hands shook a bit, not too surprising considering the stress of the past few days. She decided not to take the serotonin tabs Mother had left on the bedside table next to a glass of water. Maya did have to admit that the tabs had carried her through the ordeal in admirable fashion. She just didn't want to risk becoming dependent on chemical mood elevators.

Her mother had acted thoughtfully, all things considered. Maya resolved to treat her with more patience and extend the effort to notice little changes around the house. Maya had trouble imagining her mother's life, so different from Maya's, with no career or clear purpose. Doubtless Mother still had the churning thoughts and creative urges, but no outlet for them like Maya had at work.

To avoid waking her parents, Maya prepared for the day quietly. She bathed and medicated the tattoo, much less painful, thank goodness. She dressed in a black blouse and an aqua jumpsuit then added small turquoise and gold earrings. She carried her running shoes and debated whether or not to take her boots. Maybe she'd throw them in the car, just in case. She'd have to shop for a new phone after work. This time she'd buy the model old ladies carried in a purse.

Maybe she could keep that kind running. Lately she'd gone through several because they mysteriously quit working. It occurred to her that the force of her mind broke them, but that seemed too farfetched to be true.

The polished wooden staircase extended through all four stories, its rubber treads muted all footsteps. When Maya trekked down to the second story, she heard voices in her father's office. She assumed he already have a patient with him. The man inside sounded agitated, and her father tried to soothe him, using the comforting voice on which Maya had come to depend.

Tiptoeing past the door, she turned at the landing and glanced out the deco glass window in the hall. Snow swirled, softening the glare of the streetlight. With the polished railing for support, she hurried down to the hall closet. She grabbed her canary ski jacket and checked the pockets, confirming that gloves and muffler still lay inside from last season, then she headed to the parking garage.

After starting the engine of her pumpkin-colored Tango, she pulled into the street. She had laughed when she bought the little car because of the allusion to Cinderella, always waiting for Prince Charming. Not much different from Maya.

Snow clouded the windshield, and she started the wipers. If this kept up, traffic would surely be in a snarl by evening. A motorist behind her leaned on his horn. People got so crabby in bad weather.

Maya hated going to work alone in the dark. She wished her sense of confidence would return, but for now, she must attend to any possible danger. What if the sniper came after her? How could she protect herself?

"Warning, warning," said the efficient male voice of the Tango's computer, "check gasoline levels. We're running low."

"Oh, that's ridiculous. I just filled up a couple of days ago." Maya glanced at the visual gauge, which showed over half a tank.

"Warning, warning, engine overheat a possibility. Check fluid levels."

Fluid level gauges all appeared normal. Maya wondered what in hell had happened. The computer's information seemed at variance with the dashboard. She flipped the computer voice switch to the off position.

By the time she arrived at the NexTech parking garage, Maya felt a bit crabby herself. She would have to deal with car problems after work, something she never liked to do. She scanned the garage for any person she didn't know before getting out of the car. Seeing no one suspicious, she hurried into the elevator and up to her office.

With an audible sigh, she finally took off her shoes and walked into the familiar crystal of her computer terminal. She slipped on her headset and spoke softly, "Good morning, Fairy Godmother."

"Good morning, Maya." The computer's voice sounded like a kindly grandmother's. "Welcome back. I hope you had a productive weekend."

Thinking of the fundraiser and the funeral, Maya said, "Somewhat spotty, I guess. Let's get to work."

"Terrific idea," the computer said.

"I've some thoughts on enhancing Fluttering Fairy. Open the file, please."

The wings appeared on the screen before Maya. She imagined the tiny face and pointed ears of a girl fairy. When she saw them, she added a gauzy aqua gown and long golden hair. "Now add texture and depth," she said to herself and the computer. "This is going to be good. I'm coming in."

In her imagination, Maya transported herself into the screen with the fairy. She held out her hand, and the fairy lit on her palm. "Hello, you pretty thing. Shall I give you a name?"

"You could, I suppose," the fairy said with a wry grin, "but I already have one."

Delighted, Maya laughed. "You do? Tell me what it is."

"It can be dangerous to give out that information. Someone might steal my soul."

"You can trust me. I'm your creator. I would never harm you. You could think of me as like a mother."

"Yes, I know." The fairy curtsied. "My name is Daffodil."

"Aha, that's what I was going to name you."

"Looks like your program works," said the computer.

"Looks like!" Maya had not felt more encouraged in all the time she'd been programming. She couldn't wait for the next product meeting to suggest going into the toy market. Little girls all over the world would love such a toy as this pretty fairy to play with, and each would have its own name chosen by the owner.

"Terrific idea," said the computer.

"All right, good-bye for now, Daffodil." The fairy waved as the file closed.

Soon Maya's day filled with normal details and catching up from her absence. After lunch, Frank called a meeting that lasted for hours. Finally, when it was time to go home, she had the chance to get back into her computer and said, "New file."

The amorphous field surrounded Maya. She felt at home in the place of raw creation and excited at a new prospect. Her powers were growing, and she wanted to express more of her inner vision.

On her one visit to the West Coast, her parents had taken her to California for Christmas. She'd been sixteen at the time. Maya could still close her eyes and remember the white beach at La Jolla, the high cliff with divers, sailboats passing, and best of all the warm sun. Just the thought of wearing a swimming suit in December brought tears to her eyes. She could hear the cries of the gulls as they dipped into the crashing waves and feel the caress of an ocean breeze.

How lovely it would be to live there, a modern paradise. The picture needed one more thing to achieve perfection. She must have a handsome man to hold her. She imagined how that would feel. His strong arms around her, her head nestled under his chin. The skin on his arms smelled of suntan lotion. The sturdy texture of denim brushed her bare leg.

Maya opened her eyes to see a blue jeans-clad leg next to hers, touching hers. She didn't want to disturb the image even though startled by its verisimilitude. She looked up to see who held her. She recognized the man from the fundraiser, the one she thought the off-duty cop, and whispered, "Dylan?"

The figure of the man receded as if he faded into the past or grew shorter or maybe both. Maya fancied him in an old-fashioned baseball uniform or something similar. Unable to get a clear fix on him any more, she stood alone on the beach. Perhaps she needed to clarify in her own mind what she found attractive in a man before trying to create one in the software.

The program needed work, no doubt, but she felt satisfied with her progress. Soon she would complete a robotic man with human performance capability. Maya blushed at the possible applications, glad to be alone in her cubicle. Maybe she would read some romance novels, as research. Definitely she'd have to read those novels away from home, but they might help her expand the repertoire of what the robotic man might perform. If she could create a man in her program, she wouldn't ever have to feel unattractive or unworthy again.

"Save this file," Maya said. "Let's call it Big Girl Toy."

"Terrific idea," said the computer.

Maya laughed. "We're on a roll here. New file."

This was just the kind of thing Lola would find hilarious, and Maya couldn't wait to tell her. Maya paused, remembering the bitter fact. Lola was dead. The nurturing cloud of mind-altering drugs had completely worn off.

A flood of grief engulfed Maya. She felt pain so great it stabbed at her belly. Her head throbbed. Her heart felt as if it would explode in her chest.

The enormity of the loss overwhelmed her. All the years of her remaining life, Lola would not be there. They couldn't share their troubles. They couldn't cry together, laugh together, tell each other dirty jokes. All Maya's girlhood had expired, buried with Lola's ashes in the urn.

Still within the amorphous field, Maya heaved a great sigh and allowed the darkness of grief to come over her.

She shuddered, and the computer shuddered.

She wept and the computer cried out, "It is time."

"This is too much," Maya sobbed. "I can't go on."

"You must," said the computer, not in a voice but in her mind. "The time has come."

Maya didn't understand or care what the computer meant. She didn't want to live in fear. Dropping to the floor neither in nor out of the screen, she cried and cried and cried. To go through life without her friend was a horrendous option. Not without Lola. Maya could not bear the pain. It was too great to endure.

The computer went dark. The room lights winked out.

"What the hell is going on?" said a male technician in the next cubicle.

"Turn on the lights," yelled the woman down the row.

"I can't. They don't work."

"Go flip the switch, you moron."

"I did."

Maya wiped her tears. Her head felt as if someone drove a hammer into her skull. She'd cry later. Right now, she had to get the computer humming again. In darkness, she stumbled out of the cubicle, felt around in a drawer for an old keyboard, and typed in commands. Nothing happened. "Where are you, Fairy Godmother? Come in, please."

A siren wailed outside. In complete darkness, Maya scrambled to the window. She could not see a single light all up and down Eighty-Sixth Street or along the avenues. There'd been a major power outage somewhere. What on earth had happened?

Chapter Four

In darkness, Maya sat back against the office wall beneath the window and listened to the clamor of her alarmed co-workers. Voice rough from crying, she shouted, "We can just wait this out. The electricity will be back on in no time."

No one responded to her.

"Where the fuck are the emergency lights?" a male voice shouted.

Frank's voice bellowed above the others. "All right, you guys. Settle down."

No one paid any attention to him.

Frank roared. "I'm your boss, damn it. Shut up and listen to me."

"Quiet down," Maya shouted.

Momentarily they stopped talking.

Frank sounded more commanding in the darkness. "I don't want to step on anybody, but I'm feeling my way to the window. Maybe I can make out something in the street that will help us figure this out." His clothes swished as he moved along the wall.

Sirens wailed in the street and cars honked. Maya would never have thought it could be so dark. Only the flickering shadows of headlights outside relieved the blackness.

Maya heard several people breathing and figured all six of the technicians remained either in the area outside her cubicle or close by. It was surprising that so many techs were still been working at seven in the evening. She must have gotten lost in the program because she'd believed herself to be alone in the building after five.

How many people had heard her crying? Maya felt embarrassed that she'd lost control. She never did, particularly at work. Now she must behave more maturely and responsibly to help get herself and her co-workers out of this situation.

"Excuse me." Frank smelled of the licorice he usually kept in his pocket.

"Ouch," came the sound of a female voice. "You stepped on me."

"Sorry." Frank grabbed at Maya's arm.

"It's me, Boss." Maya guided his arm past her, and she could feel his heft as he leaned toward the window.

"Well, I can't see crap," he said. "Anybody got a match?"

"We've all quit smoking," a fellow called out. "Remember, you said we had to. Otherwise, we'd have a light now."

Several people snickered.

"Okay," Frank called with, for him, a conciliatory tone. "There's no doubt this'll be over in a few minutes, so in the meantime, how about a song?"

"Oh, please," a girl called out.

"What is this, summer camp?" asked another.

Everyone laughed, and the tension broke.

A girl said, "Look what I've got. I forgot I had it." A pin light flashed across the wall momentarily then winked out. "Anybody got a battery?"

"Anybody got a radio?" Frank yelled out.

They laughed again and someone asked, "Who has a radio any more?"

"Nobody," a young male voice said, "but I know a ghost story. Want to hear it?"

After some boisterous slapping, they settled down.

With all the commotion, Maya had temporarily forgotten her grief and the strange comradeship she'd felt with the computer just before the blackout. It was almost as if her emotions had caused the computer to malfunction. Her imagination must have gone berserk. Surely she'd only experienced a very strange coincidence, and she would laugh about it tomorrow. She felt exhausted and wished she could go home and go to bed. She'd have to get to her car first. "You know, if we could get to our cars, we'd all have radios."

"Hey, that's right." Frank sank down beside her. "One video band converts to a radio signal for GSS emergency evacuations. That might be working."

"Only one way to find out," the young male technician said. "I want to get out of here. I called my wife, and she's okay, but she's home alone and very pregnant."

"Let's go." Frank sounded energized with an idea so Frank-like. "Everybody pull out your shirttail so the guy behind you can hold on."

"Or girl."

With general laughter, they all complied. Frank took the lead with Maya behind him. The eight people formed a queue and set off, feeling their way along the wall.

"Let me get my coat." Maya found her footlocker. She pulled out her coat and purse then grabbed Frank's shirttail.

They stopped at each of person's station in turn and collected coats, keys, and other needed items. At the end of the row of cubicles, Frank turned toward the elevators.

"Hey, Frank, don't you think we ought to take the stairs?" the young girl called.

"Oh, yea, I guess you're right." Frank laughed with them.

Maya felt proud of him. He could take a teasing, after all. He'd turned out to be rather heroic in a smalltime way.

The journey down the stairs became painstaking, with people falling into each other and stumbling. They found a few people from other floors in the stairwell, cleaning personnel and late night workers. Their good humor frayed.

Maya kept hoping the lights would soon come back on, and none of this would be necessary. She felt alarmed at the fact that the emergency backup power had failed.

Once they reached the parking garage, Frank unlocked his car and turned on the headlights. Everybody headed for their cars with shouts of "See you tomorrow" and "It's been real." Someone hummed *Auld Lang Syne*.

With great relief, Maya jumped into her car and turned on the ignition. Earlier, the video broadcasted the Morning Show on NBC, but only static came over the channel. She changed to the GSS emergency evacuation channel where nothing appeared to be broadcasting. Flipping on the heater, she headed toward the exit. Her co-workers honked as they drove out. Their headlights brought comforting illumination.

When Maya passed the guardhouse, she noticed someone had kicked down the wooden turnstile. Everyone probably felt a lot more scared than they let on. But no more than she.

Someone had tried to kill her. Someone had murdered her friend. Now someone or something had caused this terrible blackout.

Maya dismissed the ludicrous thought that she had caused this awful mess. What on earth had she been thinking? She inched along to exit the parking lot and merge with vehicles that filled the street. Everyone wanted to get somewhere in this bizarre blackout. The buildings around NexTech appeared abnormally dark. Had their backup systems failed too?

With chilled fingers, Maya tuned the dial on the emergency video band. The snow had stopped earlier in the day, leaving white crust on the ground and slush in the street.

A crackling preceded the precise, unemotional voice of an announcer. "This message was recorded at 7:32 p.m. and will be repeated every fifteen minutes until a new message is available." The dashboard clock read 7:49. "The power outage has spread throughout all New York. The backup power grid is down, too. It is believed the source of interruption came from the general area of the technology sector in Manhattan."

Maya gasped. She realized the problem could have originated in her building, but she couldn't imagine fully blaming this on her computer. Perhaps it had been a victim of the blackout, which happened for another reason. That seemed the only logical explanation.

The announcer continued, "If your emergency power does not come on, please notify GSS at one thousand, one hundred, one thousand. Stay tuned for new messages."

Frustrated, Maya sat in bumper-to-bumper traffic and watched vehicles move at a snail's pace. With the stoplights out, the intersections had become four-way stops, backed up as far as she could see.

She found the lack of a phone most annoying and inconvenient. Although it was a poor second best, she thought an email to her parents through the undependable Nanobot. *I'm all right, but caught in traffic. Be home as soon as possible. Don't worry.*

There was probably zero possibility that Father would read the email when the power came back on, even if it did get sent. Doing so always set him off, complaining about the use of cyberspace for personal gain. With great relief, Maya jumped into her car and turned on the ignition. Doubtless, Father would worry about her. She hoped her parents had fared all right and she intended to turn her car toward Walnut Street as soon as possible. At this rate, it would take her hours to get home. It occurred to her to leave the car and walk home even if it was a very long way. The memory of walking home with Lola changed her mind.

In the Sheraton Baghdad, the voice of the interpreter droned in Jason Carrick's ear, the accent so heavy as to make the English almost unintelligible. Carrick nodded respectfully to the president of Iraq and waited for him to finish his remarks. That worthy leader looked like a goon in his long robes. In fact, from the view at the head table, Carrick noticed that hardly a man in the banquet hall presented a manly appearance. They might as well wear dresses.

Carrick glanced down at the sharply pressed crease of his uniform trousers. He had gone over each detail of his attire before the ceremony and knew himself to cut the perfect military figure, down to the smooth combing of his wavy hair. Since he had been up at four, he'd even shaved a second time. He held his beret in his lap and sat at attention. These fools couldn't finish soon enough, although he'd be glad he'd showed up when the news services reported his award.

"Gentlemen," the interpreter said, "we are greatly honored this morning to award the Medal of Iraq to the man who has done so much to protect our democracy, General Jason Carrick, Commander in Chief of ORION, Operational Readiness / Intelligence On Nations."

With a smile, the president bobbed his head and moved one arm up and down. The long white sleeve of his *disha dasha* flowed with the saintly-looking gesture as if he blessed Carrick.

Polite, but probably genuine, applause issued from all parts of the room. Everyone rose, including two ORION colonels, stationed locally.

Snapping to attention, Carrick strode toward the podium with just the right mix of appreciation and superiority revealed in his expression. He shook the president's hand with strength and noticed the president's return felt limp. The man was probably a puppet of that Ayatollah in the south. Carrick had little tolerance or respect for the insanity of these people to mix religion and politics. Their fervor, no matter how misguided, did make them fearsome. He'd never underestimate their power and felt glad to have them in ORION's pocket.

Some people argued in English in the back of the room, but Carrick didn't dare turn around to look. At all times, he should appear unflappable.

Carrick stood before the microphone and spoke in a clear, low voice. He'd practiced the speech to make his inflections impeccable. After all, the video cameras were rolling. They almost always were when he spoke in public. "I thank you for this award and accept it in the name of my brave operatives in the field. I am humbly grateful that they carry out my orders and keep the Anaz-voohri threat at bay."

The voices in the back of the room grew in intensity. The ORION sergeant who guarded the inside of the door argued with the corporal Carrick had stationed outside the door. He concealed his anger at their rudeness. What in hell could cause his own men to interrupt him?

The corporal hurried toward the head table, waving a paper over his head.

Carrick decided he'd better finish quickly. "The security of Iraq is a high priority for ORION and will remain so. I thank you all."

"General." The corporal thrust the paper in front of Carrick, a worried expression on his face. "I'm sorry, General, but this is important."

It better be or your ass is grass, Carrick thought but said, "Excuse me, Gentlemen." He nodded to the audience. "Duty calls." He adjusted his glasses and read the signature, President Grant of the United States. The message said

Entire eastern seaboard in blackout. Your personal attention needed. "What the—?"

The corporal said, "Sir, your jet is waiting. I'm sorry I interrupted your speech."

"You did the right thing, Corporal."

"Thank you, sir," the corporal nearly shouted and flashed an I-told-you-so look at the sergeant by the door.

Carrick advanced through the room, carriage composed. He didn't want to upset these Iraqis just yet. He needed more information. Paparazzi hurried after him, video cams tucked under their arms. They wanted to know what had happened. He didn't have a clue himself, and that bothered him. He didn't like surprises.

While the sergeant held the door, Carrick passed through and addressed him brusquely. "So, you didn't want to disturb me?"

The sergeant blushed. "I thought...uh...we should wait till after the ceremony."

"You believe you can think?" Carrick glared at the dumbass. "Oh, the irony in that supposition. You can take those stripes off and give them to that capable young man." He indicated the corporal.

The sergeant's face crumpled. "I'm sorry, sir."

"Thank you, sir!" shouted the newly anointed sergeant.

Carrick passed through the Sheraton lobby, followed by his soldiers and the Paparazzi. He ignored their shouted questions.

Outside a helicopter hovered above the street, the buildings in the area too close set for a landing. Carrick stopped beneath the copter, shielding his eyes from morning sun. The wash the blades created felt good on his cheeks.

These were the moments he lived for. He waved to the pilot, who dropped the rope ladder. Carrick stuffed his beret inside his jacket and grabbed hold, securing himself with both legs and one hand. As he rose in the air beneath the rumbling blades, the soldiers saluted.

With his free hand, Carrick acknowledged the salute. What a photo op! At least one photographer had gotten a picture, he felt certain, before the ladder pulled him into the chopper.

Carrick crouched in the helicopter bay for the six-block ride to the airport above Baghdad's new high rises dotted among bombed-out buildings. He barely noticed the familiar landscape, so fixed was his mind on the stark message from Grant.

Something big had happened, but Carrick would be equal to whatever mission presented itself. The moment he arrived on the tarmac, he dashed into the waiting jet.

Even before they were airborne, his secretary, the ever proficient Flavia, appeared. She spoke with a slight Greek accent he had always enjoyed. "Sit down, sir. I'll brief you."

Flavia had the big tits and raw-boned look of a farmer's daughter. With such an appearance, one might expect her to be stupid, but Flavia's mind dwelt in logic with a phenomenal memory for detail. Carrick liked that unusual combination of qualities in her. In fact, he took comfort in them. Flavia allowed him to have a woman in his sphere without any consequences. No demands, no needs, just business.

Carrick sat in the captain's seat and strapped himself in what they called the cockpit rotunda, a circle of five seats directly behind the forward cabin, situated to facilitate interaction with the pilot in flight. Opposite him, Flavia pulled the belt across her flat tummy.

Tonight, with only two seats filled, Carrick wondered whether he might have allowed himself to get caught off guard. He had considered the errand to Iraq just politics and intended to return to the Headquarters Flotilla directly afterward. As a result, he hadn't requested his usual complement of advisors. To be wrong on that assessment was unforgivable, inconceivable. "What's up?"

Flavia gave her head a woeful shake, not a black hair moved within the bun. "The whole eastern seaboard blew. The power's been out for..." she consulted her watch then clasped her hands in her lap, "...two hours and fifty minutes."

"What about the backup battery grid?"

"It's down, too. That's probably why we've been called in."

This situation could deteriorate rapidly, a chance for Carrick to shine. "GSS emergency kicked in okay, didn't it?"

"Yes, but the hospitals are hard hit, and there's enormous traffic congestion."

"They can handle it."

Carrick had a lot of faith in GSS, ORION's parent organization, when it came to mundane chores like traffic and people moving. He couldn't trust it to track down Anaz-voohri or hybrids though, infested with them as it was. The task of killing those enemies of the Earth fell to ORION. Carrick felt proud of the successes the organization had had in the eight years he'd been at the helm. Thousands of dead hybrids around the world and even a few hundred Anaz-voohri.

"What's the likelihood that it's a terrorist attack?" he asked.

"None. I contacted CIA before you got here. They claim negative possibility of something this magnitude. The outage originated on Eight-Sixth Street in New York."

"Computer town. No surprises there. Any chance it's just technical difficulties? You know, Grant's pretty quick to jump in these days with the election less than a year away. Wants to show he's protecting the people."

"We've got it tighter." Flavia gloated. "It's NexTech."

"Fuck. An Anaz-voohri mole!"

"Exactly." Flavia unclasped her hands in a gesture that for her indicated excitement. "This is huge. Nobody else could have done it."

When Carrick took command of ORION, he'd read the files on seven women whom the Anaz-voohri abducted as children and genetically altered. The Anaz-voohri then planted the women in human society to disrupt in ways not as yet clear. He'd always known they were a bad business. Although with no timetable for their activation as moles, more pressing matters took his attention. He wished he'd never allowed this mole to live.

Carrick asked, "How in hell did she accomplish this?"

"With her mind, of course." Flavia's tone conveyed how impressed she felt. "I wonder if even she understands how powerful she is."

"Those Anaz-voohri bastards are clever, no question about it. This mole of theirs could do a lot of damage if it got in all the computer systems of the world." Pushing his glasses up on his head, Carrick rubbed his eyes.

"Implant bothering you?" Flavia's voice carried polite professional concern.

Whenever he got tired, his eye hurt even though he'd not admit it. Carrick would never forget the day he'd lost his left eye to a hybrid in a firefight. He pulled down his glasses and blinked to focus on Flavia. "I'm fine. Now, let's see. What's the mole's name?"

"It's Maya Rembrandt. Super brain, degrees from Yale and MIT in AI. She's been at NexTech almost two years."

"That one?" Carrick felt jealous. He wished he could remember those facts. "Hell, I thought she was still in college. I didn't connect the dots."

"That's what you've got us for."

Carrick couldn't imagine who she meant other than herself. No one else knew about the moles. Maybe Flavia considered herself in the plural. He blew off the thought, however amusing two of her might be as a fantasy. He had big game to bag today.

"The seven sisters of the Pleiades I like to call them." A sincere look on her taut face, Flavia raised a hand in the air and poised a finger. "Want the names of the others? There's Celene Dupres, there's—"

"Never mind. We'll have to go after them later." Carrick tapped the phone console button and chose New York. "We've got to stop this one now."

With a faintly self-satisfied smile, Flavia folded her arms and watched him.

After one ring, Captain Hillenbrand's crisp voice came on the line. "Ready for orders, General."

"You've got an Anaz-voohri mole loose in New York. Her name is Maya Rembrandt. Works at NexTech. Lives on?" He raised an eyebrow to Flavia.

"Walnut Street."

"Walnut Street. Shoot to kill and ask questions later."

"Got it," said Captain Hillenbrand.

"You can arrest any NexTech employee, just to be on the safe side. Somebody will know where she is. Use every available officer."

"We'll not let you down, sir."

"I'm proud of you and all your men." Carrick tapped the console button and spoke to the pilot. "Head for the Flotilla. We'll take it on to New York." He'd eaten no more than courtesy required because Arab food always gave him cramps. He felt famished. "Get me some sausage and eggs."

Immediately, Flavia unbuckled and headed for the aft cabin.

Chapter Five

Sitting in the semi-darkness in Mythos Headquarters, Dylan and his boss listened to the all-points bulletin on the contraband police radio. The computer screens had all gone black.

The emergency power supply threading along the floor reflected shadows on Archer's visage. "They've put out quite a dragnet. NexTech must have three hundred employees in that building."

"Or more. They're sure as hell after Maya Rembrandt." Dylan felt excited. He needed to get moving, doing something. "This puts the Compson murder into a whole different perspective. The idea was to keep Maya alive. Why Lola had to die I don't know, but Maya's turned out to be very valuable property."

"GSS has to be running scared to issue a warrant like this." The chair creaked as Archer shifted position. "There'll be an international scandal if they arrest innocent people just because they work at NexTech."

Dylan rose and leaned against the desk. "How could one woman have accomplished such a feat, knocking out the electricity in more than thirteen states?"

"Not possible unless she's an Anaz-voohri."

"Or she's been altered by the Anaz-voohri." Dylan remembered what a pleasant woman Maya had seemed. It was quite a stretch to imagine her as a biological instrument of Anaz-voohri destructive force. "Something's not right, Archer. I think it's time I paid a visit to the Center for Evolutionary Medicine. If anyone has records on Maya, they would."

"Back to your old stomping grounds, huh?"

"I don't remember the original surgery. I was five at the time." Dylan felt a sense of melancholy. "But every year until I was grown, my mother took me for a checkup.

She had great respect for the CEM doctors. They cured congenital blindness, something unheard of. They could do no wrong in her opinion. Truthfully, the place always gave me the creeps, and I can't tell you why."

Archer lumbered up and clapped Dylan on the back. "This is as good a night to go as any, but be careful. Security will probably be tighter with the emergency power grid out too. We've only got lights here because I unearthed an antique diesel generator. It doesn't work very well, but at least we're not in pitch black."

"You mean organizations used to have individual emergency power systems?"

Archer nodded. "Businesses too. Even some individuals had them years ago."

"Times have sure changed. I think I'd have liked living in a more independent era." Dylan rummaged in the desk until he found a pair of night vision goggles and a Maglight, threw on his parka, and checked the charge on his phase gun.

How fine it must have been to have lived early in the previous century with nothing more to do than spend the day at the ballpark. In his romantic fantasy, Dylan would sit in the dugout with no worries any deeper than whether or not he would get up to bat. One day he might realize his dream to move to the boondocks and play ball.

With the elevator out, he sprinted up the stairs two at a time and stepped out into the cold air. The street looked peculiar, full of cars shining headlights, but with no streetlights or building lights anywhere, the city had lost its glow. Dylan felt charged with the inner certainty that he was about to discover something important.

Maya glanced at the display on her dashboard. The gas gauge registered three quarters empty. She'd hardly traveled five miles, most of the time spent sitting at stoplights that didn't work, waiting her turn to go through intersections. She flipped the switch on the blower off and on. The heater had quit working, and the windows had fogged up. The video channel buzzed abrasively, but she didn't turn it down out of fear of missing a broadcast.

Blowing on her hands, Maya tried to warm them. She pulled the collar of her coat against her throat, feeling more irritated every moment. She hated being cold. She hated having the events of her life out of control. Both together really put her on edge.

The broadcast update came on. The reporter's voice whined, "This message was recorded at 10:12 p.m. and will be repeated every fifteen minutes until a new message is available. The outage has spread up and down the whole Eastern seaboard. Arrest warrants have been issued for all employees of NexTech. Should you know of one or see one, call Global Security Sector one thousand, one hundred, one thousand. Again the number is one thousand, one hundred, one thousand. Remember, it is your civic duty to report any suspicious activity."

What in hell had happened for arrest warrants to be issued? How could the NexTech employees be culpable for the blackout? A memory of that little voice she'd heard inside her head returned. She never could explain it as coming from her own mind, from the Fairy Godmother, or from outside.

She had always trusted her mental acuity, her memory, all of her brain functions to operate at a superior level. Now, she couldn't trust any of them. If she was the one who had caused the blackout, she didn't know how she'd done it. Worse yet, others must think she had done it or knew who did if her company was accused.

Terrified and confused, Maya drove onto the sidewalk to turn her car around. Drivers honked at her and the trucker behind her shouted obscenities. Finally, she headed toward the George Washington Bridge. She didn't want to go to jail.

She decided to try to get to her parents' summer home outside Markle Falls. Without a key she'd have to break in, but they would understand. She'd call them when she got there since it was a long way, she'd have to find a gas station.

Near the bridge, Maya heard sirens all around. Thick traffic forced her to sit in line to get to the access road. She fiddled with the dials on the Tango's computer, but it remained silent, and she couldn't understand why.

Shivering and scared, she sat so long that the gas gauge slid down to empty. The car sputtered and died. The gauges gave nothing but incorrect readings. Was it only this morning that she'd planned to drive the car to the repair shop? That seemed a lifetime ago.

"I need you, little Tango. You can't quit on me now." But it didn't talk back to her like the computer at work. No longer able to contain tears of frustration and fear, Maya sat in the car and sobbed.

"Hey, lady." A burly man knocked on the window. "Need any help?"

At first Maya felt relieved. Maybe this man would give her a ride. Then she imagined having to talk to him, having him discover that she worked at NexTech. Next thing she knew they'd haul her into jail. She couldn't take that chance.

"No, no, I'll be fine." She held up her arm and tapped her wrist. "I'll call my husband."

In actuality she wore no phone, but the man didn't seem to notice. With a shrug, he turned and climbed into a nearby four-by-four.

Maya had intended to buy a phone tonight to replace the one she elost when Lola...the image of Lola lying dead in the street threatened to overwhelm Maya. She cried harder.

Even as her body shook with sobs, she knew she had to help herself. Strength had to come from within her being.

Resolving to act like a grown up, Maya dried her tears and considered her situation logically. The back seat held nothing except a Jackson Pollock lithograph covered by a wool blanket, and she never stowed anything in the trunk. She wrapped her muffler around her neck, buttoned the collar, and pulled on her gloves. With her purse and the red and green plaid blanket in tow, she abandoned the car and set off.

In the distance, a patrol car threaded its way through stalled traffic. A police officer walked alongside, checking license plates and speaking to drivers.

Maya raised the yellow hood on her ski jacket and drooped it over her face. She felt like a fugitive, a most unpleasant sensation. Without a clear idea of where she could go on foot, she decided to walk across the bridge and find a motel room. At least she had her credit card.

Dashing across the street between cars, Dylan passed his palm over the identity scanner then climbed on his Dial-a-Bike parked inconspicuously around the corner from Mythos. He headed toward the CEM several miles away. He didn't take time to let down the sides or put up the top. He considered flying it but, with the lighting situation so significantly different, decided not to take the chance. It might not be possible to see other small craft in the air. He set the dial for motorcycle.

The small size of his Dial-a-Bike allowed Dylan to squirrel around other vehicles and make good progress. Frustrated drivers yelled at each other and honked their horns, worse than usual.

Dylan wondered whether Maya might be stranded somewhere in traffic. Perhaps she had planned this episode and prepared a getaway. He'd be very surprised to discover that, but he wanted to keep his attitude open. Her gentle manner made him doubt she'd have evil intentions. He hoped some nutty cop didn't shoot her before Dylan got a chance to find out more and make a halfway informed judgment about her.

When he arrived at the CEM, Dylan drove around the grounds to assess the complex, with its arcades of stucco buildings barely visible on the small rise created by sloping artificial grass. None of the fountains worked, and all the windows were dark. He couldn't see any people milling around outside or know how many remained in the building.

Dylan rounded the corner, and his headlights revealed the night watchman on duty at the gate. If he took the guy out, no telling who would notice with cars going by in the street. It seemed a better bet to sidestep him and take the chance that everyone had left the building empty. Certainly, the alarms wouldn't work with all the chaos tonight.

After parking the Dial-a-Bike in the alley, he donned night vision goggles and stuffed a length of nylon rope in his coat pocket then slipped around the back side and scaled the CEM wall. He dropped down and crept along an arcade, keeping close to the building. His boots squished on the crusty turf.

The wool of his parka snagged on the stucco and he scraped his hands. He had no difficulty seeing, but the complex looked greenish-gray in the goggles. He remembered the layout and slipped around the surgery wing without encountering anyone then dashed to the door of the administration building.

Dylan felt along the smooth glass panes until he determined the exact center of the main door. He aimed his phase gun and blasted a hole through the doors. The glass splintered and crashed down, creating more noise than he preferred, but some risks were acceptable. He needed information.

As he holstered the gun and stepped inside, he heard running feet and men yelling. "What the hell are you doing?" and "Get out of here."

Two men ran toward him. One in a white lab coat appeared middle aged and in fairly good shape. The other had to be at least seventy. Dylan popped him in the face.

The old man tumbled down, tripping Dylan. The fall knocked his goggles askew.

The other man shouted, "How dare you?" and grabbed Dylan by the shoulders as if to shake him.

Off balance, Dylan threw his arms around the fellow's chest and squeezed. They fell together and rolled around, each trying to get a punch in. Glass shards crackled beneath them. Dylan pulled free and landed a solid blow on the jaw. The fellow grunted and fell back.

After straightening the goggles, Dylan whisked out the rope and tied the man's hands together and then his feet. The fellow cursed, kicked, and tried to free himself. When Dylan managed to secure him he had used all the rope.

Slinging the dazed old man over his shoulder, Dylan hurried down the hall, following glow paint on the floor. Too focused to do more than notice that his hands felt damp, Dylan kept going. If he left blood traces, too bad. When he found a linen closet, he took his groaning burden inside and set him down.

"Sorry, old man." Dylan grabbed a handful of towels, closed the door, and lashed it shut. He pulled the Maglight out of his pocket and flipped it on. He'd gotten his first piece of luck, the Maglight hadn't broken or been lost in the scuffle.

When he returned to the entry, Dylan flashed the light on the fellow on the floor. Inspection of the rope showed he'd not get free for a while although he appeared well enough because he let out a stream of curses.

"You probably won't believe me, Doc, but I regret having to do this." Dylan tied one of the towels around the man's mouth.

"You'll rot in jail for this." The fellow muttered almost incoherently.

"You might be surprised at which side of the law I'm on."

The night watchman worried Dylan, so he ran from the building and slipped up behind the guardhouse. On risking a peek inside, he found it empty. Maybe the watchman had gone home before the noise, or maybe he'd gone for help.

Dylan hurried back into the administration building and examined his blood-covered hands. He didn't know whose. In a restroom, he washed them off. He had a lot of nicks and scrapes but felt good to go.

No longer caring who heard him, he ran to the records room. He had only a matter of minutes before someone discovered him. Dylan blasted the door open and shone the light on the files.

Arranged by year they read 1995 to 2005. After that, he supposed the CEM maintained all files on computer. If the files he needed existed only on computer, this whole trip would have been a waste. He hoped to hell he found something or he'd have to come back and do it all over with much greater risk.

Not knowing where to begin, he looked first in 1995. He found no file for Rembrandt so preceded through the years. By the time he got to 2002, he doubted his reasoning that Maya had been a patient here.

The man tied up in the hall started to yell. Dylan wondered if the night watchman had returned and untied him. Who else had heard him or the shattered glass, for that matter? If the watchman had decided to go for help, it might be too late, anyway. Dylan might as well find out as much as he could.

In 2003, he thumbed to the file. Rembrandt, cross-referenced to Porter. He found it difficult to read through the goggles, set them up on his head, and aimed the Maglight at the text.

She'd been born Maya Porter in Pennsylvania then placed with the Rembrandts for re-assimilation. What had she needed re-assimilating from? There followed a list of her yearly checkups. One notation revealed it all. He muttered, "Transported to home world in 2003. Recombining of DNA successful."

Dylan had no idea why, but he sure as hell knew who. Those damned Anaz-voohri had abducted her and taken her to the Pleiades. He skimmed through other files and discovered a whole mélange of surgeries to mask Anaz-voohri characteristics, implantation of technological devices, miracle cures, all manner of bizarre procedures dating back over twenty years.

How dare these bastards call themselves doctors? Hybrids themselves or worse, human traitors. He'd been right to distrust them. They bore as much blame as the Anaz-voohri. Dylan wished he hadn't treated those two in the hall so well. Both of them probably plied the devil's trade.

Unable to absorb the impact of the words he read, Dylan grabbed Maya's file. He'd take it back for Archer to decipher. On a hunch, he emptied the whole drawer's worth of files into a plastic wastebasket.

Unable to resist looking at his own records, he returned to 2002 and grabbed the file called Brady. The words Extended Development jumped out at him. What the hell did that mean? He'd been blind. The doctors repaired his eyes so he could see. He flipped open the file and read that a "considered" decision had been made to genetically alter Dylan to give him psychic powers.

Thunderstruck, he realized he hadn't always been clairvoyant. He'd been too small to know. "Considered" must have meant the doctors didn't inform his parents about tweaking the surgery for their own purposes. Dylan felt violated in a way he'd never imagined could happen.

This was no time to dwell on emotion. He dumped his file in too, picked up the wastebasket, and dashed out the door. Back in the corridor, he turned the opposite way to avoid having to encounter the bastard he'd tied up. Next to the records room, he passed several examining rooms then went out through a crash bar at the end of the building.

Once outdoors, he hurried to the wall, threw the wastebasket over, and dropped down the other side. He climbed onto the Dial-a-Bike and pulled out into thick traffic. Curiosity got the better of him and he drove past the entrance to CEM. He pointed the headlights directly at the guardhouse. Empty still. The watchman must have gone home with the crowd.

There'd be no going home for Dylan tonight. He and Archer had a lot of reading to do, whether the electricity came back on or not. Dylan flipped on the video channel, the nearest thing to news reporting in this emergency. A pre-recorded message came on.

On Dylan's return to Mythos, he dumped the files on Archer's desk and went to clean up. He left his boss alone in the main office, reading by Maglight. No other operatives had ventured in since the blackout.

After an unpleasant shower in cold water, Dylan applied antiseptic to his hands and pulled on fresh jeans and a black t-shirt. He anticipated that Archer would want him to go out again, even though his shift ended at midnight.

Archer knocked on Dylan's open office door.

"Come on in." Dylan sat on the bed.

Archer remained in the doorway, his silhouette faintly lit. "This Rembrandt woman." He spoke rapidly, in a hushed tone. "Her genes were altered to carry plans in her body for an Anaz-voohri takeover. I don't know how they can do that, but we better believe they can."

Dylan pulled on his socks and boots. "Looks like her programming's been activated. Maya's a living time bomb. Wonder if she even knows it?" He was starting to feel very sorry for her, no matter how much she knew.

"And that's just the beginning. Your hunch about bringing the whole drawer was right on." Archer flipped on the Maglight and consulted the folder. "I found references to six more little girls who were reprogrammed. Celene Dupres, Astoria Blair, Ally Curran, Maeve Shivaun, names I don't know, but also Electra Monroe, head of Medusa's Hand, and Tierney Grant, for God's sake, the President's daughter."

Does that mean the President is a hybrid? Dylan but didn't mention his musing because he noticed a rift in his boss's normally cool demeanor. Archer might have some strong feelings on the subject, considering his long-time friendship with President Grant.

Dylan didn't know any of the women either except by reputation. Electra Monroe was a brave woman who spoke out against the Anaz-voohri and ran the dissident society, openly critical of GSS. Everybody in the world knew what Tierney Grant had for breakfast since she'd become the media's darling.

"Well," Archer sighed. "It's obvious that the Anaz-voohri plot is deep and wide. The Anaz-voohri intend to control communications across the entire world by wiping out electrical power. And they're going to try to use this Rembrandt woman to do it."

Dylan's heart hammered. "That's one short step to complete domination of humans."

"We can't wait to find out how they intend to use the others."

Grabbing his phase gun, Dylan slid it into the holster. He hoped he'd be ready to do whatever his boss said. "We've already got Anaz-voohri and undetectable hybrids in many places. They've infiltrated GSS, and maybe even ORION."

With a voice like gravel, Archer said, "I see no alternative except to kill the women, if we can find them all. Otherwise, they'll bring down world society and pave the way for complete Anaz-voohri rule."

Dylan expelled a long breath. *Do we have to?* He wanted to ask, but he'd not make a repulsive order more difficult for both of them. He'd do what he had to do.

"Find this Rembrandt woman. Now." Archer walked into the main room. His footsteps echoed away.

Chapter Six

Dylan closed his eyes. His ability to see remote places hadn't failed him, but he'd never been under so much pressure before. He'd always considered his gift as one given by God, not by alien Anaz-voohri technology. How was he supposed to feel about that? He'd give the matter more thought later, after this crisis had passed. And it would pass. It had to.

The moment he let go of worry and relaxed into a trance, he floated in his mind's eye to a park bench with frosty grass beneath it. There lay Maya apparently asleep or at least with her eyes closed. *Where was she?* He asked his subconscious mind. *Just west of the George Washington Bridge on Farouk Street,* it answered.

Dylan jumped up and headed through the main room, throwing on his parka. He didn't speak. What was there to say? Archer didn't repeat the order. He didn't need to, it still rang in Dylan's head.

When he jumped astride the Dial-a-Bike, snow spit in Dylan's face. The dashboard gauge indicated a wind chill factor of fifteen above. Not looking forward to the unpleasant ride, Dylan let down the sides, put up the top, and started the heater. As he set off, he noticed the city looked eerily dark.

Along with New York City police, ORION officers on Dial-a-Bikes wove through traffic, an uncommon sight. They generally did undercover or sensitive work, not traffic control. No doubt their primary objective was to arrest NexTech employees in general and Maya in particular.

Some drivers had abandoned their cars, and many walked the streets. Stores and apartment buildings floated in the background like hulking shadows. Candlelight illuminated occasional windows in a grotesquely festive way.

From time to time power went out when terrorists managed to strike electrical plants, but failsafe systems always came on. The city had never experienced a blackout of this duration, more than three hours, although Dylan had heard they happened years ago when he was small.

With traffic so stopped up, he drove on sidewalks and through alleys. Even so, he'd have to take care with so many pedestrians about. It would likely require half an hour or more to get to the George Washington Bridge. He had little assurance of finding Maya on the park bench by then.

That she had fallen asleep in the cold boded ill. People could freeze to death in a short time in this kind of weather. Of course, he didn't know why he worried about that since he had orders to kill her anyway. She appeared to be a marked woman by all accounts.

Dylan tried to visualize himself drawing a bead on her and shooting her. Could he see that sweet face and strawberry cream skin in the sight and still pull the trigger?

Imagination failed him. The thought of choking her seemed even worse. He'd have to touch her to do that. Fulfilling Archer's order might be the toughest thing Dylan would ever have to do. Not that he cared about Maya as an individual. He hardly knew her. He'd promised himself to avoid women, so he didn't intend to get to know her. What appalled him was the waste of a life, of the potential never realized. And this woman had incredible gifts.

Of course, her mind had been doctored by those bastard Anaz-voohri. Dylan didn't understand very well what they'd done to her, not much better than he knew how they'd tampered with his mind or his eyes. Somehow they had created his remote viewing ability, what he'd always thought a God-given gift. He and Maya had something in common; both violated at an unforgivable level.

Maya had to die because the Anaz-voohri had made a pawn of her. Dylan had the ability to find her because the

Anaz-voohri had done the same to him. In part, he had to kill her to end the Anaz-voohri's ability to use humans as pawns. Freedom cost so much sometimes that he tried not to dwell on the consequences. What else could he do?

As Dylan passed a supermarket, fluorescent lights blinked on, illuminating empty aisles. Two surprised looters dropped armloads of cardboard boxes and ran out the door. The parking lot lights began to glow yellow, first low then with stronger brilliance. For a moment, Dylan didn't make the logical deduction.

A truck behind him honked. Then Dylan laid on his horn. Vehicles up and down the street played a hallelujah chorus for the return to some kind of normalcy.

With a somewhat more confident attitude, Dylan sped across the bridge and found Farouk Street. Within a community of family homes he saw a small park with children's play equipment, braziers, and picnic benches. Nightlights from neighboring houses brightened the space. A patrol car parked in front of one looked empty.

After driving to the next block, he shut off the engine and headed back toward the park. He could see that a person lay on a bench and didn't doubt it was Maya. With the unpleasant snow wetting his face, he wondered if she were unconscious. Otherwise, how could she just lie there? He tapped his parka where the phase gun lay in the holster. To avoid drawing any undue attention to himself, he hurried but didn't run.

An NYC police officer strode toward the park bench from the other direction. He carried a phase gun and wore a gas mask.

Dylan moved into the shadows of a slide and swing set, rolling ideas for a ruse over in his mind. He needed to prevent the police from taking Maya if possible. No telling how long they might incarcerate her or whether she'd have access to computers in jail. Regardless, Mythos would have a much more difficult time preventing her from creating another blackout or worse.

The police officer walked behind the bench, but the occupant didn't move. Was she dead already? He considered slipping up behind the officer and knocking him unconscious. A glance around proved inconclusive. Other police might be in the area. They did tend to travel in pairs. He couldn't figure out how to rid himself of the man to get to Maya.

The police officer lifted Maya's hood and examined her face.

Dylan sprinted around the bench. "Darling, is it really you?" He lunged for Maya and gathered her into his arms. "Thank God, I've found you." She felt limp but not in that heavy way of dead bodies.

The police officer pushed the gas mask on top of his head. "You know this woman?"

"She's my wife." Dylan pulled back the soggy hood and wiped Maya's cheeks. "Speak to me, honey."

Maya moaned, and her eyes fluttered open. She appeared to be very cold but all right.

"Well, at least she's alive. You want any help with her?"

Fearing the police officer would ask for identification, Dylan set her up. "I've got my Dial-a-Bike nearby. I'll take her to the hospital to be checked over." He chafed Maya's hand. "Can you walk, honey?"

"Honey?" Maya looked at him in obvious confusion.

Clearly, Dylan needed to get her out of this place before she blew his trick. "Come on, let's walk. It will help get your circulation going."

"Okay." She sounded docile as a child.

Pulling Maya up, Dylan laid her arm around his shoulder and supported her waist.

"Let me help." The police officer positioned himself on the other side of Maya and hauled her free arm up to his neck.

Together they walked across the park. Although she moved stiffly, she bore her own weight. Anxious to get her to a more private location, Dylan used his remote to raise the sides of the Dial-a-Bike.

The police officer supported Maya while Dylan leaped over the seat. He reached out to her, and she took his hand like she knew what she was doing. The police officer gave her an assist, and she hoisted herself up behind Dylan.

The police officer fished in his pocket, maybe for his car remote. "I'll give you an escort to the hospital."

"I don't think it's necessary, but thanks anyway." Dylan turned the key in the ignition.

"She could be in shock, you know."

"Thanks, Officer," Maya said and leaned on Dylan's back, her coat cold and damp against him. "Let's go, honey."

Who'd have thought it? The woman had bought into the game. If she only knew what lay in store for her. Dylan hit the button to drop the sides. He couldn't get away fast enough.

Without speaking they sped through the streets and back toward the bridge. Dylan wanted to create as much distance between them and that police officer as possible.

Maya felt groggy and listless. Her clothes clung to her, and the engine of the Dial-a-Bike roared in her ears. The enclosed vehicle with its wide seat and silver horns was the farthest thing from a white horse she could possibly imagine, but this guy Dylan seemed to be rescuing her. For that, she gratefully clung to his waist, a good and secure feeling.

Earlier, she'd had an almost overwhelming urge to fall asleep. In fact, she may have done so because she thought she remembered lying down on a park bench, a stupid thing to do in this weather. The next thing she knew Dylan had called her honey. Perhaps she'd dreamed that part.

In any case, she had her wits about her now. "Where are we going?" she shouted.

Dylan shrugged and said something she couldn't hear. He pointed up ahead.

They were approaching the bridge where the local police had set up a roadblock. Many cars sat still, unable to cross over because the surrounding access roads appeared cordoned off. In water repellant overcoats, a dozen police officers, two at a time, talked to drivers in campers, trucks, and cars.

When the Dial-a-Bike came to a stop, Dylan said, "Looks like we don't have a choice but to go through the checkpoint. Are you okay with that?"

"No, not really." Maya's hands trembled but she tried to stay calm. "The last I heard I was on the most-wanted list because I work at NexTech."

"Yea, I know. Do you have your ID with you?"

Glad she'd had the foresight to conceal her purse, Maya patted her jacket. "It's in the zipper pocket."

"I doubt they'll do a body search. I'll show my ID and say you're my wife and you've lost your belongings in the snow."

"That seems a bit foolhardy, but I appreciate the gesture." Maya was touched. These past few hours she'd felt very alone. "Why are you doing this for me?"

"Don't ask."

His evasive response made Maya even more curious. He must be a member of law enforcement, after all. It couldn't be a coincidence that he had found her. He must have been looking for her. But why?

A police officer knocked on the window. "Open up, please." He looked like a St. Bernard with his gas mask hanging around his neck.

Another police officer stood behind him, holding a hand computer. "Step out of the vehicle, please."

"Of course." Dylan climbed out.

Fortunately, he held a hand up for Maya. Since she had no practice in negotiating the bulky machine, she felt certain she would descend awkwardly even with his help, and she did.

"IDs, please." Despite the polite words, the police officer's face looked wary and haggard. He'd probably had a rough time since the power outage began. Maya could sympathize.

Extracting a wallet from his parka, Dylan removed his ID and held it up with a questioning look.

The police officer with the computer took it, entered the ID number into the machine, and read the screen. "Dylan Brady, 1140 East Twelfth Street?"

"That's me."

"Pilot for Puddle Jumpers Shuttle Service?"

"My secret's out." Dylan grinned at Maya, as if he knew she'd been trying to decipher him.

Maya wished she could join the light mood, but she worried. She had no confidence at all that his deception would work. The thought of going to jail sent shivers through her.

The police officer with the computer handed the ID back to Dylan and spoke to her. "Let's see yours, please, Miss."

"Uh, that's Mrs." Dylan pulled her against him with casual intimacy. "This is my wife, Maya Brady. She lost her ID in the snow. We'll apply for a new one first thing tomorrow." He definitely looked like what he pretended to be; he looked like he could be her husband.

The first police officer spoke to Maya. "Ma'am, we need to see ID, driver's license, or work card. Do you have any of those?"

"No, I'm sorry I don't." Maya hated lying, but she didn't know what else to do.

"Then we'll have to take you in for questioning and verification of fingerprints and photo." The police officer looked more harried by the moment. "I'd do it right here, but our computer's battery is almost down, and there's no way to recharge it here."

"But, Officer," Dylan said, "can't this wait until tomorrow? You can see that my wife has had a difficult time in the storm. She's cold. She needs medical attention."

The first police officer took Maya's arm. "You'll come with me, please." To Dylan he said, "You may pick her up at Washington Station in about three hours, assuming she checks out."

Dylan bent toward her and took her face between his hands, strong but gentle beneath the leather gloves. "Let me at least kiss her good-bye."

What on earth? Was he actually going to kiss her? Maya felt fascinated by Dylan's touch. His breath was warm as his handsome face drew close to hers. Entranced by the magic of the moment, Maya forgot the ruse and opened her mouth to him. His tongue entered and flicked inside in an intimate connection that made Maya want to draw close to him. Then he brushed her lips with a kiss just a fragment longer and sweeter than a familiar husband-to-wife peck.

The first police officer gave him a withering look. "Mr. Brady, desist."

Even Maya thought the kiss carried the pretense too far, but its power staggered her. The strength of Dylan's presence awed her. She wanted to remain connected to him.

"If you cooperate, madam," said the police officer with the computer as he took her other arm, "we won't have to use handcuffs."

"Okay," she whispered, scared of what she might have to face alone at the police station. Life had become bizarre in the past few days. She felt like a pawn in a game she didn't know the rules to.

Looking dashed, Dylan raised his hands in the air in a helpless gesture. "Good luck, Maya."

"Thank you for trying to help me." Maya gave him the best smile she could muster then bit her lip to repress tears.

As the police officers escorted her to a squad car, Maya glanced over her shoulder. Dylan watched her as if she headed for the guillotine. She felt about as hopeless as a condemned person. What would they do to her when they found out she had her ID with her? Could that be called resisting arrest? Would they send her to prison?

People in the other stopped vehicles watched her. They probably thought her a criminal. She wanted to shout that she hadn't done anything wrong. She felt embarrassed, afraid, and angry all at the same time. She wished Dylan could intercede once more. She told herself to get a grip. He'd already done more than enough. Prince Charming didn't exist in real life. This would all work out. She would explain her situation to the police, and they would understand and let her go home within the hour.

Maya's teeth chattered as she sat in the chilly squad car and waited for her captors to seem organized. Finally, they turned on the heater and set off, driving a few blocks to one of the dingiest buildings she'd ever seen. She'd hardly ever been in this part of town except when on her way somewhere else. Everything looked dirty and unkempt. Trash blown against the wire fence had yellowed and frozen.

Inside, the precinct station interrogation room, or whatever they called it, looked even worse. With all the terrorist bombs going off, what a shame one hadn't hit this place and forced the insurance company to pay for renovation. The beaten up plastic desks, circa 1970, went with the steam radiators that hissed and knocked.

The police officer who brought her in directed her to sit beside a desk. When he tried to open a drawer, it creaked and caught. With an exasperated sigh, he jerked it open and took out a fingerprinting pad.

The jig was up.

"My name is Maya Rembrandt. I work at NexTech." She pulled her ID out and gave it to him.

"Rembrandt? I thought your name was Brady." The officer gave her a quizzical look.

"The...uh...marriage   is   unconventional. We...uh...my parents don't know about Dylan." At least that much was true. "The phone number on there is my parents'. Could you call them?"

After a long look at the ID card, the police officer said, "I'm sorry, but I'm going to have to hold you."

"Just because of where I work?"

"Doesn't seem quite fair." He pulled out handcuffs and dangled them in front of her. "I'm just doing my job, miss, so if you'll go quietly..."

Every part of her soul wanted to cry out at this indignity, but if there was ever a time to keep cool, this had to be it. "Don't I have one phone call coming?"

"You'll get your phone call after I fill out this paperwork."

The only good thing about her wretched situation was that the radiator heat dried out her clothes, helping Maya feel warmer. She told the policeman about sitting at her terminal when the lights went out. The blackout had surprised her as much as everyone else. She chose to disregard the fact that she had been crying as irrelevant and too personal to reveal.

The police officer seemed to believe her and, after finishing his forms, let her phone her parents. Maya told her mother about the blackout, her fruitless trip in the car, and her arrest. She left out the part about falling asleep on the park bench and Prince Charming charging to the rescue. Her mother would ask more questions than Maya knew the answers to right now.

Carolyn promised to get everything resolved and said she and Terrence would come for Maya first thing in the morning. Her mother cautioned her to get a good night's sleep.

In jail? How would that be possible?

The police officer led her back to a shabby cell, its wood floor pocked and worn. Two cots lined the wall with a toilet between, the kind with a string pull right out of a horror movie.

When the police officer locked the cell, he spoke kindly for the first time. "Get some rest. You may need it tomorrow." He tossed a blanket through the bars.

His retreating footsteps made Maya feel lonely. Unwilling to disrobe in such a place, she sank down on the cot, careless of its lumpy foam mattress. Covering herself with the blanket, she hoped neither Frank nor any of her co-workers ended up forced to spend the night in jail.

How awful everything had been all day and all night with one exception. Dylan had tried to rescue her, not once but twice, in the park and at the bridge. Would he come for her here at the jail, too, as the officer had suggested?

Why did Dylan care what happened to her? Or even know about her troubles? His refusal to say scared her. If he weren't a cop, might he be a private detective? He couldn't be a Puddle Jumper pilot. He knew too much for that. Dylan seemed so clever and resourceful he could probably be anything he wanted. His kiss, so unexpected, felt warm and exciting. It had made her yearn for him in a most unsettling way. She remembered that he had meant it only as a tactic to fool the police, and she pushed it out of her mind. Hard as that was to do, she needed sleep but doubted she'd get any in these awful surroundings.

The next morning, a brown-skinned female police officer awakened Maya. "Hey, Rembrandt, your folks are here. Get yourself together."

Maya bounded off the cot. She'd lain awake most of the night, but must have dozed off. Her back and arms ached. Bone weary, she needed first to brush her teeth and second to bring some normalcy into her life.

On standing, she realized someone else also arrested during the night. A gray-haired Hispanic woman lay asleep in the other cot. She looked familiar, perhaps someone from NexTech. Maya hoped she was mistaken. Surely, the police wouldn't stoop to arresting a poor immigrant cleaning women.

Hanging the ski jacket over her shoulders, Maya waited for the chubby female police officer to unlock the cell door then followed her into the interrogation area. The room looked even more forlorn in morning light filtered through windows that appeared unwashed.

Beneath one of the windows on a wooden bench sat her parents. They rose as Maya entered. Both looked as exhausted as she felt.

"Are you all right?" Carolyn took Maya's hands. "Has anyone hurt you?"

Terrence squeezed Maya's shoulders. "We're very glad to see you."

Seeing her parents relieved Maya. "I need to go home."

"Of course you do." Carolyn looked uncharacteristically disheveled. Her hair crept out of the beautician's careful shaping.

The policewoman shoved a paper and pen in front of Maya. "You need to sign this."

When Maya took them, her father held up a cautioning hand. "Wait. What is this?"

"A release form," the policewoman said, "guaranteeing she's not been harmed while incarcerated. It's routine."

"Pardon me." Terrence laid a protective arm on Maya's shoulder. "We don't know whether she's been harmed or not. We're going to take her straight to a doctor. If she's okay, we'll sign."

"That's not the way it works, sir." Mocking respect shone in the policewoman's eyes. She held up handcuffs. "You'd better send your doctor here. I can't release her without this signature."

Carolyn glared at the policewoman. "You wouldn't dare."

"Under no circumstances will I remain here." Maya scribbled her name on the release. "Let's go."

"Thank you, madam." Terrence ushered Carolyn and Maya out the door.

Although Maya's feet had swollen inside the snow boots, she felt glad to have them because she had to wade in slush to get to her parents' Lexus parked down the street from the police station. Her parents slogged along with her. In the warmth of the sunshine, they removed their overcoats and revealed cable knit sweaters and slacks.

Maya slid into the backseat. As Terrence started the car, her parents appeared to continue a private argument in the front seat. Her mother scowled as she whispered. Terrence shook his head. Whatever the subject of their disagreement, he would eventually come around.   Carolyn always got her way.

At the moment, Maya didn't care.   She couldn't wait to get home, bathe, and crawl into bed.   She lay back on the champagne leather and closed her eyes.   She couldn't remember ever feeling more exhausted in her entire life.

The MP13 player came on with the strains of a Bach minuet, which conspired with the warmth of the car heater to lull her to sleep.

> *Maya saw a little girl playing in a sandbox.   A very tall woman told the little girl to come inside.   The little girl began to sob.   Maya felt great pity and tried to run to help.   Her legs moved but, no matter how hard she tried, she could not cover the ground to get to the little girl.*

Carolyn's voice intruded.   "Maya, wake up.   We're stopping to eat.   Are you hungry?"

Agitated, Maya awoke.   Sweat clung to her back beneath the heavy jacket.   Her stomach growled.   They should have arrived at home by now.

"Maya, answer me."

Maya stared through the car window in alarm at farm fields passing by, a familiar landscape from previous visits upstate.   She must be mistaken.   "Where in the world are we?"

"About a hundred miles north of the city."   Terrence pulled the car into the parking lot of a roadside inn.   "Come on.   It's time we told you what we're up to."

Maya couldn't agree more.   Many times, they'd stopped to eat at the Blue Heron on the way to the cabin.

All three went inside the cozy restaurant decorated in the style of a tavern from Revolutionary War days.   Maya made straight for the restroom, swished her mouth with water, and freshened up as well as she could. Although her mother had followed her, they didn't speak because of the other women in the restroom.

Maya's parents had behaved discourteously toward her, or at least without compassion. She couldn't wait to hear why. They always knew best, at least in their opinions. Why hadn't they consulted her before driving her away from the city? Annoyed, Maya wondered if it was possible one's own parents could abduct their child.

When she sat down in the upholstered seat of the fake wood booth, Maya gazed at her parents across the table. "What is going on? Why are we here? And this had better be good."

Carolyn had refashioned her cone-shaped hairdo and looked her sophisticated self again. "You can't go home, Maya. You could be arrested again."

"This is some insane misunderstanding. It has to be."

A thin waitress in a long skirt and bodice brought a pewter pitcher and filled their cups with coffee.

Anticipating relief from the gnawing emptiness in her stomach, Maya took a long drink. Nothing had ever tasted so good, hot, and rich.

Terrence sounded solicitous. "I ordered you a quiche and salad. Is that okay?"

When Maya and Carolyn both nodded, the waitress said, "Be right up," set the pitcher on the blue checked tablecloth, and sauntered to the next booth.

"Now, Maya," Carolyn said and cast a loaded look at Terrence, "we have it on good authority that there is a warrant for your arrest. You're under suspicion for having caused the blackout."

"How could I have? I don't understand." A doubt as to whether she might have some culpability reoccurred.

Maya pushed it aside. "How can I prove my innocence if I'm not in town to confront my accusers?"

Terrence shrugged and raised an eyebrow toward Carolyn, who nodded her permission. He said, "One of my patients is an officer in ORION. He told me that you're wanted. We can't take the chance that they will jail you. We'd not be able to bail you out then, like we did at the local police station."

"ORION? Why would they want me?"

Carolyn cried, "Maya..."

Terrence cut in. "ORION is the branch of GSS that tracks Anaz-voohri and hybrids."

The situation dumbfounded Maya. "I'm not from another planet. I've never even been out of Earth's orbit. And I'm certainly not a hybrid. How could I be? You're both humans."

"Whew!" When Terrence picked up the pitcher and refilled the coffee cups, his hands trembled and he splashed coffee on the tablecloth.

"Maya, listen." Carolyn looked exasperated. "Your work at NexTech is very valuable to, well let's just say, to a lot of people. If you keep working on the interface program, you'll likely come into more and more jeopardy. There are...uh...groups that want the capability you're developing with artificial intelligence."

Maya thought her mother sounded more like a spy than a parent. Pushing a daughter around at home was one thing, horning in on Maya's work quite another. Where did Mother get off? Maya didn't try to keep annoyance out of her voice. "We've got a lot of competition among companies, I know, but, there's nothing secret about my work. I mean conspiracy-type secrecy."

Terrence smiled at her. "You might be surprised."

Carolyn's eyes glinted. "Some of those people are willing to kill to get it."

"Kill?" The thought that anyone would want Maya dead horrified her. She'd never harmed anyone in her life. "Is that why the sniper shot at Lola and me? Was he trying to kill me?"

"I wouldn't be a bit surprised." Carolyn gave Terrence one of her don't-interrupt-me looks. "There's a good possibility that he was after you, not Lola."

The prospect tore at Maya's heart. Her friend had died because someone wanted the Fairy Godmother program? Nothing could be more unjust.

Sighing, Terrence leaned back and rubbed his forehead. He didn't look one bit happy.

Maya felt like her life had become completely unmanageable. "I don't know what I should do. Maybe I should just go to the police with the information I have."

Terrence shook his head so that his jowls flopped. The waitress set a quiche in front of him. He moved it to Maya's place. The waitress set the second quiche before him. He snapped at her. "I get the ribs. They get the quiche."

"Sorry." The waitress righted the orders, glanced inside the empty pitcher, and held it akimbo. "Anything else?"

Maya grabbed her fork and started eating, too hungry for good manners.

"Going to the police is not a good idea." Carolyn took a dainty bite. "We're taking you to the summer cabin. I packed a suitcase for you. It's in the trunk. You'll be safe there at least for a while. You can continue to work on the program and stay in contact with your boss through email."

Since when did Mother tell Maya how to do her work? "How secret can that be? Any half-wit hacker can tap into email."

"Oh," Carolyn looked taken aback, "I never thought of that."

Well, one has to have at least half a wit, Maya thought but said, "I'll figure it out myself." She'd never voiced the idea but to herself acknowledged that her mother was not a mental giant, more a dwarf. A dwarf with a giant's mouth.

Basically a kind man with no perceptible backbone, Terrence seemed to want Maya's approval. "Once we get you installed in the cabin, I'll rent a car for you. I don't want you stuck up there by yourself with no transportation."

"Wait a minute." Maya choked down a bite of quiche without tasting it. "How will I be any safer there? If these ORION people can track me in New York, why can't they find me just as easily in Markle Falls?"

"I worried about that, too," said Terrence, "but my patient assured us that he would garble our name in the database. He'd change it to something similar to Rembrandt, or maybe just a different spelling. I guess if you take a name completely out, a flag goes up somewhere. He said he'd tweak our name just enough to throw off any searches and keep them from figuring out where you are."

Doubting the ploy would work, Maya asked, "Father, how have you gotten so involved with this man?"

"You know I can't tell you. That's doctor/patient privilege." Terrence dropped a rib in his lap, tossed it onto his plate, and dunked a napkin in his water glass. He furiously dabbed at his trousers.

Shrugging off her suspicions, Maya actually began to feel human, at least in body if not in mind. She finished the quiche and started on the salad. "How will I get the program?"

"You mean the software for the parent program? Oh, that's no problem." Carolyn relaxed against the booth with a smug grin. "It's in the trunk too."

Perhaps Maya had underestimated her mother. How had she gotten pull at NexTech? "You got it from Frank?"

"Of course not." Carolyn's laugh got away from her and turned into a snort. "I received it from the source. I'll not tell you more."

"What source?" Maya mentally ticked off the company execs, none of whom might willingly deliver the program, especially to an employee's relative. They were very sticky about software theft in general, not just AI software.

"NexTech has a parent company, doesn't it?" Carolyn examined her fingernails in a classically phony way.

"Carolyn," Terrence barked, "eat your lunch."

Maya had definitely underestimated her mother. "It's hard to say who owns NexTech. A conglomerate holding company. Mother, tell me where you got the program."

Terrence raised his arm and peered around. "I'm ordering pie. You two want anything else?" He glared at Carolyn.

"Mother?" Maya didn't like sitting in the middle in parental crossfire, but she really needed an answer.

With a gulp, Carolyn ducked her head in an act as close to contrition as she ever got. "Yes, thank you, I'll have lemon."

"Maya?" It seemed very important to Terrence that she order.

"Pecan, please. With whipped cream." Maya thought of the fluffy, crunchy taste she loved so much. Ordinarily, she'd dwell on the coming delicacy. She so loved subsuming her mind in the senses. She enjoyed them all, but taste was the best.

Now she forgot about anticipation, lost in resentment of the dynamics between her parents. They always jockeyed for power. She'd been the major pawn between them as long as she could remember. She wished she understood what had transpired between them today.

Her mother had gone too far, but how? And why couldn't they forget their bickering at a time when Maya's life might be in danger?

More than anything, Maya hated the feeling of being a dunce. She needed to figure things out for her own psychological comfort. Perhaps that characteristic had spurred her on in high school and college. She'd far surpassed her classmates in every level of school. She scored as a genius on IQ tests. Somehow her parents didn't seem to notice, always caught up in the transgressions of each other.

At some level, she knew she'd made too harsh a judgment. Always, her parents had rejoiced with her, for passing eighth grade at the age of nine, for graduating college at fifteen, then graduate degrees. Mother and Father had never seemed surprised by her stupendous intellectual achievements. They expected her to excel, as if they knew in advance she would.

Maya had not known. As far back as she could remember, she felt an abiding self-doubt and a great need to excel that fueled her life with purpose. She continually amazed herself with her grades, her achievements, and her intellectual accomplishments. Important as they were to her, awards from schools took second place to the delight of living in her own thoughts, not when she tried to parse out her parents or figure out the meaning of some comment a boy made. No, the real delight of life came when she considered a mathematical or computational problem.

Glancing down, she regretted that she'd eaten the whole piece of pie without tasting it. Maya postponed any further attempt at answers and waited as her parents finished their desserts. No one spoke. Perhaps they all sensed that too much had been said, and not said, in the past hour.

Chapter Seven

The supersonic jet approached ORION's Headquarters Flotilla moored in the Atlantic off the coast of Nova Scotia. In the forward cabin, Carrick watched the array spread out beneath them. He ignored the ringing in his ears from decelerating out of Mach Two into the vertical descent pattern.

Pride filled him as always at the magnificence of four battleships and his transport flagship, the *George W.* Beneath the waters hidden from Anaz-voohri eyes waited six submarines. Along with this armada, Carrick's army units, nearly a hundred thousand troops around the world, stood always at the ready for his command. They would respond efficiently to this crisis. Carrick promised himself to make wise choices that would dispatch the Anaz-voohri mole and make up for his error in judgment. He had to do that to remain honorable.

When the jet touched down on the flight deck of the battleship *Clinton* and lunged to a stop, Carrick unbuckled and hurried onto the rotunda. Already in her regulation overcoat, Flavia handed him his, which he threw on as he deplaned. He yawned to break the buzzing stuffiness in his ears. Flavia hustled along beside him.

A freezing wind blew from the east. The officer of the deck saluted. "Welcome aboard, General."

"Full speed ahead. New York." Carrick popped the sides of his head with cupped hands.

"Aye, aye, sir."

Carrick and Flavia strode to the elevator and rode to the hangar deck, then to the officer's accommodation ladder where they climbed down into a waiting boat. Within minutes, a sailor had rowed them between the ships. Carrick gestured for Flavia to climb onto the ladder of the *George W.* When she started up, he kept a scowl on his face so no one would imagine that he was thinking how much fun it would be to have that ass bare and sitting on him.

Flavia must not have gotten the vibes since she didn't turn around to look at him. Intuitive she was not.

Once on deck they entered the flagship conference room, which held several leather armchairs around a rectangular table, a computer wall, an electronic map of the world, and conference phones.

Although Carrick often needed to talk with all his captains at the same time, today he cared only about getting to Hillenbrand in New York. A quick glance at the map showed green lights in Baghdad, Moscow, London, Peking, and Rio. Only New York projected a red light.

Flavia threw off her coat and punched in buttons on the conference phone. "I'll get Captain Hillenbrand for you, sir."

"Thank you, Lieutenant." Carrick sat in a navy blue overstuffed chair.

On the computer wall, the grainy image of Captain Hillenbrand appeared. Tired and drawn looking, he stood at attention.

Carrick doubted Hillenbrand could rise to the challenge, but he'd give the dumbass one shot to get it right. Carrick asked brusquely, "What do you have, Captain?"

"Well, the good news is that the lights are back on around here." A small grin played along Hillenbrand's thin face.

Carrick disliked mixing any levity with business, but sometimes he felt he had to tolerate it in others, especially when he might have to depend on some flunky to bail him out of this mess. "I hope to hell there's no bad news."

"Not really. We've arrested over two hundred employees of NexTech and are in the process of questioning them. One's the mole's boss, a Frank Atkins. He wasn't much help. Just kept saying what a wonderful, smart, brave girl she is and how she'd never cause any—"

"Have you found the mole?"

"Could be." Hillenbrand's face brightened. "A report came in that a Maya Rembel had been incarcerated in Washington precinct, a local police station. It could be nobody, or it could be just a typo and we've got her. I'm going to send Sergeant Schwartz to check it out because he can ID the mole."

"Going to?" Carrick's leniency was ebbing fast. "Why haven't you already?"

"Schwartz is off duty, and we've not been able to find him," Hillenbrand's voice carried a higher pitch, "but we're on it. Don't worry."

Carrick rose and walked along the row of chairs while Hillenbrand watched with an anxious look. "How about the relatives or parents or friends? Turn up an Anaz-voohri, and you generally find hybrids hiding under the same rock."

"Well, it appears this Rembrandt person is a human."

"She's been modified with Anaz-voohri technology. She's an Anaz-voohri." Carrick banged his fist on the back of a chair. Why didn't this dolt of a man understand? "She's the enemy, goddamnit."

"Yes, sir. She was adopted. Her adoptive parents are hybrids. We've learned that much. Carolyn and Terrence Rembrandt."

"Use your kill order for them." Carrick's good humor returned because he enjoyed ordering the extermination of hybrids, knowing the world would be a safer, better place without them.

"Yes, sir."

"Call me as soon as you know anything."

The computer image went dark after Hillenbrand's salute.

Carrick took a brisk walk around the deck to settle his mind and to put in an appearance for the sailors on duty. Later he went into his apartment. Nothing sat on the tile floor except a twin bed and a folding chair. He paced, staring at the bare gunmetal walls, and berated himself over and over for not going after that mole sooner.

How in hell had he let her slip by, much less all seven of them? Any of those bitches might appear at any moment. He wished he knew what the Anaz-voohri had planned for them, about their triggers, so to speak. There was so much he didn't know, but what the fuck? He hadn't acted on what he did know. Now he was forced to depend on that wimp Hillenbrand. Well, not for long.

Lying on the bed, Carrick listened to the hum of the engine and felt the ship's vibration as it slid through the water. Filled with remorse, he promised himself he would make this right. He would take out those moles and a shitload of hybrids with them before the end of this operation.

Carrick must have dozed because a knock on the door jolted him.

Flavia's voice said, "I have a message from Captain Hillenbrand."

Leaping up, Carrick called, "Be right out." He smoothed the coverlet with a deft movement and opened the door.

Flavia sounded the tiniest bit disappointed. "The sergeant didn't make it to the jail in time. By some fluke, the mole was released to the custody of her parents. Hillenbrand is instituting a manhunt for all three of them."

"Damnation." Carrick slammed the door in Flavia's face and dialed a phone number so private only he knew its combination. No image appeared on his wrist phone.

"Yo," came the scratchy voice.

"I've got a job for you."

"Say who."

"Lester Hillenbrand, captain of the New York branch. Take him out and make it look like an accident."

"You got it, boss."

When Maya and her parents arrived in Markle Falls, they stopped at a grocery store and bought the items she might need for several days. They rented her a Buick sedan, and Maya felt a pang, wondering how the Tango had fared. Impounded by now, she assumed. She drove the Buick three miles outside town to the A-frame pine cabin and parked beside the Lexus.

She wondered what had really happened with that blackout and why the authorities had connected it with her. Nothing made sense. Her parents had acted very strangely, particularly with regard to her work. Why did they think it so important to continue in the face of all this?

Quite unsettled and fearful, Maya looked around the grounds. She made certain she locked the Buick then went inside the cabin. The paneled downstairs, one big room, contained a living room/kitchen combination, decorated in orange calico slipcovers. The furniture, from Maya's childhood in the brownstone, had gone out of style and been removed to the cabin.

Her parents had already turned the heat up and put the groceries away.

As Carolyn fixed ham sandwiches, she said to Maya, "I've unpacked your suitcase and arranged your things. Let your slacks hang until tomorrow, and you'll not have to iron them."

Terrence stood beside the tiny plastic table, arms folded. "If you get lonely, call me. I can talk you through it, but if you're afraid call nine-one-one."

"I've left some tabs upstairs for you, in case you get tense." Carolyn wrapped the sandwiches and stored them in a grocery bag. "I can just toss this bag after we eat, right, Terrence?"

"Sure." Terrence sounded surprised, probably because Carolyn never asked his advice on anything, important or unimportant.

Maya tried to calm her nerves and act brave in front of her parents. She didn't particularly want to spend any more time with them but dreaded staying alone. "Why don't you sleep over and get a fresh start in the morning?"

"No." Terrence squeezed her shoulders. "I'm anxious to get back. I've got appointments all day tomorrow."

"Where is the software program disk, Mother?"

"I left it with your computer on your bed in the loft." Carolyn set a six-pack of soft drinks beside the bag. "Now, Maya, you've got a great responsibility to develop that program. I know you'll do your best."

"Of course, I will." Maya wondered why her mother had taken such an enormous interest in the AI work all of a sudden. It didn't make sense. "Now, would you please tell me where you got it?"

"Drop this subject," Terrence demanded. "We can't tell you." Scowling, he picked up the bag and soft drinks then laid his palm on the doorknob. "Talk to you tomorrow."

His anger surprised Maya into letting the subject slide, at least temporarily. She hugged Carolyn, who looked a bit embarrassed and broke away with knitted brow. "Promise me you'll tell me when this is over, Mother."

"It will be obvious to you then." With a worried look, Carolyn threw her purse strap over her shoulder and hurried outside.

What an inexplicable thing to say. Standing in the cabin doorway, Maya watched her parents climb into the car. She'd had a lot of trouble reading their emotions today. They treated her more like a ward than a daughter. She didn't feel loved so much as protected. Both parents wished her well, no doubt, and she felt a duty to them but little fondness.

The business about getting the software program disk made her suspicious of them. They had connections in high places they'd never told her about. What a weird family! If they ended up getting her fired, she'd never forgive them.

After this horrible business with the blackout ended, she'd have a talk with her parents and try to come to a more complete understanding of them and their feelings about her.

Maya waved as the Lexus pulled out of the driveway. The pines and bare maple trees smelled tangy and looked pretty with a light coating of snow on their branches. Down the road the falls trickled, the faintest of sounds. They'd soon freeze completely for the rest of the winter. She loved this place.

Suddenly shivering, Maya glanced around with the fear that someone might be lurking but saw nothing worrisome. Undisturbed snow lay in the driveways of the four other cabins visible in the lane, all their occupants gone for the season. She felt abandoned and quickly closed the door. It was as quiet inside as outside.

For company, Maya turned on the plasma TV and changed the station to the news while she boiled water. The stories all revolved around the aftermath of the blackout. The smiling young reporter told of traffic snarls, deserted cars, crippled hospital power systems, people without heat, one pitiful situation after another.

The idea that she might be to blame for all of this by turns made Maya depressed and outraged. Never would she intentionally inflict harm on anyone.

Wanting no more reminders, she changed the channel and saw the image of a Christmas tree covered entirely with angels. When the camera panned back, there stood Tierney Grant, explaining the history of the tree decorated every year by a local church. Beautiful and poised, Tierney walked about, describing gifts given to her father and presidents before him by world leaders.

As a general rule, Maya didn't follow the lives of political figures or entertainers. It seemed like voyeurism, but she made an exception for Tierney. Maya had never met the President's daughter but felt a bond with her, the most fragile of feelings. If she and Tierney did meet, Maya believed they would embrace like old friends.

Remembrance of the loss of Lola washed over Maya. That was her true friend, one she would never laugh with or embrace again. No one close to Maya had ever died, and she found dealing with the sadness that swept over her at the thought of Lola unbearable.

If Maya didn't do something, she'd cry. She wanted to gain some equilibrium. Who knew what troubles she might face here in the woods? She had to keep cool and let logic reign.

After clicking off the TV, she selected a peppermint tea bag and dunked it in a cup of hot water. She turned off the stove and climbed the stairs to the loft. Nothing else but work could come close to keeping her mind from filling with ugly emotions.

Beside her laptop computer lay the AI software and a packet of serotonin tabs. The magenta sheets and blankets were already turned down efficiently in the manner of a hotel maid.

Again, Maya found it odd the fact that her mother had gotten hold of the program. Maybe she'd been able to con Frank. How else? If so, why didn't Mother just admit it?

In any case, Maya would enjoy working on the program again, even with the limited access the laptop afforded. She inserted the disk into the drive. Intrigued, she wanted to discover the extent to which she could merge with the computer program. She didn't know if she could overcome the confines of the laptop. This was not the Fairy Godmother computer at work, after all, with all its bells and whistles. While the computer booted up, she sipped and let the spicy tea linger in her mouth.

First she would try to create little Daffodil again. If that worked, she'd attempt to reconstruct the man. A shudder passed through Maya. In all the drama and tension of the past twenty-four hours, she'd not really considered what she thought about Dylan, besides his undeniably good looks.

Maya appreciated his efforts to help her but feared he could be a hybrid because of his uncanny ability to track her down. Her father had taught her to be respectful of hybrids because, he said, they were as nice as humans. But Maya didn't really know any hybrids and felt suspicious of their special abilities. Something about them spooked her, and she didn't know why.

On the other hand, she had enjoyed putting her arms around Dylan. He felt stable and warm, homey in a way, as if they belonged together in some framework she didn't understand. When he kissed her in front of the police officers, she was already in shock and fear of potential arrest. Now she remembered how nice his lips had felt on hers, gentler than Mark's.

The only guy who ever really kissed her, Mark had always had an edge, been insistent, almost impatient with her. Believing as he truly did that all of his dates should become his lovers, he'd told her on the first date, "By the third date or I'm out of here."

She had definitely made a mistake falling into his intimidation. When they had intercourse on that third date, he acted like she ought to know how to do things, but she didn't. Reading about the act and hearing about it from Lola had not prepared Maya at all.

As soon as he took her clothes off, fear filled her. She'd never suspected she could feel so vulnerable, a disconcerting emotion. When he asked her if she was a rape victim, she'd felt shocked. She told him of course not, no one had ever raped her. Then he finished fast in what Lola called the missionary position. He hadn't hurt her, and she never felt afraid of him so didn't understand her own reactions. It still caused Maya shame that Mark stopped calling after that.

Surely, having intercourse could be a much more pleasurable experience or everyone would give it up. Lola had regaled Maya with stories of thrilling encounters. Lola had loved having sex. It was better than eating cheese and crackers, she always said. And that girl had dearly loved cheese.

Maya wondered whether Dylan would act like the men Lola described. Would he be as edgy as Mark? They certainly kissed in different ways. In fact, she remembered how dry she had been when Mark had kissed her and even when he had entered her, but just thinking of Dylan's kiss made her feel moist. She'd read enough to recognize that as a normal female response to arousal. How clinical that sounded.

It would be lovely for Dylan to hold her and kiss her. At least in her mind he could become the perfect lover, warm, sensual, sweet, and exciting. Maybe in the computer program she could experience a romantic encounter with him. Dylan wouldn't ever have to know. Were artificial intelligence specialists at risk of falling in love with their creations?

Would she see the real life Dylan again? Probably so. He'd turned up twice already, oddly puzzling. How had he known where to find her? Why had he been looking for her? Did it have anything to do with the blackout? Or Lola's death? If it weren't for questions, Maya would hardly have a thought these days. She had such a restless mind today. It seemed to skitter off anything she tried to consider except Dylan's lips on hers.

Since she'd missed her shower that morning, Maya decided to take a bath and try to relax. Then she would see if she had the ability to conjure what she had come to think of as her handsome hybrid. She would try to return his kiss in the computer program. That should be a worthy enough goal to keep her on task.

Chapter Eight

According to the advice given at the time of Maya's arrest, Dylan had returned to the police station three hours later, at one the next morning. He doubted the officers would let him take Maya. They didn't.

One police officer gave no information except to say that her one phone call had been to her parents, not to any husband. Obviously, the cop had seen through the subterfuge. Dylan felt relieved that she gained permission to call her parents. Even if they managed to get to her before he did, at least it should be easy to track her down. He felt a little guilty for having failed to keep her out of jail. He wanted to find her before she realized what she'd done to the power grid, or maybe she already knew.

After a few fitful hours of sleep, he returned at noon to find the police station in an uproar. A female officer sat crying, another yelled at her, and a police officer shouted into an old-fashioned phone with a cord.

None of them took any notice of him. Dylan peeked into the side offices but didn't see the two men who had been in charge the night before. He wished he knew what had caused this turmoil.

The police officer on the phone held up a hand toward Dylan. "Hold on, buddy. I'll be with you in a minute." He rolled his eyes at whatever the person on the other end of the line was saying then plopped into a chair, his back turned.

Since Dylan couldn't get anyone's attention, he walked back to the cells without permission and satisfied himself that Maya had gone. Whether she had obtained a release or been transferred to another jail he didn't know. He only saw one prisoner, an old woman who ignored him and picked her teeth, then he returned to the office.

The police officer hung up the phone and shouted at the two policewomen. "He says we're all fired! How the hell should we have known ORION was after her?"

"Give me that phone," the black policewoman said and wiped her tears. "I'm getting a lawyer. They can't do this to us."

They couldn't have ignored Dylan more if he were invisible. He hurried outside to his Dial-a-Bike. When he called Maya's house, the answering machine came on, so he drove by and noticed drawn curtains at every window.

Thinking he might get a new take on the situation, he went back to Mythos. The records of the police radio confirmed that Jason Carrick had ordered ORION to kill Maya on sight. She must have great power. Otherwise, why would Carrick want her?

Finding Archer and some other operatives in conference, Dylan took the opportunity to have a second look at the reports stolen from CEM. He needed to figure out more fully what Mythos was up against. Spreading the files on the desk, he read through them again.

First, he wanted to understand the implications of the variety of surgeries performed there. From the medical chart summaries, he learned that children born of one Anaz-voohri clone and one human parent had a wide range of characteristics, something he'd never realized. He had hardly ever seen a hybrid that looked anything but human. Nothing so far could modify height, and as a result many hybrids were tall. But skin grafts performed on creased craniums to create aesthetic value, and elongated ears were often easily remedied with a well-placed clip. If skin looked too red, bleaching procedures made hybrid skin pinker like white people's or tanning to create a black skin look.

As a result, hybrids operated in society at every level. Anyone could be one, and who would know?

Those revolting Anaz-voohri had absolutely no regard for the lives or well-being of others. They probably considered humans and hybrids more like animals. Otherwise, why the experimental surgeries, particularly those accomplished without permission?

A common procedure involved implanting devices in both humans and hybrids. The purpose seemed to be to assert control from outside of the body. Actually altering DNA caused some subjects to act in ways totally at odds with their biology. Humans and hybrids, for that matter, who were partially human, should never have the mission to destroy the human race, but Dylan feared much programming already executed for that purpose. Those cold-hearted Anaz-voohri considered humans and hybrids alike useful and expendable, like weapons in a war.

He knew they'd subjected Maya to this diabolical technique. An alteration of her DNA amounted to a device of enormous power, which implanted in her brain, rendered her pliable to Anaz-voohri control. Either overtly or covertly, Dylan didn't know which. He didn't think they'd literally blow her up, but the metaphor worked.

She was a time bomb about to go off. Or, maybe she already went off and that's what caused the blackout. Maybe she didn't realize what had happened to her or what she had done last night. If she knew, did she consciously work for the Anaz-voohri? Or was she their unwitting dupe?

Reading the reports on cures saddened Dylan. Over the years, the human public seemed sucked into cooperation because the Anaz-voohri taught and probably bred doctors who could cure all manner of ailments. At CEM, they specialized in children. Of course, parents wanted their crippled child to walk or their blind child to see.

Perhaps his own parents had begun to suspect what had happened to their son; what they had unwittingly allowed. They may have complained or questioned too much. Dylan wished he knew the details of why the Anaz-voohri had murdered them.

Maya's case propelled him into unknown territory. Maybe he'd find answers for her and for himself. They had a whole lot in common. Violated by the Anaz-voohri, not rape of the body but of the mind, of the soul.

That he used the gift the Anaz-voohri had given him to help hunt them down gave Dylan great satisfaction. He hoped to hell they knew that about him. They deserved whatever he could accomplish against them.

Occasionally Dylan felt some ambivalence, particularly about the hybrid doctors, because they had given him his sight, but the fact remained that the Anaz-voohri and their hybrid confederates, those that didn't support the human side, remained a threat to human existence. Dylan had no choice but to fight on the side of Mythos.

The Anaz-voohri bastards had given Maya an incredible power to become one with a machine. In the process, without caring one whit, they had taken away her autonomy. They had turned her mind into a bomb that she carried around but that someone in a spaceship could detonate. He needed to find her to deactivate her first, no matter what that involved.

After gathering up the files, Dylan returned them to Archer's desk drawer and twirled the tumble lock. He went into his room and closed the door, as he had done so many times before. Mythos had built the room for him because Archer valued Dylan's ability. Dylan intended always to deserve the confidence.

He grabbed a pistachio ice cream bar out of the fridge, bit it in two, and sat down on the bed. He pulled off his boots and lay down, biting the nutty crunch and letting the mellow cream fill his mouth. After he'd eaten the whole bar, he let his mind relax.

Once his breathing evened out, he said, "I want to find Maya. Wherever she is in the world, let me see her."

Waiting in the empty silence, he found one of the most satisfying aspects of the remote viewing experience. In the past, there had been moments of great vitality when his mind had traveled outside his body.

Once as an experiment, he had astral traveled to Gettysburg and looked down to see the battle of the Civil War in progress. He could almost feel the rough wool of a Yankee uniform and a cold rifle in his hands. He had sensed other times, particularly the 1950s, as if he could look down into them, without such a specific image. Drifting through time seemed no more implausible than drifting through space, and that he did successfully. Some philosopher had once said that it was no more remarkable to have lived twice than to have lived once. Dylan assumed he had lived other lifetimes and wished sometimes that he could draw more precise memories to him.

Now he wanted to find Maya and had no doubt that he could find her wherever in the world she might be. Lying on his cot, awaiting the onset of astral travel, Dylan felt completely contented and set his consciousness free. With ease he seemed to float out of his body, up to the ceiling, then out over the city. He skimmed along over buildings and trees with a feeling of exhilaration he never knew in waking consciousness.

When he felt the inclination to stop, he looked down at a cabin set deep in a wood. In his mind, Dylan descended through the roof of the cabin. He hovered at the ceiling of what he took to be a bathroom. From the counter, the flame of a large candle cast shadows on the walls and shower stall.

Before the sink stood Maya, naked. She had a perfect body, curving and soft, skin so pink it glowed. Without self-consciousness, she moved her arms to brush her wavy hair. Her beautiful, round bottom flowed with the movement of her arms.

She had a tattoo on the small of her back. Dylan strained to identify it. A flower or an angel? No, it was a fairy. A charming little fairy with delicate aqua wings that fluttered as Maya moved. He wanted to run his fingers across the fairy's wings and press his naked flesh to Maya's.

Shocked at himself, Dylan popped back into his body back at Mythos and shook off the trance. He had violated his own taboo against the use of his gift. Never would he become a voyeur. He chastised himself for such carelessness.

Still, he couldn't stop a smile. Maya had looked lovely.

Dylan did not know in what direction he had traveled during the remote viewing or how far. The cabin could have been anywhere in New York State, in the Carolinas, even as far away as Ohio. He had no sense of place this time, but he did have an erection.

Over the years with Mythos, he had learned that he could trust his remote viewing of locations to a considerable degree, accurate eighty percent of the time. The twenty percent failure happened either because of imprecise knowledge of the subject's appearance or some emotional reactions on his part. In this case, he definitely knew the appearance of the subject, beautiful.

This session would have to be logged as part hit and part miss. He dreaded increasing his failure rate.

Dylan had shut out the memory of the little kiss they had exchanged as merely doing his job. Suppose they really had been husband and wife separated by a police arrest. That kiss wouldn't have been any more delicious.

To become emotionally involved with this case could be disastrous. Dylan would not do so. He would find Maya and carry out his directive.

The bath had not only failed to relax Maya, it had made her more tense than ever. She must be getting paranoid because she felt as if someone watched her while she brushed her hair.

No way could that have happened. She opened the loft window to make certain no one prowled around outside. She didn't want to go crazy and reminded herself of her parents' reassurances that no one would discover her here at the cabin. They had taken care of the details. Maya had to trust something and someone

Any attempt to work was out of the question until she could get her fears under control. Mother would say to take some tabs, but Maya didn't want to. She wanted her mind clear and alert.

With only two weeks before Christmas, she couldn't tolerate the forlorn-looking cabin. In past years, she and her parents had trimmed beautiful cut trees in the living room and strung holiday cards from the previous year around the landing. How safe they had been then, and Maya had not even thought to be thankful for her security.

Her depression over Lola's death deepened. They had always exchanged little gifts, like purses or charm bracelets. From now on, there would be nothing but loss.

Maya dried her hair, dressed in sweater, jeans, boots, and ski jacket, and headed outside, despite her fears and grief, or maybe because of them. She had to avert descending into the abyss of negativity.

She took hedge clippers along for two reasons. One, she could cut boughs for decorations. And two, hedge clippers made a good weapon.

Setting off at a brisk pace, Maya breathed in the fresh, clean fragrance of air devoid of gasoline fumes. Her breath frosted before her mouth. The wind chill might already be as low as fifteen or twenty, so she wouldn't stay out long.

Maya hiked by the trickling falls and admired the ragged ice formations freezing rivulets made. She entered a section of the wood with close-set pines. Cones crunched beneath her feet. She clipped some fir boughs, enough to trim the mantle and make a spray for the door.

Cutting decorations from trees instead of buying them at Macy's held a certain nostalgic charm. She imagined everyone followed that tradition fifty years ago. On second thought, maybe a hundred years ago.

The wan sun sank below the horizon, leaving a white afterglow in the sky. Having cut as many boughs as she could juggle while still carrying the clippers, she hiked back to the house. The temperature had dropped. She guessed the wind chill would probably go to zero soon. Maya couldn't wait to get inside and build a cozy fire in the fireplace.

Just as she walked off the road and into the lane that served the five cabins, she stopped. Something had changed, but she didn't know what. Quickly, she moved back into the shadow of the nearest neighbor's cabin. She could see her own and realized what had disturbed her. Footprints in the snow, boot prints, in fact, and big ones. Someone had been walking around the area.

A man strode from behind her cabin. Tall and thin, he wore an ORION uniform with a phase gun holster. He peered into the downstairs window. She had left in daylight and hadn't turned on any lights. Now at twilight, the house appeared empty, albeit with open curtains. She feared he'd notice that as a sign of habitation.

Thankful that she hadn't blundered into his sight, Maya tiptoed behind the neighboring cabin. He looked very familiar. Maya knew she'd seen him before. Maybe he had attended Lola's funeral. Many police officers had. The thought occurred to her that he could have been the sniper.

As carefully as she could, aware of her trembling hands, she laid the boughs down behind the cabin and sat on top of them. She put the hood up on her ski jacket and determined to wait it out, no matter what.

The man walked around the cabin three times then leaned against the Buick and felt the hood with his hand. It had been several hours since Maya had driven it. She wondered how long the engine remained warm to the touch.

He watched the house for what seemed an eternity. Complete darkness fell, darker than the city ever seemed. Maya huddled against the neighbor's cabin and chafed her hands, but she still felt incredibly cold. At least she wore warm gloves and boots, and it was not raining or snowing. If she believed in a god, this would be the time to pray. Praying might help to calm the wild fear that surged up in her.

Stars winked on. Maya wondered how much intelligent life existed out there, with gods or without. She knew some galaxies had life on them. Anaz-voohri had even come to visit Earth. Maybe other aliens had, too. She wondered what they were like and whether she would ever meet any. Wildly, she thought, if ever there was a time for an alien abduction, this would be it. At least they would take her away from this man who stalked her.

Perhaps because no lights came on inside the cabin and the officer thought no one was coming home, he strode up the lane and passed out of Maya's sight. She wondered why he had left at all but had no doubt that he would return. Moments later a car engine started, and she heard it drive away.

Terrified, Maya slipped up to the door and slid the key in the lock. Once inside, she huddled against the door, afraid to turn on a light. He might come back and find her. She felt even more depressed and as helpless as a child.

Finally, after many hours of peering out the windows and sitting in the dark, she crawled into bed, still in her clothes. As she lay awake, unable to sleep, it dawned on her where she'd seen the officer. He had not worn a uniform at the time, but he had come to the house. He was one of her father's patients.

Tomorrow she would call her father and tell him. And find a safer place to stay.

Every time Dylan considered trying to remote view to find Maya, the image of her gorgeous body blocked him. In this particular instance, he'd zeroed in on a private moment and felt embarrassed and more lustful than he wished. How he wanted to press himself against her nakedness and cup her soft breasts in his hands, to take his time touching every inch of her flesh. What would it take to bring her to climax?

Dylan didn't trust himself or believe that he could have a successful remote viewing right now. No point in trying again unless he had to. He'd find Maya another way.

When he awoke the next morning, he decided to do the obvious and go to her house. She might actually be there although he doubted it because those ORION henchmen would have already covered that base. Perhaps her parents would tell him how to find her. He had a hunch they had taken her somewhere after they left the police station. He knew she was in a cabin in the woods somewhere, but where?

With nothing to lose but the effort, he set out for Maya's house. The weather had become unseasonably warm, so he wore a leather jacket. Once on his Dial-a-Bike, Dylan put the top down and the sides up then took off driving. Most of the snow had melted. It wasn't spring weather, but for December quite warm and sunny.

Turning onto Walnut Street, he braked and stopped. Police cars and ambulances lined both sides of the street, some with red lights whirring. People stood on the stoops of brownstones up and down the row, their faces turned toward the Rembrandt house.

Dylan parked the Dial-a-Bike and strolled along the sidewalk. A stocky man, probably in his sixties, sat on the steps of the brownstone directly across from the Rembrandt house. He stuffed a pipe with tobacco and lit it.

Dylan leaned on the wooden railing. "What's going on?"

"Don't look good." The smoker talked in a muffled way around the stem of the pipe. "Heard a lot of shouting about an hour ago." He held out his bent index finger and pointed it. "Then…zip…zip."

"Did you call the police?"

"Me, naw. I keep to my own business, but somebody did." The smoker pulled on the pipe and coughed.

They waited a long time while Dylan cast around for something more to say. The smoker's pipe burned out, and he lit it again.

Finally, a police officer exited the Rembrandt's house and called to the crowd. "Everyone, stand back."

While he held the door open, two medics carried out a gurney with a shrouded body on it. Then two more brought another one out. They lifted the bodies into the back of an ambulance and closed the door.

Troubled, Dylan wondered whether Maya were one of the dead. As close as he could guess, both bodies looked bigger than hers. Maybe his hunch had been right.

"Officer," a woman down the row sobbed. "Tell us who is dead, please."

The police officer spoke to the crowd. "I have no information except that the bodies have been identified as Carolyn Rembrandt and Terrence Rembrandt."

"Oh, no," the woman cried. "Carolyn was such a nice woman. A good neighbor."

The young man standing beside her patted her back, and the woman sobbed aloud.

Dylan asked the smoker, "Did you know those people?"

"Naw." The smoker grinned. "Probably a homicide and suicide. That's the way them hybrids do, you know. Violent by nature."

The remark surprised Dylan. Although the public had some awareness that hybrids existed, they had few details on identifying them. "How do you know that they're hybrids?"

The smoker shrugged. "They act all hoity toity, like they're better than the rest of us. That's a sure sign."

"Think so, do you?" Dylan thought fondly of the fellow who'd helped him assault the spaceship. "Well, I've known some hybrids who acted more human than some humans. At least they didn't bad mouth."

Dylan left the old coot looking chagrined and headed toward his Dial-a-Bike. There would be no possibility of getting into the house right now with police investigating the crime scene.

ORION had done the murders. They would do whatever it took. Now they'd be looking for Maya even harder because she'd gotten away again. Maybe they'd discovered a clue to her location in the house. She could be anywhere, holed up in a hotel or staying with friends out of town. Damn, how would Dylan ever find her?

Chapter Nine

First thing in the morning, Maya tried to call her parents from the cabin. The fact that they didn't answer over a period of an hour made her exceedingly nervous. In order to execute her plan, she had to remain calm.

She considered taking the tabs but remembered how spacey she felt on them. Not willing to take a chance, she flushed them down the toilet and dressed for physical work.

After making absolutely certain that no one lurked outside, she dashed to the Buick and took off for Markle Falls where she bought a sleeping bag, some blankets, a lantern with a five-year guarantee, a battery-powered space heater, some packaged puddings, chips, cookies, and a new video phone.

While leaving the phone store, she called her parents and left a message with the answering service. Her father had said to call every day. He always had a patient by nine or nine thirty. Someone should have answered. Weren't they worried about her? She feared for them.

Her first plan had been to take off driving west as far as the Buick would take her. Then she realized her rental records had her name on file. Anyone trailing her could check them and trace the car. She'd have to spend her money credits, and dump any traceable cards. In fact, the details of her life seemed far too public. How free people must have felt years ago when they actually carried dollars that couldn't be traced.

Maya didn't know how to get away, so she came up with the second plan, to hide in the cave.

When she returned to the cabin, she parked the Buick in exactly the same place. If the man returned, she hoped to make him think nothing had changed. Maybe he wouldn't lean on the car. Grateful that the snow had melted, she didn't have to worry about leaving tracks in it.

Maya willed her hands to stay calm and her mind focused. She carried the purchases straight to the cave a little over a mile from the cabin and stashed them outside.

She made two trips; one to bring the clippers, her computer, pillows, and clothes, another to haul all of the food she could carry. She became so anxious when she neared the cabin each time that she didn't return again even though she wanted to look around for anything she'd forgotten. She just hoped she'd brought everything important.

The cave, an oddity in the area, formed millions of years ago, she supposed, probably by erosion and other strange forces of nature. Blackberry bushes had overgrown the mouth of the cave. Maya worked her way around the back of them to avoid disturbing the natural shape of their brittle branches and thus give the appearance of an uninhabited cave. She carried her supplies inside the oval space, approximately ten by fifteen feet. The domed top of gray rock was about five feet high in the center. Maya had to stoop to move around inside now. As a child she had no trouble walking in.

The cave represented the most privacy she ever knew, a world apart from schools, teachers, assignments, parent-teacher conferences, and study. She had spent wonderful summer hours here, so much time that finally Father had carried down an old trunk to stash her belongings. She'd not been here in recent years, but the trunk still stood at the back of the oval.

Raising its corrugated wood and metal top, Maya found books she had loved. Since she'd been an extremely fast reader, Mother had bought many series for her - *American Girl, Harry Potter, The Lord of the Rings, Post Haste No Waste,* and *Flowers Abounding.* She had no interest in botany in general but always loved flowers—their shapes, their scents, their delicate beauty.

Maya arranged her belongings in as organized a way as possible. On the hard-packed dirt floor, she spread a wool blanket for a rug. She feared the cold. If she had any luck at all, the break in the weather would hold until someone rescued her or she thought of some place else to go.

In a way, the most bizarre part of her plan involved the computer. Whatever the outcome, she could think of nothing else to do.

In her extremity, more terrified than she'd ever imagined she could be, Maya determined, just for the moment, to suspend her disbelief. Suppose she really did cause the blackout. What did that say about her and her link with the computer?

What she thought it meant was that, in some way she as yet did not understand, she and the computer had entered a symbiotic relationship. The logic of that fact eluded her so she went with the feeling. But in the moments before the blackout, it had seemed that the computer shared her pain. The computer grieved with her. She wanted to find a way to recapture that event.

Sitting cross-legged in the middle of the cave, she logged onto the laptop, inserted the software disk, and waited for it to boot up. She opened a package of chocolate chip cookies, the bite size kind, with double white chips, and slid one in her mouth. It tasted delicious, so full and rich.

She let her emotions guide her. What did she want most? To feel safe. Who could guarantee that? No one, but Dylan had tried to rescue her two nights ago. Maybe he would try again. Or maybe someone else.

It was important for her to trust that the mental energy she needed to help herself would come to her. She laid another cookie on her tongue and let the yummy white chocolate melt there.

The grainy black of the computer screen enticed her. It wanted her to come into it. Her left brain screamed *this is preposterous*. Her right brain said *let it happen*.

After leaving the police investigation site at Maya's house on Walnut Street, Dylan drove directly to the NexTech building. In the corridor, he scanned the list of names on the directory, trying to deduce which one Maya worked in. Not that he anticipated finding her at work. ORION would already have covered that, but he needed a lead of any kind.

A female security guard sat at a table near the elevator doors. "May I help you?" Her voice conveyed her unwillingness to do so.

"I'm looking for Maya Rembrandt. Could you tell me which department she works in?"

The security guard folded her arms across a bosom as full as her nose was flat. "She's not here."

"Then maybe I could talk with her supervisor."

"Let me see your ID."

When he pulled out his pilot's license, she grunted, "I thought you was police."

Dylan held his arms wide so his jacket fell open to show jeans and t-shirt. He hoped his smile conveyed boyish charm. "Do I look like police to you?"

"What do you want?"

"Hopefully to get a date…"

The security guard's homely face brightened.

"…with Maya." Dylan thought he'd surely blown it now.

Pressing an intercom button, the security guard gave him a dour look and picked up a privacy phone. "Mr. Atkins, there's somebody here for Maya. Yes, again. Nope, not police this time…says he's her boyfriend or some such.

All right." She returned the license. "Eighth floor. Frank Atkins."

"Thank you, ma'am. You've been very helpful." Dylan pressed the elevator button. When the doors opened, he gave her a genuine smile and stepped inside.

On the ride up he hoped to hell this Frank Atkins would turn out to be as helpful. Dylan's luck had to change, or he'd never find the woman. Archer would have his ass, and with good reason. The longer she remained at large the greater the risk that she would harm human society.

The doors opened on the eighth floor lobby, an empty expanse of beige walls and office cubicles. Before them, a holly red, artificial Christmas tree occupied most of the tile floor. It bore three or four green glass ornaments. Dozens more lay at the base of the tree, still in packing boxes. With the hall so quiet, Dylan wondered if anyone had come to work today. Considering they recently suffered unfair arrest, who could blame them for taking personal leave? And for losing Christmas spirit?

A dumpy, middle-aged man sauntered toward the elevators. "You looking for Maya?"

"Frank Atkins?" When the fellow nodded, Dylan said, "Yes, I'm a friend of hers. I'd sure like to find her. I've got some bad news to tell her."

Frank shook his head. "That's about all that poor girl's had these days. She's not here, but you can tell me."

"Well, I'd rather tell her. It's personal."

"Sorry. Don't know where she is and, even if I did—"

Dylan saw no reason to conceal what was probably already on the news. "Her parents have been murdered. I've got to find her."

Frank looked like someone just punched in his considerable stomach. "Sorry, man. I don't know where she is. I've not heard a word from her since the blackout."

"If you do, call me." Dylan laid a card in Frank's hand. "And thanks."

Until the time the elevator doors opened, Frank studied the card, as if it contained far more than a phone number, email, and address. He looked queasier by the minute. As Dylan stepped inside he heard Frank mutter, "It musta been her."

Yep, you're right, buddy, Dylan thought, hard as it was to believe. He followed the only other lead he could think of and backtracked to Maya's house.

On Walnut Street, yellow tape surrounded the Rembrandt house and two NYC police officers stood guard. Dylan knocked on the door of the brownstone next door where the woman had cried earlier. She looked through the keyhole then opened the door to Dylan. Her jet-black hair hung loose and showed gray roots so wide she looked like she had a zebra stripe down her head.

Behind her, the plasma wall blared the newscaster's voice over videotape of the bodies now carried out of the Rembrandt house.

"I'm sorry to bother you, ma'am," Dylan said. "I'm looking for Maya Rembrandt."

"Who are you? I thought you were a friend of my son's. That's why I opened the door, but I don't know you." She grabbed the door as if to close it.

Dylan held the knob so she couldn't. "Maya doesn't know about her parents. Can you help me find her?" His voice sounded a bit desperate, not a phony emotion. He held out his pilot's ID. "I'm not police or anything, just a friend of Maya's."

The woman glanced back at the news program. She seemed compelled to stare at the images and spoke with her back turned. "This is just so awful. Nothing like it has ever happened around here. This is a nice neighborhood and now we've got so much trouble." Her shoulders drooped when she looked at Dylan, and her eyes betrayed cloudy confusion.

"I know. Very nice neighborhood." Dylan wished he could think of something appropriate to say. "I'm sorry. I know you're sad."

The woman grimaced as if she were about to cry then took a great breath and blew it out like a weightlifter. "I don't know where she'd go."

"How about a friend's house? Did Maya have a friend she might be staying with?'

Letting out a cry, the woman pointed to the brownstone across from hers. "Her friend Lola is dead, too. She was shot."

Dylan felt sorry for the woman, traumatized by events over which she had no control. "Such a tragic loss. I went to the funeral, did you?"

The woman nodded, and her eyes filled with tears. Perhaps she began to trust him because he'd gone to the funeral. "I don't know where Maya is, but they do have another residence. You could look there. They always go for a few weeks in the summer."

"Do you know where it is?"

"Maybe in Connecticut, I can't remember for sure." She took a tissue from her housecoat pocket and wiped her nose.

"That's all right." Dylan wished he could pat her or comfort her in some way, instead he shook her hand. "You've been a great help. Thank you."

While he drove toward his loft, he phoned Mythos and asked for an aide to do a search for homeowner files for Terrence, Carolyn, or Maya Rembrandt, in Connecticut, New York, Pennsylvania, anywhere outside the city. "Email me with the info as soon as you can." He felt a sense of urgency and feared his time was running out.

If Maya fell into ORION'S hands, there was no assurance that they would kill her. They might torture her or turn her to their purposes, only slightly less odious than having her under the thumb of the Anaz-voohri. Far better for the safety of the world for her to be in the hands of Mythos.

If the killers had had a chance to search the house, they might have come across the address of the summer residence. Dylan remembered a detail of the remote viewing before he saw Maya's image. He'd passed over a lot of trees, too many for a city. He felt certain that had been no coincidence.

In the cave, Maya had heard no sound from outside for quite a while. She expected at any minute the ORION officer would stick his head in. After trying several times to make the email Nanobot in her brain work, she gave up. She'd wasted her time and her money on that item.

Too afraid to turn on the flashlight, she worked in filtered light from the afternoon sun. Even though chilly, she hesitated to turn on the space heater. Its battery might not last long, and she would need it if she had to remain in the cave for very long. She felt nervous about spending the night here, but maybe she wouldn't have to, if she managed to obtain some help.

Maya laid her hand on the grainy screen of the laptop. It felt warm to the touch, and her fingers made depressions that rippled out in a satisfying way, as if true life dwelt within. She willed herself to believe that it did for the sake of the experiment. Her life might depend on whether or not she could convince the computer to help her, or at least to send a message to Dylan.

The Fairy Godmother, in her computer at work, acted much like an expansive, loving grandmother, who tempered knowledge with wisdom and could be present with Maya for the fun of creation.

This laptop had a different kind of energy – youthful, restless, and excitable. She had hardly used it except to run her father's business accounts, generate invitations for her mother's parties, and email from home. She had invested all her AI efforts at NexTech.

For artificial life, relationship with the creator was everything. Maya needed to establish one with the laptop. Gaining its trust would be her challenge. Otherwise, it would not hear her requests, let alone do her bidding.

She focused her attention on the screen and willed herself to connect with the intelligence inside. She emptied her mind of everything except the desire to meld with the laptop. She flexed her fingers and pressed down. Her fingers disappeared up to the knuckles. Maya quelled her surprise.

Where her hand went, her body could follow. Logic required it. Only the consideration of size remained. Maya pressed the palm of her hand against the screen and it yielded. She slid in up to her wrist, a satisfying merging. In a moment of panic, she thought of pulling back. What might happen to her in a place where an unruly AI invented the rules?

What would happen to her if she didn't go? She could get killed by the sniper, or by ORION, or she could die of the cold. Not one desirable scenario among them. She had to gamble that she could manage the new AI and convince it to communicate for her. In fact, at the moment that risk seemed like the only reasonable option. She touched the viscous texture inside, warm and willing.

Closing her eyes, Maya imagined herself a river flowing into the computer. She waited and nothing happened and so decided to rethink her attitude.

She thought, somebody here calling herself Maya tried to get into a nothing space. That's where logic broke down. This Maya person thought she was somebody, somebody trying to meld with a computer, somebody trying to escape extinction.

What a laugh. Nobody escaped death. In Hindu tradition *maya* meant nothingness, illusion, form without substance. Maya must become *maya*, like the old yogi said, "Nobody doing nothing."

Just for the moment, Maya let go of being somebody, let go of all fear, of all longing. Just for the moment she entered the force of life, the force of creation itself, the Divine power.

Her head followed her mind and slid into the screen. Her breath came more labored in the gelatinous interior, so she couldn't stay long. She had imagined it would be dark but on opening her eyes could see in dusky light. Crystalline structures like colorless snowflakes floated about the tunnel-shaped cyberspace. Maya felt warm and welcome.

Create a messenger, she thought and waited in the humming silence.

Finally, with her patience all but exhausted, she heard a thudding sound at even intervals. From the end of the tunnel a movement matched the thuds, which came closer to her. Maya squinted to make out the shape, small but human, amongst the floating particles. The sound took on more definition.

A boy trotted toward Maya, bouncing a basketball. He moved through the transparent maze of thought patterns as if it were empty.

When he drew closer, she saw that he wore tennis shoes and a New York Knicks t-shirt. He looked about eight or nine years old with brown hair and eyes. He jumped up and tossed the ball at an imaginary basket. "Three pointer," he shouted in a high-pitched voice.

"Hello," she whispered. "I'm Maya. What's your name?"

The boy cocked his eye in a familiar way and grinned. "You know." He twirled the ball on his finger and it turned into a football. He ran and tossed it for a long pass.

"I do?"

"Hermie!" The boy leaped up in the molecules of mind and caught the football. "You named me, didn't you?"

Maya smiled. "I guess I forgot."

Hermie leaned toward her with a silly leer. "Bozo."

He looked very much like Maya, in fact, just what she would have looked like had she been a boy. No doubt, she had manufactured a part of her own subconscious mind. Analysis would have to wait until later.

"Who're you calling a bozo?" she teased.

With a shrug, he dropped to a three-point stance and yelled, "Set, two, three, hike," then dashed back up the tunnel.

Maya feared he would disappear. "Wait, come back. I've got a mystery to solve, and somebody told me you're the only one who can do it."

Pausing, Hermie obviously thought about it then returned to her. "Well, I am pretty smart, smarter than just about anybody, I guess. Who told you?"

"That's a secret, and I won't give you the answer until you see if you can solve the problem for me."

"Thought you said it was a mystery."

Maya chuckled at his quick wit. "Well, I don't know which it is. So I'll tell you my...uh...situation and you can decide. Let's see if you can solve it, okay."

"Shoot!" Hermie tossed the football up, and down came a tennis racket, which he began to swing as if serving imaginary tennis balls.

"There are these people outside the cave, and they're trying to kill me."

"Cool!" He looked like any kid excited to play a fantasy.

"I need to get a message to Dylan Brady, to tell him where I am, but I don't know how to get hold of him. I don't know his email address or his phone number. Even if I did, I'm afraid to try to use the phone because the guys that want to kill me are very dangerous and smart, and they can track a phone call."

A look of stark terror crossed Hermie's face. "I don't want to do this. Maybe the bad guys will track me down and kill me."

"Oh, no, you're completely safe. I promise." Maya realized he was picking up on her fear. She took some deep breaths and calmed herself. "And, if you're successful on your mission, I'll get you a secret decoder ring."

"You will? All right! This is a job for Messenger Man," Hermie shouted and crossed his arms over his chest. "Ta da!" His tennis shoes grew wings, and he scuttled down the tunnel.

Maya's jaws weighed heavily as they worked against the molecular field. She called after him, "Remember, I need Dylan Brady. Come to 46 Haven Road, Markle Falls."

Hermie's shape grew smaller as he hurried into the distance toward two others, who appeared to be a man in a baseball cap and a woman in a full skirt. No matter how Maya tried to clarify her vision, she could make out no more details of their appearance. The man looked familiar, but she couldn't remember where she'd seen him.

The three figures dissolved into undifferentiated form. Only the molecular snowflakes remained.

A wave of exhaustion overcame Maya. She felt as if she'd breathed in lead. With a sudden push, she expelled herself from the computer environment and lay on the makeshift bed. She absolutely had to rest but felt pleased with the contact.

Suddenly cold, she struggled up and turned on the space heater. Even if she couldn't have good light, at least she would feel warm for a while before either the sniper or the ORION officer who was stalking the cabin found her. *They might be one and the same.*

"Please, darling boy," she murmured. "Get through to Dylan and tell him where I am."

Chapter Ten

Dylan dashed up the stairs and into the loft, throwing off his coat. His computer, always running, sat on the tablet arm of a replica of a 1950s student chair. Not taking time to sit, he checked his messages.

One from the Mythos clerk read *Sorry, no Rembrandt, Terrence, Carolyn, or Maya listed as property owners anywhere in any of the states.*

How could that be? Dylan supposed it was possible that they didn't own the brownstone but not likely. He plopped down to type in a request to find out who owned their brownstone. As he did so, he saw a faint image on the screen. Perhaps he had a malfunction and his screensaver had come on too soon.

Taking a closer look, he realized he saw a woman's face. The image seemed odd, very imprecise, and grainy, not like the normal resolution on his screen where people looked exactly like they did in person. The woman's face contorted, as if she spoke with great difficulty. He turned the volume up to high and strained to hear her voice.

"I need Dylan Brady. Come to 46 Haven Road, Markle Falls." The words, though faint, sounded clear, the voice familiar.

Dylan bent close to the screen in an effort to decipher the image. "Maya?"

The woman repeated the message. How in hell had Maya gotten through to him on his email program on his antiquated Internet hookup? In addition, she had managed a visual instead of typing words. Amazing.

Maya had given a demonstration of her power with computers, and he was damn well impressed. She had an incredible intelligence for them, but not for self-preservation or intrigue. She had given her location away.

Markle Falls, Dylan knew the area, north of Ithaca. He called Archer and explained the situation. Archer offered the use of Mythos backup. Hurrying into the bedroom, Dylan packed an overnight bag.

After he brought up a flight plan on the dashboard screen, Dylan dialed the knob for propellers on the Dial-a-Bike and flew it to Markle Falls, arriving at sundown. The blades whirred evenly, and the cockpit felt warm.

While he circled above the clump of cabins, in one of which he believed Maya to be hiding, he searched for lights. If she were there, she'd probably have a light on. She obviously expected him to come for her, otherwise she wouldn't have tried to contact him on the Web. And she trusted him to help her.

That could work to his advantage. She would not expect him to kill her and would be off-guard. At the same time, he felt like a low life taking advantage of her trust in him. He had never disobeyed an order and didn't intend to this time, but he would talk to her first and attempt to ascertain which side of the war she was on. Or, talk her into changing sides, if necessary. She might be willing if she recognized the Anaz-voohri as the real enemy. Humanity could sure use someone with her ability.

Off to the east he could see a glowing Anaz-voohri ship headed toward him, low in the evening sky. He hoped to hell it kept traveling. For the most part, he felt satisfied with the Dial-a-Bike. With its function switched to flying, it was similar to a tiny helicopter but more efficient because it ran on electricity.

Unfortunately, the manufacturer hadn't overcome some technical shortcomings that involved susceptibility to electrical interference. If a pilot came too close to a microwave tower, he could lose a lot of altitude rapidly. A high voltage line could pull him like a magnet and hold him prisoner. Only hardy souls flew Dial-a-Bikes very far. Dylan considered his a challenge.

The Anaz-voohri spaceships constituted a moving electrical barrage. Dylan thought it ironic that so few people had actually seen the ships, or would admit to it in public. Some people still called them a hoax, including the Dial-a-Bike company president, a terrific technological engineer but a throw-back conservative of the first water.

Worst of luck, the spaceship went into hover mode a mile or so away from Dylan and turned on its beacon. The damned Anaz-voohri were after somebody. They hunted human beings like animals and abducted them anytime they wanted to. Seldom did Mythos have advance information detailed enough to intercept the abductions. ORION got all of the headlines about alien busts.

At least the rate of abductions had slowed in the past few years, small consolation for the poor son of a bitch the Anaz-voohri took tonight. He was in a lot of trouble and might never return to Earth.

Too worried to fall asleep, Maya lay on her pallet, the hedge clippers close beside her. When twilight came, the space heater whirred, and an occasional semi-trailer truck rumbled by on the highway, far enough away that the drone of passenger car traffic didn't carry. She thought she heard an airplane engine, odd because Markle Falls lay far from any airport flight path.

An intense, focused beam suddenly poured through the opening and infused the cave with light. The whirring grew to a deafening strength. Maya felt paralyzed so that she could not close her eyes or move her hand to shield them from the brightness.

Down the beam of light floated a tall being with a bald cranium. Her cloak flowed out behind her. Dust motes danced about as she extended an arm to Maya and spoke with a clicking sound. "Come with me."

No, I don't want to go, Maya thought in terror, but she couldn't speak. *Please don't hurt me.* Against her will, her hand rose and clasped the hand of the being.

Together they floated out of the cave on the beam of light and up into the air. Maya could see the tops of the pine trees with the cluster of cabins beneath.

An Anaz-voohri spaceship hovered above her. She recognized it from drawings in the newspaper. A great force pulled her toward the ship.

Nearby circled some kind of an odd-looking helicopter. Maya wondered who might be flying it, whether ORION had come to arrest her or Dylan to rescue her. Since she didn't know, she feared crying out for help. Not that it mattered. If she tried to free herself from the being, she would fall to her death. Maya panicked like a newborn pulled unwillingly from the womb.

The engine of the Dial-a-Bike began to miss, and Dylan searched for a place to land without crashing into a cabin or trees. By the light from the spaceship's beacon, he spotted a country market parking lot and steered toward it. The electrical current surged, and the Dial-a-Bike picked up enough speed to get close then misfired again.

Dylan didn't want to bail out. These machines cost a great deal, and Mythos needed to practice frugality at home in order to fund the high-rolling operations in England and Russia. This Dial-a-Bike had been a high performer, and Dylan would save it if he could. In any case, he pulled his parachute across his back. He turned off the lights and heater to slow the drain of electricity and steered by the light of the spaceship's beacon.

The bare limbs of trees came rushing toward him as the Dial-a-Bike lost altitude. This could be a nasty landing.

At the same time, Dylan felt an adrenaline rush. He might land safely if he choked up the throttle. "Come on, baby, you can do it."

When he approached the block wall around the parking lot, he let the landing gear down and eased into handlebar control. With a loud grating, the wheels clanked on the wall as he went over. The force pitched him forward, bruising his forehead, and threw the bike into a spin when it hit the sludge-filled pavement.

Squeezing the handbrake, he leaned into the skid. The tires crackled as he bumped along toward the country market and came to a stop within a few feet of it. Thankful that he'd not killed himself or anyone else, Dylan leaned against the windshield and took deep breaths.

The wooden door of the market opened, and a large man stepped outside. As he pulled on an overcoat, he shouted, "What the hell's going on? You tryin' to kill us?"

Raising his door, Dylan called out, "Man, I'm sorry. I had an electrical failure in the air."

"Those damn machines ought to be outlawed."

"Maybe so." Dylan chuckled and turned the key in the ignition. Not even a sputter. The battery had died. "Mind if I leave it here till I can get some help?"

The man glanced up at the spaceship's light and shook his head. "What the hell's going on around here?" He went inside and slammed the door.

Dylan took that as a yes. He felt a sense of urgency to continue his mission.

As a fearful Maya and the Anaz-voohri guide floated toward the spaceship, its meshed doors, decorated in an ancient Indian motif, slid soundlessly apart. The light beam they traveled emanated from the ship's beacon and held both travelers in a force field that Maya didn't understand. Torn between admiration of the magnificent ship with its technological superiority, Maya let outrage of her abduction flow over her..

Still afloat, they passed through the domed bridge where several beings with wrinkled pates and elfin cheeks stood or sat at controls. When the beings tipped their heads, as if to disregard the new arrivals, the machinery inside their transparent craniums glistened.

The guide and Maya entered a second room that resembled an operating room with monitors and scanning devices around the perimeter and an examining table in the center. The guide laid Maya on the table, and she stared up at a ceiling mural of a stylized purple eagle, its feathers fading into a mango sunset.

By the time the terrible paralysis left Maya, the guide had begun to strap her arm down. Two helpers, equally ugly, reached for her legs.

Their unwelcome touch mobilized Maya's indignation. She kicked at her captors and screamed, "Let go of me. Leave me alone." She struggled to a sitting position despite their efforts to restrain her. "Don't touch me."

If Maya hadn't remembered the entire trip up the light beam, she would believe she had somehow awakened within a dream. The three beings looked like creatures from a bad sci-fi film. What might they do to her? They glanced at each other with looks of alarm, lights flickering in their heads.

Unable to decipher their meanings, Maya suspected they communicated with each other telepathically. She slapped at one who tried to make her lie down again. "I said don't touch me and I mean it." If she were about to die anyway, she might as well get in some good licks.

"Thank you for your efforts." A tall Anaz-voohri with a feminine voice entered from what appeared to be an office on the side of the room away from the bridge. Her voice sounded metallic. "You may go."

"Yes, Captain Kavak." The guide bowed her head.

"As you wish, exalted leader," said one helper.

All three let go of Maya and filed out through double doors that zipped open when the beings approached. Their dejected posture indicated their unhappiness with their dismissal.

Relieved to at least have mobility again, Maya jumped off the table. Its white covering felt like human skin. The thought of using skin for upholstery made Maya shudder, and she wondered if the Anaz-voohri indulged in such disgusting practices? She rearranged her twisted clothing, filled with trepidation and curiosity about the Anaz-voohri leader.

Captain Kavak looked almost regal in her long silver gown, her head narrow at the chin and wide at the top. The absence of hair on the cranial covering gave her the look of a combination woman and machine. Her almond-shaped eyes had no brows or lashes, only glowing black irises.

A scanner in her hand, Captain Kavak spoke with an even cadence. "I apologize for my colleagues' treatment of you. They thought only of doing their work well, not of your comfort."

Despite the kindly tone, Maya didn't trust this female at all. "What work? Why have you brought me here?"

"Why, you asked to come, did you not?"

"No, I did not. Your minion abducted me against my will."

Captain Kavak didn't exactly smile but her features softened. "Think back to a moment when you wished we would come for you last night. You wanted us to get you out of a dangerous situation."

Maya hadn't a notion of what the captain meant and started to say so. Then she remembered waiting in the dark for the ORION officer to go away and how afraid she had felt. "You heard my thoughts?" Despite her amazement, she realized that telepathy didn't explain why the other three beings had wanted to examine her. This one held a scanner, so they had another agenda. Maya should stay on guard.

"You must forgive me for my poor manners." Captain Kavak laid the scanner on the table and hovered above the floor as she moved to a glass panel in the wall. "We are unaccustomed to receiving visitors here and so I am somewhat out of practice. I would like to offer you some refreshment."

The artificial courtesy seemed bizarre to Maya. "Take me back to Earth."

Two fluted glasses filled with royal blue liquid slid out of the panel. "All in good time, but first..." The captain took one and offered the other to Maya.

"I don't want any."

"You may as well drink it. You'll have to cooperate if you want to get back."

Despite the Anaz-voohri's obvious efforts to sound civilized, Maya sensed an insidious undercurrent of evil in the captain. "What do you want from me?"

"Sit down. Let me explain."

Maya felt too warm with her ski jacket on, but she folded her arms anyway in an effort to protect herself. "I'd rather stand, thank you."

"Very well." Captain Kavak downed her drink in a long swallow. She closed her eyes and sighed then drank the one she'd offered Maya.

Evidently the drink tasted pretty good. Maya may have made a mistake by not taking it. Several hours had passed since she ate the cookies, and she felt hungry and thirsty.

After the female set both of the glasses back into the container, the base retracted into the wall. "It will be necessary for me to examine you, but I won't hurt you. In fact, my device will not even touch your skin. Please lie down on the table."

"I don't see the purpose in this."

Captain Kavak pointed at Maya's forehead with a four-fingered hand that had no thumb, an oddity since the other Anaz-voohri had human-like hands.

Maya began to experience vertigo. As she slid toward the floor unable to control the muscles of her arms and legs, the captain raised her hand. Terrified, Maya felt her body rise without her willing it and stretch out on the table.

Picking up the scanner, the captain passed it over Maya's body and read the digital display. "Very good. Your Recombinant DNA registry reads perfectly, as it should be. We feared something had gone wrong when your trigger went off unexpectedly."

What trigger? Maya thought.

"Very well, I'll explain. You heard a voice in your head that may have sounded like mine. The voice said something like 'it is time' and then you merged with the computer."

That is my exact memory of the moment before the blackout. This alien bitch acts like she had something to do with it.

"There's no need for insults and profanity." Captain Kavak gazed down at Maya.

Dear God, she's reading my thoughts.

"God has nothing to do with it. I'm trying to tell you how the error happened. You humans are so thickheaded it's almost impossible to explain to you, but I will make one more effort."

The captain floated back and forth a few inches above the slate floor, arms swinging wildly. Maya had felt a lot of fear in the past few days but nothing approaching her terror of this creature, who could eliminate Maya with a wave of that deformed hand. *I'd better keep my thoughts docile if I want to get back to Earth alive.*

"It's about time." Captain Kavak waved an exasperated hand in the air.

Maya felt a tingling sensation she recognized as her foot going to sleep. That she felt something at all allowed her to deduce that the paralysis had ended. She sat up, pulled off one boot, and rubbed her foot vigorously.

"Your shutting down the electricity in so much of the eastern United States actually was an error."

"I did cause it then?" Maya felt humbled by the knowledge. She could no longer doubt the suspicion but failed to understand how she had accomplished it.

"We thought something might have gone wrong with your DNA and that accounted for why your trigger went off prematurely. In point of fact, your bumbling parents were the cause. They jumped the gun on your inner trigger." Captain Kavak stopped pacing and stared at Maya. "Well, aren't you going to laugh?"

Confused, Maya couldn't think of a reply.

"That's as close as you'll ever get to a joke from an Anaz-voohri."

"I'm having a difficult time seeing any humor in this situation." Maya wanted to make the comment snide but found sincerity in her heart instead. She had become involved in forces far exceeding her experience. "I'd appreciate it if you'd tell me what my parents have to do with this."

The captain shrugged. "Nothing any more."

Maya thought that an obtuse answer. "And me? What do you expect of me?"

"You are healthy and capable of helping us achieve our mission. We have designed you to assist us and you have no choice in the matter."

"I? How will I assist you?"

"We intend to eliminate the human element from Earth." Captain Kavak's tone took on the quality of one who had recited the words many times, one who had professed beliefs for so long she had lost any revulsion for their content. "You and your ilk make the planet unstable. It is dangerous to neighboring solar systems for you to remain in control of this planet. You ransack the natural resources. You subject the biosphere to all kinds of contaminates. You tamper with energy forces that could disrupt the orbits of planets. You are stupid, greedy, and incapable of responsibility or refinement."

Astounded by the discourse, Maya recognized in the captain the psychology of the zealot. Father had spoken of such people many times and the danger they posed to others. He had in fact counseled some and had resorted to medicating others to make them harmless. Perhaps he had encountered an Anaz-voohri at one time or another.

The captain apparently took no heed of Maya's thoughts and went on. "In short, we intend to take over the stewardship of the planet once we eliminate the human scourge." Pinching Maya's cheeks painfully with long fingers, Captain Kavak said, "You, my pet, will aid in this endeavor. Even though you have no choice, we shall reward you by allowing you and your sisters, assuming they help too, to remain alive after the transfer of power. You all must remain childless. We shall make certain of that. Human reproduction will be illegal, but you will be allowed to live out your natural life span under our supervision."

Her words, fueled by such ruthlessness, overwhelmed Maya with their power. She could not imagine such motivations. From what did they stem? It didn't matter, these Anaz-voohri intended to eliminate the human race. The threat was clear, and Maya knew it. She had no idea what the reference to her sisters meant.

This alien appeared to think that Maya would go along with the program and even help make the disaster happen. Just as Maya's thoughts turned to anger and revenge, she realized that the captain would read them in a heartbeat.

Maya used all the power of her mind to focus on innocuous subjects. She couldn't let this maniac read hostile thoughts. "Captain Kavak, your words have overwhelmed me. May I have a drink now?"

"Why, of course." The captain walked to the drink machine.

What had happened to require the Anaz-voohri to walk on the floor instead of hovering? Maya filed that in her memory as something to think about later when she returned to Earth. Whether safe or unsafe, it would be better to be there. She followed the captain and retrieved her own drink. When she held it up, she prayed that her hand would not shake and offered a toast. "To the future."

"To Anaz-voohri rule."

The glasses clinked, and Maya sipped hers. With a touch of alcohol and a delicious blueberry flavor, it tasted wonderful.

"It is wonderful, isn't it?" Captain Kavak appeared to smile for the first time.

"How do you make this?"

"I know it uses rum. I'll get the recipe for you."

After another round of drinks, the captain seemed almost jovial. Maya knew it wouldn't be wise to continue to drink alcohol. Its effect might prevent her from repressing every emotion that arose within her. Repress them she must in order to return. "Thank you, Captain Kavak, for explaining things to me."

"You deserved to know. Your role is very important to us. Once you've merged with the computer systems, they obey your whim. In fact, they become you." The captain must have noticed the doubt creeping into Maya's thoughts. "The technique will become clear to you after some practice."

Maya affected an innocent look. "What exactly do you expect me to do once I've merged with the computer systems?"

"You are to overload the computer systems and shut down the electrical power to the entire world. Once it is plunged into complete and total darkness, your part will be done. Others have assigned duties to execute the takeover."

Maya hoped her words sounded logical, devoid of the panic she forced down. "I see. Thank you for your faith in me. I need to get back if I'm to carry out my mission."

"Yes, I'll arrange it." Captain Kavak slipped a hand in her pocket and retrieved a figurine of a purple eagle. "Here, take this. I know how humans love their toys."

Maya took it gladly as tangible proof of the encounter. "This is beautiful. I appreciate your...uh...generosity."

The female guide who had escorted Maya to the spaceship entered through the doorway. "You called?"

Captain Kavak tipped the glass toward Maya. "You may return her."

Maya felt like jumping and shouting in delight. She didn't care that ORION or the sniper might await her back on Earth. Those enemies seemed far less intimidating than they had only a short time before. At least they were humans. Maya felt almost kindly toward them.

As two of the beings took her by the arm, Maya gave the captain a small smile that she hoped looked trustworthy. "Thank you, Captain."

"You may call me exalted leader."

"Thank you, exalted leader." Maya repressed a thought about the bizarre nature of the title.

Captain Kavak reached out and patted Maya on the head with the deformed hand. That Maya avoided recoiling was a small miracle. The captain returned the smile, "Good girl."

After stashing the parachute and locking the Dial-a-Bike, Dylan took off to retrace his flight path, or rather the descent. When he called in his report, he learned he'd have to wait for Mythos to get back with him about replacing the battery.

Dylan turned up the collar on his parka and set a brisk pace, glad for the warming trend that had melted the snow earlier in the day. The spaceship turned off its beacon, and dark settled as he hiked down the two-lane country road. He felt very uncertain about the danger that lay ahead.

What had Maya gotten herself into that forced her to turn to him? She had appeared very stressed on the computer screen, desperate even. Some primal desire to protect her arose within him. He must guard his emotions and keep his options clear.

Dylan automatically touched his phase gun. He had no idea about Maya's loyalties or state of mind. She might not even be aware of her abilities. Archer wasn't crazy about the kill order either, so Dylan would check in with Mythos later when he had better assessed the situation.

Moonlight revealed the Rembrandt cabin, and he could see open curtains framing the dark windows. Crouching he slipped up to a Buick parked in the driveway, but no one hid inside. He saw no visible tracks and thought that he was probably alone. He stepped up on the porch and found the front door locked then went around the cabin where the windows and the backdoor already secured.

From there, he noticed the garret style bathroom that he had visited in the remote viewing, conclusive proof if he'd needed any that he'd come to the right place. He remembered how beautiful Maya's naked body looked in flickering candlelight. With a sigh, he realized he had to push the image away and focus on his task.

The unmistakable cold barrel of a phase gun pressed against the back of Dylan's head. A man's gruff voice said, "Don't move or you're dead meat."

Pissed, Dylan wondered why he had allowed himself to become distracted. Oh well, at least now he'd find out who else wanted Maya. Then he'd figure out some way to get the upper hand.

"Turn around very slowly and open your coat."

When Dylan complied, he recognized the ORION soldier from Lola Compson's funeral. Thin, wiry, early forties, graying hair with sideburns longer than folks usually wear them. No way to mistake him. Dylan had made a good decision to go to the funeral. It had borne fruit tonight.

The soldier took Dylan's phase gun, stashed it in a jacket pocket, and patted Dylan down. He had no other weapon, except for the knife in his boot where the soldier didn't search. "Where's Maya Rembrandt?"

"You tell me and we'll both know."

With a scowl, the soldier shot through the lock and opened the back door. He indicated with his gun that Dylan should enter. Once inside the main room, the soldier flipped on the kitchen light and said, "Remove your coat."

When he complied, Dylan noticed that the cabin felt warm. Someone had been here, probably Maya, and had left without intending to stay away long. Otherwise, she would have turned the furnace down.

Wouldn't it have been crazy if the Anaz-voohri had taken her? But that couldn't be the case. Their ship had stopped at least a mile away from here.

The soldier forced Dylan to sit on a plastic kitchen chair and tied his hands behind his back with rope. Dylan tried to flex his fingers to keep the knots loose, but the soldier cinched them tighter, searing the taut skin.

"Who the hell are you?" The soldier took Dylan's ID out of his pocket. "Brady, huh? A pilot? What are you doing here?"

"Just came to check on Maya. She's a friend of mine."

"If you're such a good friend, why didn't you speak to her at the funeral?"

"Well, uh…Maya was an emotional wreck. I didn't want to bother her, you know?" Dylan recognized the soldier might become a fearsome enemy. Whatever he wanted remained to be seen. He wouldn't likely be forthcoming, but Dylan read the name Schwartz embroidered over the ORION constellation with a sergeant's insignia. That knowledge increased Dylan's confusion.

It wasn't like ORION to send one officer on something as big as this. Carrick must think it big or he wouldn't have ordered Maya's parents killed. Usually ORION sent a whole swarm of troops on such details.

Taking a close look at the sideburns, Dylan believed them way too long. They could hide scars that made a hybrid look human. That would mean the Anaz-voohri had infiltrated ORION. This whole thing could become very big indeed.

Dylan didn't buy the idea that Schwartz had come here to kill Maya. He'd had the chance in the street when he shot Lola. Why had this fellow acted alone, and what did he intend? Dylan had nothing to lose by asking. "Why are you looking for Maya?"

"Shut up or I'll put a gag on you." Schwartz opened a kitchen cabinet and surveyed the shelves.

From Dylan's perspective across the small kitchen, it appeared that the shelves held nothing but some spices and a packet of teabags. However, some apple peels had not decomposed in the trash where they lay with plastic sleeves for meat or cheese. If Maya had been here, why would she take the food and not turn down the heat? Something didn't make sense.

"You want some tea?" Schwartz asked.

Dylan nodded with the faint hope that Schwartz would untie him to drink it.

With a snigger, Schwartz filled one cup with water and set it in the microwave with a teabag in it. "Tough shit."

Chapter Eleven

Alone and back in the warm cave, Maya sat exhausted on the pallet. She couldn't tell whether she had fallen asleep or not. Her perception of time had altered while aboard the spaceship. Fifteen minutes or fifteen days might have elapsed. She could only be certain that night had fallen and that the heater's battery still worked.

Her purse lay where she'd hidden it in a niche in the cave wall. From inside the purse, she pulled out the hand-held videophone to read the watch embedded in its face. As soon as she grabbed the phone, the digital readout crackled and went dark.

"Damn." Maya threw the blasted thing against the cave wall. She could no longer ignore the facts. Something about her energy disrupted electricity, the worst part of it being that she never knew when or what sort of things she might affect. She needed conscious control of the process, if for no other reason than to keep from ruining her equipment.

Whatever the Anaz-voohri had done to her must have caused this nasty result. Those sons-of-bitches. When had they recombined her DNA? She had no memory of ever seeing them before. She had to conclude they had tampered with her memory, a very scary thing. What else didn't she remember about herself?

When Maya picked up the laptop, the screensaver blanched in an odd way. She glanced at the tiny readout at the bottom of the screen. December 14, 2022, 7:12 P, EDT. The whole abduction had happened in real time. It surprised her to realize her entire life had changed so dramatically in somewhat over an hour.

The monitor sizzled and went dark. Just like the phone. What had happened to her aboard that dreadful ship?

How much danger did she face and from where? The Anaz-voohri seemed incredibly powerful, and they intended her to do their bidding. The night of the blackout, she'd heard a small voice, almost her own thought but not quite. Rattled at the time, she'd forgotten to analyze the voice. No doubt it came from the aliens, maybe from that bitch of a captain. Well, no more.

From now on, Maya intended to control everything about her life, including so-called triggers in her head. She would do only what she wanted. The Anaz-voohri had given her an unusual ability that she would turn against them. She would go so far as to kill them if she had to, to maintain her integrity.

From outside the cave she heard no helicopters or airplanes. It appeared that neither Dylan nor ORION had found her hiding place. She wondered again who had been flying the helicopter and whether that boded ill or well.

It had been a long shot to try to contact Dylan anyway. Maya admonished herself to give up the romantic fantasy of rescue by a handsome hybrid, no matter how enticing he seemed. She must end any intellectual sidesteps in illusion and depend on her own efforts. Strictly speaking, people probably considered a hybrid of some sort, too. What a repulsive thought.

Her father had assured her she would be safe here in Markle Falls, but he'd obviously not reckoned on the ORION soldier's stalking her. Why had Father been so cryptic? He probably thought what she didn't know wouldn't hurt her. He'd said so often enough over the years.

That had turned out to be the big lie of her life. What she had not understood about her mental abilities had hurt her a great deal. She knew now that her mind was a powerful resource and could not turn away from the truth. She would learn how to use it or die in the effort. Others would never use it for their gain.

Apparently, her parents had known all about her Anaz-voohri connection. Snidely, she thought they'd surely had enough time to tell her in twenty-two years. It could have gone something like this, "Look, Maya, the Anaz-voohri rigged your DNA. You're a walking bomb. We're sorry, but don't worry, we'll take good care of you."

Right now she didn't see how she'd ever be able to forgive them.

Starving, she made two ham and cheese sandwiches, shoved her purse in her zipper pocket, then stuffed a Coke in one side pocket and some chocolate chip cookies in the other. She had worn the yellow ski jacket so long it felt like second skin. Once this horrible business ended, she'd throw the jacket in the trash and buy herself a scrumptious new turquoise one. She pulled on a black knitted hat and gloves and picked up the sandwiches.

Maybe that man from ORION had given up. She'd never know if she didn't go back to the cabin. She had to find answers if she possibly could and set out, eating as she hiked in the crisp night air. Her anger with both her parents and the Anaz-voohri fueled her. She hated being used.

With her stomach full and her wits sharp, Maya reached the cabin grounds to see light shining from the kitchen. She didn't remember leaving any lights on but may have done so in her anxiety to get away fast.

Not willing to take any chances, she remained in the shadows of the trees and crept along the edge of the property. Around back she found a portion of the door missing. Only a rough edge remained where the knob had been, and the door hung open at the hinges.

Moving as quietly as possible she arrived opposite the kitchen window, three-quarters of the way around the house. Through the open curtains, she saw an ORION soldier moving around inside. Her worry increased with the realization that he looked like the one who had been stalking her. She could see the shoulder of a person who sat at the table but couldn't tell whether or not he was another soldier.

When his head moved into the frame made by the window, he seemed familiar.

Maya would satisfy her curiosity then get out of here. She edged on around the perimeter to stay out of the line of sight of the window and slipped up beneath it. With her mouth covered to keep her breath from becoming visible, she waited, fearful of rising and exposing her location.

All was quiet inside. How odd that these two housebreakers didn't talk to each other. Intending to drop back down immediately, she inched her eyes up to the window ledge and took a quick peek.

On the chair sat Dylan with a gag over his mouth. He twisted his shoulders, obviously trying to free his hands. He looked straight at her with panic on his face. He moved his head wildly, trying to communicate something to her. But what? Then she realized she couldn't see the other soldier any more.

Taking a deep breath, Maya dashed to the back door and rushed inside.

Dylan didn't speak but gestured with frantic black eyes for Maya to untie him.

The other man had to be somewhere within earshot so Maya didn't dare even whisper. She grabbed a serrated knife from a drawer and started to saw the ropes.

Nodding, Dylan tried to tell her something with low grumbling.

The toilet flushed upstairs.

Terrified, Maya laid the knife in Dylan's sweaty hand. When their eyes met, she mouthed the words, "I'll be back."

The clomp of boot steps descending the stairs energized her with fierce resolve. She hurried out the back door, glad she'd thought to bring her purse, which contained the car keys.

Dylan had come to help, and look at the mess he'd gotten into because of her. She had to save him, no matter what.

Moving along the trees, she retraced her steps. Once around front, Maya crept to the Buick and opened the trunk. Conscious of making as little noise as possible, she worked until she freed the tire iron, careless of scrapes to her hands.

With tire iron in hand, she ducked under the living room window. Strains of the Channel Eleven theme song drifted from inside. The soldier might be watching the news. She moved to the kitchen window and saw Dylan struggling to free himself. He glanced toward her.

"I'll be right there," Maya mouthed while she removed her gloves and stuffed them in her pocket.

Maya had to either knock the soldier on the head or free Dylan so he could attack the soldier. Neither prospect seemed possible. Even if she managed to slip in unnoticed, she doubted she had the strength to render anyone unconscious. On the other hand, the downstairs was a very small space. She couldn't imagine she'd successfully get in and cut Dylan loose without being discovered.

The moment she stepped into the kitchen, Dylan let her know he'd been considering the same problem. He motioned with his head toward the living room. Maya felt relieved that he had taken the decision out of her hands.

With the TV blaring, she slipped beneath the stairs rather than walk directly into the living room. She could see long sideburns on the side of the soldier's head, which lay against the recliner. If he moved his eyes even a fraction, he would see her.

Maya raised the tire iron high above her and lunged at the soldier. He gave her a surprised glance and moved forward as she struck him across the nose.

Blood spurted out of his nostrils. "What the fuck you doing?" The soldier looked stunned as he grabbed at her waist and stood up. The chair rocked forward against his legs, toppling him toward her.

Grunting, Maya hammered him, landing two blows on his shoulder before the soldier wrestled the tire iron from her hands. He pushed her down and reached for his phase gun just as Dylan came flying into the room.

Dylan knocked the gun out of the soldier's hands and dropkicked him in the groin. With a yelp, the soldier grabbed his crotch and crumpled to the floor. Maya scrambled to the phase gun and picked it up.

Jumping on the soldier's back, Dylan pulled his arms together and yelled, "Get a light cord or something to tie him up."

Frantic, Maya jerked an unlit lamp off the side table and unplugged it. She yanked at the socket and pulled the black cord free of the base. "Here." When she handed the cord to Dylan, he bound the soldier's hands.

Blood pooled around the soldier's nose, and he groaned. "You'll regret this."

Maya pointed the phase gun at the soldier, feeling awkward. She'd never used one, but nobody had to know that.

"See how you like this, asshole." Dylan kept a tight grip on the soldier. "Now get up."

The soldier struggled to stand and stumbled toward the recliner. When Dylan shoved, the soldier dropped into the chair with a grunt.

Dylan's broad chest heaved, but he smiled at Maya, indicating the phase gun. "Want me to take that?"

Happy to be rid of it, Maya passed the gun over. She had no doubt Dylan would know how to use one. She noticed blood on her palms. "I'll be right back."

Maya's back and arms ached as she trudged up the stairs to the bathroom sink and let water run over her hands.

The TV went silent below as she dried several small lacerations then applied antiseptic and Band-Aids.

Thank goodness, Dylan had been here. Otherwise, she knew how easily she could end up killed. He seemed like such a good man. She didn't think he'd been hurt in the fracas but grabbed the medical supplies just in case. She could hear his commanding voice from below as he spoke to the soldier.

When Maya entered the living room, Dylan had removed his parka. Wearing a black sweatshirt and a medallion shaped like a crystal, he sat on the coffee table and held the gun on the sniper, who looked grim and angry.

Dylan said, "Our friend here, Sergeant Schwartz, has decided to answer a few questions."

"Can I go first?" Maya leaned against the stairs.

"Sure."

"Why have you been stalking me?"

"I haven't." Schwartz nodded toward Dylan. "Maybe you better ask him what he's doing here. If there's a stalker involved, it's him."

Maya doubted that and said to Schwartz, "You waited outside the cabin for hours last night, and here you are again."

"Sounds like stalking to me." With a shrug, Dylan pushed up his sleeves, revealing raw rope wounds on both wrists.

Maya offered the antiseptic. "You need this."

"I can wait." Dylan raised the gun in a threatening way. "Now, answer the lady, and don't make us wonder what to ask."

Schwartz sounded like he had a very bad cold. "I wasn't stalking you. I came up here to warn you to be careful because it was just a matter of time."

"Warn me? About what?" Maya doubted he'd tell the truth about anything. Contemptuously, she threw the empty Coke can and plastic wrap in the trash and stuffed the supplies in her pockets. She didn't feel disposed to offer medical help to Schwartz at the moment.

"I wanted to warn you and your folks, but it's too late now."

Goosebumps went up Maya's neck. "Are my parents in danger, too?" Maybe this guy knew the reason she'd not been able to contact her parents. Where on earth were they?

Blood dripped from his nose as Schwartz spoke. "Yesterday, I came to tell you that I garbled your names in the ORION computer. I didn't know whether Terrence had told you or not, but it was just a temporary thing. I knew some officer would figure out Rembel was really Rembrandt and come after you here."

Schwartz's tale jived with what her father had said. Fear crept into Maya's heart that something awful had happened to her parents. "What's it too late for?"

Dylan held up a warning hand to hush Schwartz. "You better brace yourself, Maya. I've got bad news." Dylan chewed his lip, and his eyes looked haunted. "ORION killed your parents."

Schwartz snarled. "That's what the killers expect everyone to believe."

"Killed? My parents are dead?" Staggered, Maya didn't know what to feel, but she couldn't give vent to any emotion right now, not with her life at stake. Choking down bile, she sat beside Dylan, and he gave her a sympathetic look.

Schwartz's cough distorted his words. "I came back here today to try to help you get away. I still will if you want me to, but we've got very little time."

Dylan raised an eyebrow. "If ORION didn't kill them, who did?"

"The Anaz-voohri." Schwartz spit out the words.

"Why would they want Maya's parents dead?" Dylan sounded convinced of the guilt of the Anaz-voohri.

Maya decided she ought to believe Schwartz, after all, because the Anaz-voohri captain had alluded to her parents in a telling way. The captain must have known Maya's parents were already dead, maybe even ordered it herself. "Why would they do such a terrible thing?"

"They were pissed that Terrence and Carolyn messed up their plans for Maya." Schwartz bent over with a coughing spasm. "Help me. I'm choking."

Dumbfounded, Maya found a kitchen towel, moistened it, and hurried to the recliner. Dylan held Schwartz's shoulders while Maya swabbed his nose. The coughing subsided.

Dylan released him. "Tell us all you know, and we'll let you go."

"The Anaz-voohri," Schwartz said, "had programmed Maya to go off on a preset emotional trigger that they would supply. I don't know what it was or when it was supposed to happen. But Lola's death upset the timetable. I guess it was that because Maya's trigger went off right after."

"You killed Lola, didn't you?" Dylan asked.

Looking more resigned than guilty, Schwartz nodded.

"Why?" Maya caught a breath. Schwartz was the sniper.

"I did it because Carolyn insisted." Schwartz's voice betrayed a lot of frustration. He must have known her for a long time to have that kind of reaction. "I told Terrence it was a bad idea, but he always appeased her. He was afraid she'd get pissed and turn him in. I figured if I didn't do what she wanted she might turn me in, too."

"Mother wanted Lola dead?" Horrified, Maya rejected the idea. "I know she didn't like her, but to plot her murder?"

"Your mother was a very jealous woman. More than you know."

Looking impatient, Dylan rose and stepped toward Schwartz. "Tell us how you got involved with Maya's parents."

"They weren't her parents. You might as well know that."

"Not my parents? That's insane." That couldn't be true, else Maya had indeed jumped down the rabbit hole.

"They were hybrids, like me," Schwartz said. "We've all been trying to do our duty by the Anaz-voohri. Their job was to protect Maya. Mine was to infiltrate ORION. Now, those Anaz-voohri bastards have killed my friends, and I'm pretty sure they're after me."

"If they weren't my parents, then who are?" Maya doubted she could absorb any more revelations without turning to stone.

Dylan gave Schwartz a cock-eyed grin. "No doubt Jason Carrick will take a dim view of your parentage, too, once he finds out. No wonder he set his flunkies on Maya."

Helicopter blades whirred in the distance.

"That's them!" Schwartz tried to wiggle out of his bonds. "They've figured out the computer glitch. Untie me, please."

"We've got to get out of here," Dylan said to Maya.

"I know a place."

Maya didn't question the wisdom of taking Dylan to her hiding place. She needed to trust somebody, and she might as well take a chance on him. Dylan grabbed his parka.

"Don't leave me here!" Schwartz screamed. "They'll kill me!"

"Are you up for letting this guy go?" Dylan asked. "I did say we would."

Ruffian that he appeared to be and Lola's killer in the bargain, Maya couldn't leave Schwartz for certain capture. He had been her parents' friend. When she nodded, Dylan slashed the electrical cord away, and Schwartz leaped up.

Helicopter searchlights fanned the cabins as Dylan flipped the lights off in the kitchen and ran out the backdoor with Maya. Schwartz scrambled out behind them and fell down the steps.

Maya and Dylan ran into the tree line where they ducked down behind a fallen pine. Once back on his feet, Schwartz took off in the opposite direction, stumbling toward a neighboring cabin.

Dylan tapped the medallion. "Apollo reporting. They're here." He said to Maya, "It's ORION all right. I recognize the logo."

Maya wondered who he contacted on that gadget around his neck, definitely not ORION or the police. Who was this guy, anyway? And by what irrational reasoning did she trust him? "The place isn't far, a cave. I think we'll be safe there." At least she hoped so. Nothing seemed certain any more.

"Lead the way." Dylan took her hand and they dashed down the lane and out to the road amid the beams of crisscrossing light, the gyrating wind, and the rattle of chopper blades and engines.

Chapter Twelve

Dylan watched the swarm of helicopters circle the cabin. When all but one landed, he concluded that the ORION efforts focused there, at least temporarily. That gave him and Maya precious minutes.

Keeping in the shadows, Dylan and Maya ran parallel to the road for about three quarters of a mile. His heart began to pound with the cold and the exertion. He welcomed the trickle of the falls, a respite from the receding noise of helicopters.

"This way," Maya murmured. She left the road and headed deeper into the woods.

When Dylan followed, brambles caught on his parka and scratched his face. "How much farther?"

"We're almost there." With labored breath, Maya ducked beneath the limbs of a tall oak and pointed toward a thicket. "See."

With the light from the helicopters dimmer, Dylan saw nothing except a large outcropping of some kind of bushes, probably berries, but he didn't know much about horticulture. "Where's the cave?"

"Here." Maya circled around the bushes and pressed against the wall of an outcropping. A faint red glow issued from it. "Watch your head." Then she ducked and entered the cave.

The hiding place pleased Dylan. They were right on it before he saw the cave at all. From the air, he doubted anyone could recognize it. The top would look like a low hill.

Ignoring the thorns and woody stems, Dylan edged behind the bushes, stooped, and followed Maya inside the muted interior. Its warmth surprised him until he noticed a battery-powered heater. From its glowing red core, he could make out the shapes of piles of clothes, blankets, and food.

Fearful or not, Maya had evidently given some thought to provisions.

Maya sat on the blanket and caught her breath. "I have a lantern, but I doubt we should use it."

"Not now. We'd better be cautious."

"You think they'll come after us?" Maya sounded scared.

"I don't know. Depends on what Schwartz tells them. He seemed to want to protect you, at least at the start, but I wouldn't count on him. ORION has some very effective ways of making people talk."

"I hadn't thought of that." She shivered. "Guess we'll just have to wait it out."

Dylan picked up the heater by its casing and hid it behind the trunk, but it still created light. "Well, that's not working."

"Here." Maya handed him some pillows. "Will these help?"

After he stacked the pillows up in front of the heater, Dylan scurried out the cave entrance to check but could still see red light. He crawled in and sat down. "I think we've got to douse the heater, at least for now."

"All right." Maya removed the pillows and reached for the heater then sat back. "Maybe you better do it."

Surprised, Dylan wondered just how powerful she had become. Her interface with technology might have gone haywire. He turned off the switch.

Complete darkness settled on them, and Maya gave a ragged sigh.

Dylan felt sorry for her and wanted to reassure her. Losing her parents and running for her life were not things she signed on for. He had at least known the extent of his commitment. "It'll stay warm in here for a while." Sitting beside her, Dylan took off his parka and felt his sore wrists. His efforts to free himself had battered his skin. Then the kitchen knife had caused several lacerations. "Think I'll take some of that ointment now."

Maya laid the tube in his hand. "Are your wrists bad?"

"They're all right." Dylan knew he should clean the wounds, but this would have to do. The medicine stung when he rubbed it in.

"Band-Aids won't work. I didn't bring any gauze, but I can…" Maya rustled around, feeling for something. Then she made a ripping sound.

"What are you doing?"

"Making some bandages. Hold out your wrists." When he did, Maya wrapped soft cloth around each of them.

"That feels better." Dylan felt touched by her concern. "Thanks."

"You're welcome." Her voice sounded soft and sad.

"And thanks for rescuing me." Dylan wished she could see him smile. "I was in a hell of a bind back there until you came along." What an understatement. He'd felt most annoyed with himself for falling into Schwartz's hands. The man was a trained professional, but just the same, Dylan would take more care from now on. He'd not get another reprieve with the stakes so high.

Maya's voice brightened for the first time. "That's all right. I owed you."

"For what?"

"Finding me in the park? Trying to stop the arrest?" Her tone indicated surprise that he'd had to ask.

"Oh, right." Dylan realized she had a whole different take on his actions. She had no idea about his orders or even about his true identity. Naturally, she felt gratitude toward him. He wondered how much she did know about the blackout and the Anaz-voohri. She at least seemed less confused than she had at the funeral and in the park.

"I might have frozen to death if you hadn't come along. How did you know where I was?"

What should Dylan tell her about himself or the mission? Assuming they got out of this mess with ORION tonight, if he took her back to Mythos, any options he'd have would go out the window. Archer didn't give orders lightly.

Before he would even consider disobeying them, Dylan felt compelled to determine whether or not Maya really presented a threat. If he could make her understand what the Anaz-voohri had done to her, she might react like he had and turn on them to fight back. Bottom line, if he had to kill her, she might as well know the truth about why.

"Dylan?"

Shifting so that he sat opposite her, he tried unsuccessfully to see her face. He felt awkward talking to her in complete darkness and took a casual tone in the hope of contradicting the melodramatic nature of his words. "I work for a secret organization called Mythos. We expose government corruption whenever we can and we fight the Anaz-voohri."

"You fight them?" Maya sucked in a breath. "They took me up to their ship."

Remembering her file, Dylan assumed she referred to her abduction at the age of two. "You know about that, then?"

"Tonight. Before I came to the cabin and found you. They took me up to their ship, actually abducted me, and the captain told me I'd caused the blackout."

Maybe she didn't know anything about her childhood trauma, but at least she was up to speed on the blackout. "I'm glad that's out in the open. At Mythos, we knew that you were the cause. That's why I was looking for you."

Maya sighed. "I didn't think it was a coincidence."

"Do you understand how you did it?"

"Not completely, but I've got some ideas. The fact that you came after me tonight shows me I'm on the right track."

"How?" Dylan wanted to tell her she could trust him, but he didn't feel right lying. "I saw you on my computer at home. You gave me your address."

"Oh," Maya whispered.

Dylan wanted to understand what thought processes she had used. "How did you do it?" When she didn't answer, he thought maybe he should give her some bolstering. "I've done some computer espionage. I've got some background. Go ahead and tell me."

Maya remained silent for so long that Dylan began to worry. He hated not being able to see her. He had a new appreciation for the value of body language in communication and decided on a new tack. "You were actually in a ship? What was it like? Man, I'd love to pilot one of those babies."

"Very high tech. I didn't ride in it, but I saw the bridge. They are powerful people, or beings, or whatever you call them. Their feet don't always touch the ground when they walk. They can read minds and they can paralyze people." Maya's voice cracked. "They had me completely under their control, and I don't want to ever feel like that again. They scare me. I don't want to go on living if they're in charge."

"Did they tell you their intentions?"

"To take over the planet. Under what circumstances I don't even want to consider." Maya sounded livid.

Dylan realized she knew quite a bit. Whether she could control her actions or whether the Anaz-voohri had made her a helpless pawn remained to be seen. He felt certain she didn't have any desire to do their bidding. It surprised him how relieved he felt to know that. Maya seemed like an honest person caught in a bad situation. The least he could do was help her think it through.

"They said I had sisters, but I'm an only child. Oh…my parents weren't my real parents…maybe I do have sisters somewhere." Her breathing took on an uneven cadence, and her subtle movements indicated that she was crying.

Dylan reached out in the hope of touching her cheek but found her shoulder. Wanting to comfort her, he trailed his hand down her arm and squeezed her hand.

Her voice sounded frail. "I'm so cold."

Picking up his coat, he scooted back against the trunk. "Come here." When he held up his arm, she moved into it with a sob. He pulled the blankets over them and put his parka on top. "Is that better?"

Her fresh-smelling hair brushed his cheek when she nodded. "My parents are dead." She trembled against him. "At least I thought they were my parents. They're all I had, and I'm so mad at them, but I can't be angry now because they're dead."

Dylan's heart went out to her. It really didn't matter how rotten her foster parents had acted, at least not tonight. She'd get more perspective later. "I know how you feel. My parents were murdered by the Anaz-voohri, too."

Maya shook for a long time with soft sobs. Dylan didn't know what else to do but hold her.

When she finally stilled, she said, "This day has been so long, I can't even remember its beginning. I am just so tired."

While Dylan considered a response, she relaxed in his arms. He felt glad to let her sleep in his arms, it was the least he could do. He knew far too well what a nasty, lonely business grief could be.

Unquestionably, Maya was desirable. He had seen her naked, so he had first hand knowledge of that. He had trouble visualizing having sex with her and then killing her. On the other hand, things could change fast. Maybe he should keep his options open. Not tonight though. Maya seemed far too upset and vulnerable.

Not that he wanted to get involved with any woman in an emotional way. He needed space to do his work. Besides, attachments brought the risk of loss. The deaths of one's parents and two failed relationships ought to teach anybody.

There was no denying how good Maya felt cuddled in his arms, like she belonged there. He could go on holding her for a long time. Dylan shoved aside any sexual imaginings along with gentle thoughts toward her as a person. He admonished himself to stay on task.

Did Maya's abilities operate like his did, without physical manifestation? Maybe hers required machinery. She'd not wanted to touch the heater no doubt because she feared interactions she couldn't control. She represented a huge threat to the world if she couldn't harness the energy or if she chose not to. He'd kill her if he had to, but damn, he liked her. He just couldn't get past her sincere and trusting manner. The fucking Anaz-voohri had jerked her around big time.

Dylan tuned his ear to the outside world. While they'd talked, the helicopters had gone away. Strain as he did, he couldn't hear anything. Not a car on the highway or a duck left behind for the winter.

Dawn soon would mask the heater's light, so he decided to take a chance. Otherwise, they might not survive till morning. Carefully, he nudged Maya out of his arms and laid her down. She didn't stir. Dylan crept to the heater and turned it on then returned to enfold her, ski jacket and all.

After tugging the blankets around them, he gave his sleeping assignment a fond hug and silently agreed with her.

He couldn't remember when the day began either. Worried about discovery, he wished he could muster a prayer.

Somehow any religious belief had deserted Dylan the night he'd broken into the hospital records room. He wished he could regain the simple comfort he had experienced sometimes during prayer. Now he felt a great emptiness instead. The fucking Anaz-voohri had robbed him of the one solace that remained from his mother's teachings, faith in God.

Seated on the edge of the oak desk in the New York office, Carrick read the files recovered from Terrence Rembrandt. Windowless for security reasons, the room looked like its counterparts around the globe with video screens, phones, and gunmetal filing cabinets. Two pictures adorned the walls—one a large photo of Carrick and Hillenbrand shaking hands the day of the captain's promotion, the other of an ugly, fat woman and two little boys dressed in the baggy styles of twenty years ago.

Carrick's anger boiled up at the realization that those hybrids had gotten away with raising that little Rembrandt bitch right under Hillenbrand's nose. He had deserved to die for that alone, never mind that the dumb son-of-a-bit had been duped by one of his own officers.

Flavia's voice came over the intercom. "Sergeant Schwartz is here to see you."

About goddamn time, Carrick thought. "Send him in." He picked up the placard that read *Captain Lester V. Hillenbrand, ORION Commander of New York* and dumped it into the wastebasket. The world was a safer place without that incompetent fuckoff in it.

Sitting in the regular issue Navy blue leather chair, Carrick smoothed his hair and composed himself mentally for this important interview.

Schwartz entered and snapped to attention. A homely man in the best of condition, he looked trashy with a rumpled uniform, a swollen nose, and one eye blackened. "General, sir, please forgive my appearance. I've come straight from the landing pad." He held his felt hat crushed beneath an armpit and gazed at the photos. "Sorry to hear of Captain Hillenbrand's drowning. I felt proud to serve with him."

Carrick tapped a ball point so hard its point broke on the desk. "Your assignment was to ID Maya Rembrandt. Did you find her?"

"Yes, sir. At 46 Haven Road, Markle Falls."

"And did you apprehend her?"

Schwartz shuffled his position and glanced at the floor. "She was a lot more difficult to handle than I'd supposed."

"Attention!" This traitor wouldn't get the chance to relax in Carrick's presence. "So you're telling me she got away?"

When Schwartz snapped back, he said, "Yes, sir. I'm sorry, sir."

"Where is she now?"

"I don't know, sir." Blood oozed from Schwartz's nose. "She had a car. She may have gone on foot. I just don't know, sir."

"Why not?"

"The helicopters made so much noise I couldn't hear. She may have started up the rental car. I couldn't see because the other officers whisked me away so fast. She could be anywhere, sir."

"You're a mess, Schwartz. Are you trying to make me believe one little girl inflicted so much damage on you?"

"No, sir. They…uh…tied me up. She had an accomplice. I don't know who he was, maybe a boyfriend. I can give you a description. He's about six feet tall, Caucasian, black hair..."

"We already know his name and occupation from the police report."

"Thank you, sir." Schwartz saluted.

Not for one minute did Carrick believe Dylan Brady to be a pilot for hire, as the report had said. He was a Mythos operative, protected by the President's crony, that bastard Lawson Archer, whose all-powerful ranks Carrick had so far failed to crack. It pissed him off mightily that Mythos was off limits. In his fantasies, that idiot American President and other presidents around the world begged Carrick to forgive them for their stupidity and to take over the functions of incompetent Mythos.

While he reviewed the scene in his mind, Carrick glanced away. He enjoyed forcing Schwartz to hold the salute an uncommonly long time just for the hell of it. When he saw Schwartz's right hand trembling, Carrick returned the salute and said, "Sergeant, I have one more question." He pressed the intercom button. "Has the medic arrived?" It pleased him to notice that Schwartz had become even more agitated, wiped his nose with the back of his hand, and restlessly twisted his hat.

"Yes, sir," came Flavia's voice.

"Send him in." Rising, Carrick turned the full force of his disapproval on Schwartz. "Tell me, why do you wear sideburns?"

Schwartz looked like a sonic blast hit him between the eyes again. "Just...uh...my lady friend likes them. That's all."

The medic opened the door and stepped inside. An expression of terror crossed Schwartz's face at the muscular Latino man with a syringe in his hand.

"To be more accurate," Carrick said, "those sideburns hide scars from surgery, done to add fullness to fucking Anaz-voohri cheeks." He picked up a mini CD and tapped it. "Don't bother to deny it. I've read the files we recovered from the Rembrandt house. The good doctor was your shrink, I believe."

Schwartz blanched and tried to get out the door like the scared and cowardly hybrid he was. The medic blocked the way and sunk the syringe into Schwartz's stomach.

When Schwartz cried out, the medic said, "It's gonna be all right, Sergeant. We can talk all you want. I think you'll be with us for a good, long time."

Sagging almost to the floor, Schwartz nodded docilely at the medic. "Okay." He laid his arm over the medic's shoulder and allowed himself assistance.

"Oh, and, Doc," Carrick sniggered as they went out the door, "Dr. Rembrandt's diagnosis was persecution complex. Maybe you can work on that and help the sergeant resolve it."

Carrick walked to the doorway and watched the two cross the reception area and head toward the elevators. Given a choice, he'd just as soon murder the traitorous son of a bitch, but no telling what information they'd need later. Better to keep the hybrid bastard alive. The medics would keep him incapacitated for as long as necessary, incarcerated, and medicated into mindlessness, a fate too good for a hybrid, anyway. Later, he suffer extermination when Carrick felt certain the hybrid had nothing more to contribute to the search for those bitch sisters.

Sitting at the outer desk, Flavia appeared to have her attention on a computer monitor but surreptitiously glanced at the hybrid and the medic.

"Lieutenant," Carrick smiled down at her, "double the guard on the Rembrandt house on Walnut Street, and I want a full contingent redeployed to Markle Falls. Kill orders remain in place."

"Yes, sir." Flavia's broad face bore a look of vindication.

"No, make that shoot to stun. I want to talk to the bitch myself before she dies."

"Right away. Anything else?"

"Make some recommendations for special task forces. I want to appoint one to search for each of those seven moles."

Holding his head high, Carrick marched back into his office. Others, including Flavia, had to see him strong. Once he'd closed the door, he sagged against it, holding his stomach. He wanted to throw up at the thought that his precious ORION infiltrated. For years, he'd railed against GSS for their failure to keep their ranks pure. Now, it had happened to him.

"Dumb fuck, you let some little girl best you," he whispered to himself. "Dumb fuck, you let some idiot hybrid sneak in." He beat on the sides of his head. "Dumb fuck, dumb fuck! You gotta get them all, or you'll lose your power and your authority. Then where will you be? Dumb fuck!"

Chapter Thirteen

A mixture of sensations awoke Maya. Her legs felt cold on the back sides, the rest of her warm. Her head moved ever so slightly with the rhythm of Dylan's breathing as she lay against his chest. Even through the fabric of their clothing, she was incredibly aware of his presence. The length of his muscular body touched hers in repose beneath the blankets.

So this was the way it felt to actually sleep with a man. Cozy, protected. She dared not move, else he would awaken, requiring her to say something. For the moment, she cherished the sense of belonging, of feeling at home in the arms of a good, strong man. She didn't want to think of the turmoil in her life.

Too soon, emotions and images crowded her memory – the fear that drove her into the cave, her helplessness before the Anaz-voohri captain, the fight with Schwartz, running from ORION, the deaths of her parents and Lola.

The only good Maya could see in those events was that they had brought Dylan to her. How much more difficult it would all have been without him. What would this day offer them? She didn't know how to retrieve her parents' bodies and arrange their funeral without exposing herself to danger. She thought it pointless to worry. Nothing could be worse than yesterday.

When Dylan yawned and stretched, she pretended to sleep. After a moment, he gently extracted himself from beneath her and crawled to the opening of the cave. She opened her eyes and noticed by wan morning light that he had a very nice butt.

Once he'd gone outside, she could see only his jeans as he stood up to his full height. She imagined how good that felt, after the requirement to sit or stoop inside the sloping cave, hardly bigger than a walk-in closet, much worse for him than for her. He was about six inches taller than she, and they had slept in almost a sitting position.

Together! They had slept together! The joy of that simple pleasure she'd never experienced before returned to her, refreshing her. She hoped someday to find a place of belonging with a man. *Why, it might even be Dylan. If they got out of this alive!*

The crunch of his boots on frozen ground receded. Maya found a Coke, her toothbrush, and toothpaste then hurried outside into the cold, damp air. The water bottles were buried under other stuff in the cave already.

Dylan stood several yards away, looking up at the sky. She glanced upward also but saw nothing except gray clouds.

Heading in the opposite direction, she relieved herself then brushed her teeth, rinsing with the Coke. Actually, it turned out to be less horrible than she imagined. Just as she finished, she heard a helicopter approaching. She wished to hell she didn't have on the bright yellow jacket and ran for the cave entrance.

Waving, Dylan jogged toward her. "Get inside."

Maya edged behind the bushes, dropped to her knees, and crawled in the cave with Dylan following. "Is that ORION?" she asked

"I think so, but it looks like their main force is gone. Hopefully this copter is just doing a wrap-up sweep. My guess is they'll start a ground search later."

Worried after all, Maya asked, "Should we stay or go?"

"Since we've got heat and food, I'd think we should stay here for a while. It's almost nine now. Some help will be coming at two."

"More soldiers?" Nearly five hours? How could they possibly find enough to talk about to fill that much time together? Would he make a pass at her? Maya had not thought of that dimension at all last night. Surely not, with people out to kill them.

"No, some buddies of mine are going to send me a new battery."

The situation seemed more desperate to Maya now that they were talking about it. "I've got a rental car back at the cabin. I know the car would be easy for the police to find, but at least we could go some place warm." She ducked her head to compose herself, unwilling for him to see her any more flustered than necessary. He'd been so considerate last night when she cried.

"Later, we can go check on the car." Dylan's voice softened. "Right now we need to stay out of view." He tipped her head up with a smile. "Have you got anything to eat?"

"Oh, of course." Glad to have something to occupy herself, Maya pulled some bagels and a Nitrogen-Pac of cream cheese out of a shopping bag. "This okay?"

"Great." He took out two Cokes and sat down facing her, matching her cross-legged position. "How'd you sleep?" His smile of familiarity made her self-conscious.

"Better than I thought possible." It would be so immature to blush, but Maya could feel the heat rising along her neck. "How about you?"

Dylan nodded. "It's a good thing you found a hiding place. How'd you happen across it?"

Greatly relieved that he had changed the subject, she said, "This was my hideout on summer vacations when I was a kid. I spent a lot of time here." The irony struck her. "Now, it really deserves the name of hideout."

"Will anybody know to look for you here?"

"I doubt it. The owners of the land gave me permission to use it years ago, but they're only here in the summers." Maya lifted her soda can. "How does the saying go? 'Eat, drink, and be merry, for tomorrow you die.' Or maybe today." She took a long swallow and tried not to shiver. She did want to live, more now than before, if she could spend her time getting to know Dylan better. She found him easy to talk to and kind, despite his exotic occupation.

After chewing thoughtfully for a moment, he asked, "So what did you do in this cave to entertain yourself?"

Maya gestured toward the trunk. "I read a ton of books and used it as a base to explore. In the summer, there are a million varieties of flowers and weeds and butterflies. Actually, bugs were my first love. The summer I was eight, I was out looking for bugs and found this cave. That's my first memory of life."

"Really?" Dylan gazed up to the right at the cave wall. He seemed comfortable with silences in conversations. "I'm trying to remember my first memory of life. It probably was listening to *Shrek* series music. I loved that when I was a baby, even before I could walk."

"You can remember before you could walk?" Maya had never heard of such a thing. She licked the delicious cream cheese off the bagel and noticed Dylan had eaten his in only a couple of bites.

"Well, I was probably almost two when I walked on my own. I was late getting started because I was blind until I was five years old, but I'm positive I remember voices and music long before then. I can remember my granddad had a very coarse voice, and he coughed a lot. You know, how a smoker's sounds? He died when I was four."

"Amazing that you can remember so far back. I've always had a feeling I'm missing a good portion of my childhood. And now that I know my parents adopted me, I'm even more certain." The enormity of the conclusion hit Maya. "It's amazing to discover that I was adopted. Why, that means I might have another mother and father somewhere. Do you think they're still alive?"

"I don't know, but I wouldn't count on it. The Anaz-voohri don't leave too many loose ends. They murdered my parents, I think, because my mother began to ask questions about…"

"About what? Tell me all you know, Dylan. It's important for me to understand your situation and mine. I've got to grow up fast here."

"I think my mother became suspicious of some of the doctors at CEM, not because they restored my sight. She was ecstatic about that, but because I developed some rather unusual abilities afterwards."

"The Central for Evolutionary Medicine? You went there?" When he nodded, Maya said, "That's where I went every year for my checkups."

Dylan grinned. "I think you'd better get a new doctor for your future checkups."

Laying down her bagel, Maya took his hands and turned them over. Although their texture felt rough, probably chapped from the cold, with long slim fingers, like she imagined a pianist would have. "I'm sorry the Anaz-voohri killed your parents. How old were you?"

"It was seven years ago. I was nineteen."

"Just three years younger than I am, and now they've killed mine. Maybe both sets. We've got a lot in common." The loss stunned Maya. She was beginning to understand that sorrow could be as paralyzing as the Anaz-voohri. Maybe they used it as part of their technique. Her grief over Lola had triggered the blackout. She didn't completely understand the link between grief and paralysis, but she had no doubt it was there, and maybe intentionally exploited.

"The Anaz-voohri are a tough crowd. You've got to remember they'll stop at nothing to get what they want."

The memory of the fanatical captain and her speech about her mission returned to Maya. "They intend to rid the earth of human kind."

"I don't know how much time we humans have left." Dylan withdrew his hands and rubbed his chin, his beard making a rasping sound. Then he laid his hands on her shoulders. They could have been two kids playing cops and robbers, except for the anxiety in his dark eyes. "I remember my surgery, but you don't. I can probably help you remember, if you want me to try."

"How can you do that?"

"Hypnotherapy."

"You're a pilot and a secret agent and now a hypnotherapist? What other occupations have you got up your sleeve?" Maya grabbed the bag of cookies, opened it, and offered it to Dylan. She felt fascinated again by this darkly handsome hybrid. With what she knew now about her own history, she should stop thinking of him in that way.

"Oh, I love these." Dylan bit into a cookie, and it was a joy to watch him eat it. His face relaxed and he so appreciated its flavor. He couldn't have looked happier if he'd won the lottery.

"Have some more." Maya smiled, bit into one, and let its sweetness sink onto her tongue. She wanted to feel what he was feeling. "Tastes good, huh?"

"Sure does." Dylan ate two more then laid the sack down. He smiled at her with mock sincerity. "If I was stranded in a cave in the winter, I'd want chocolate chip cookies for every meal."

"Me, too." Watching him eat had given Maya a sense of intimacy with Dylan. They'd shared something wonderful, far more than cookies. For once she didn't feel embarrassed to acknowledge the fact, at least to herself. They were becoming friends.

Poor Mother would be outraged if she knew what Maya was up to. Poor Mother, indeed. How had she dared to lie to Maya and conspire to kill Lola with that awful Schwartz? Mother and Father both, Carolyn and Terrence rather, were no longer parents to Maya. How could they have kept the details of her life secret from her? For that, she could never forgive them. Maya owed it to herself to try to uncover her past.

"If you seriously think hypnosis will help…" Maya felt nervous about trying. Father had used hypnosis in his practice and always called it a good tool, but she had never experienced it. Maybe she wouldn't be able to go under. After all, they were in a highly stressful situation.

"You can trust me on this, Maya. It's all right to remember in my presence."

"What about the helicopters?"

"I've not heard one since we came inside. I think we're safe for a while. Just lie back and make yourself comfortable. I'll do all the work."

With the sun higher in the sky and the heater on, Maya felt warm enough to take off her ski jacket. Wishing she'd changed her rumpled sweatshirt to something more flattering, she lay down, her head cushioned by a pillow.

Dylan moved closer, but not enough to touch her, and sat cross-legged. He looked so earnest that he charmed Maya. She wondered what he thought of her. Did he like her? Or was she just a job to him?

Removing his medallion, he swung it back and forth before her face. His voice carried a softer, more mellow tone, just above a whisper. "Let your eyes follow the medallion. Don't think about anything except the medallion and how completely and totally relaxed you are. Nothing can interfere with your willingness to fall into a quiet, peaceful trance, a place inside your own mind where you have never gone before. Yet this is a place with answers.

You can trust this place in your mind. It will uncover truths that you need to know."

Maya sighed and relaxed. She could make out the crystal shape moving before her. She liked his hypnotic voice and allowed it to soothe her. If he talked like this, he could talk to her all day.

"Your eyes are getting very tired, in fact so tired that you will be unable to hold them open much longer. When you finally let them close, you will fall down and down into a profound slumber. No sound will distract you. You will hear nothing except the sound of my voice, and you will always respond to it, no matter how deep you go."

Although Maya tried to keep her eyes focused on the medallion, her lids simply became too heavy and they closed.

"I want you to imagine that you are lying in a beautiful white sailboat and you are drifting far away from land. It is a warm, sunny day." The spaces between Dylan's words became longer and longer. It seemed an eternity between them. "You can see San Diego Bay in the distance. You love floating on this ocean of serenity and yo let it take you deeper and deeper down, deeper and deeper down into trance. As you float, your mind becomes more alert while your body becomes more and more drowsy."

Maya's breathing became somewhat erratic. She flushed and her eyes fluttered beneath the lids. She felt curious and capable of creation, just like with the Fairy Godmother back at work. Expelling a long sigh, Maya sank into the sailboat and let the warm breeze blow over her. In her mind's eye, she saw the perfect California blue sky overhead. Sails flapped in a gentle wind.

Speaking in his mesmerizing way, Dylan focused her attention. "Imagine you have a book in your hand and you let it fall away. As it lands on the deck of the sailboat, a breeze ripples the pages. Those pages are the years of your life, and they are blowing back. You find that you can look at any of those years and remember clearly and distinctly. You are going back, twenty-one, twenty, nineteen, eighteen. You stop at your eighteenth birthday. All you need to do is wait, and a scene from that day will drop into your mind. When you see it, you will describe it."

Maya waited in an empty space, still and quiet and comfortable. Then a memory came to her. She had come home from college for the weekend. Mother prepared a dinner for several guests but had not invited Lola, so Maya did. Mother couldn't act outraged in front of the others. "Lola and I are laughing because we fooled Mother, and we're drinking spiked punch."

"Very good," Dylan said. "You are floating on the ocean of time and going back, to seventeen, sixteen. On and on back, to your tenth birthday. All you need to do is wait, and a scene from that day will drop into your mind. When you see it, you will describe it."

Maya scanned her memory but couldn't find anything like she had before. She followed the suggestion and waited. Then she heard barking. "I'm standing in the backyard at home, and Buster comes bounding toward me. He's hungry and he knocks me down."

"Who is Buster?"

"My Airedale puppy."

"Okay, we're moving back, leaving the puppy and going back. You are nine. Eight."

After several moments, Maya whispered, "I'm in the cave. The ceiling is so high I can't even reach it."

"Good. Very good. Now we are going back to seven, going back to six, going back to five, going back to four. Time is slipping away. Wait for a scene to come into your mind."

Maya reached down into her mind. At war with herself, she wanted to retrieve a memory but feared what she would find. Huge hands grabbed her around the waist and pulled her up. Terrified, she tried to squelch a rasping scream.

"It's all right, Maya, you're safe. It's all right to remember, and you can do so quietly. You won't feel any pain. You will be able to look without passion on your past and know that you are beyond it."

Helpless and vulnerable, Maya sobbed. "Don't take me. Don't put me in there. It hurts me."

"Describe the scene as if you were an observer. Pull back and tell me what you see. You can do so calmly."

With a shiver, Maya said, "The big people strap my head down on a table. They punch my neck with sharp things. They cut my head open. I don't want them to hurt me anymore, but I can't stop them. This is a bad place. I want to go home. I want my mommy and daddy."

"Are there any good people in this place?"

"Just the other little girls. We play together on the playground." Her voice broke with the overwhelming sadness she felt. "But they all want to go home, too."

"It's all right, Maya." Dylan rubbed her hand. "We're leaving this place right now and going back again, to when you were two years old and you lived with your mommy and daddy. You will remember a good thing. Tell me when you see something from your life as a two year old."

Reaching back into her memory, Maya waited but saw no pictures from any time before she lived with the Anaz-voohri. She sighed and wondered what might come next. Emptiness settled over her. All dread left her. She felt happy and content. She spoke without a sense of having formed the thought. "Mommy's very proud of her big girl. I can go potty by myself now."

Dylan's chuckle broke into his voice. "Good for you. What's your name?"

"Maya Elaine Porter, and my teddy is named Pinkie."

"Glad to meet you, Maya Elaine Porter. I'm very proud of you, too. I'm going to bring you back now. On the count of five, you will awaken, feeling refreshed. You will remember everything that transpired, but you will remain calm about it. Five, four, coming awake…

Excited at the prospect of remembering her real mother, Maya awoke and stared at Dylan, whose smile showed approval. She said, "Please, take me back down. Ask me for the names of my parents."

"That won't be necessary. We have their names and their address from twenty years ago."

"What! You mean you knew already and made me go through this?"

"You had to remember for yourself. Otherwise, the information wouldn't be nearly so meaningful to you."

Maya struggled to a sitting position, so fascinated by her experience that she felt no annoyance. "Perhaps you're right. That place where the tall person picked me up? I've dreamed about it, so I guess the information had been there in my mind all along."

"It just takes the right circumstances to break into consciousness. You're a very good subject."

"Thanks. I've a lot to think about, but one thing I know already. The Anaz-voohri violated me far more than if they had raped me. They took my soul programming, the DNA my real parents gave me, my humanity. I want revenge on them somehow."

Dylan's voice cracked. "I feel the same way. I've dedicated my life to their destruction."

Maya had a feeling he didn't like the burden that mission entailed. "What did they do to you?"

"About the same thing they did to you only it didn't hurt as much. I remember very little pain, but afterward I was an oddball." Dylan spoke in a matter-of-fact tone, one he might use when analyzing someone else's behavior. "I knew when things happened in other places without even trying. Kids at school teased me and called me weirdo. They didn't know it, but they were making me tough enough to be a soldier. I didn't understand the value of my gift until I joined Mythos. Now, I can use the way the Anaz-voohri screwed me over to help defeat them. That gives me a good deal of satisfaction." His wan smile showed more of the schoolboy than the soldier.

Maya wondered if she could find a home in his cause and his concern. They were hers also. "Do you think Mythos will take me in? I'll help you any way I can."

Dylan took her face in his hands and gazed at her as if he searched her soul for answers. He had a dark and musky scent that matched his eyes. His heartbeat pulsed through his hands, electrifying her.

Was he going to kiss her? Maya wanted him to. He had an air of adventure about him and a homey tenderness, the combination tantalized her. What did he hope to find in her?

Dylan's lips grazed Maya's, they felt warm and sweet, then lingered for a more urgent kiss, one that made her tremble. She sensed the possibilities of passion or love or friendship, all available in the moment.

No one had ever kissed her with so much promise. She wanted to go on kissing Dylan. Maybe from him she could learn how to love.

Breaking away, he sighed and sat back, giving a sense of finality to the moment. "That wasn't a ruse for the police, and I'm not trying to seduce you. You're a very nice person, Maya, and I'll protect you if I can."

Maya wished he hadn't stopped. Emboldened, she wanted to feel close to him and return his kiss. She touched his cheek to draw him close, but Dylan looked so melancholy that she changed her mind and asked, "How did you know I love San Diego? Were you really there with me in the computer program? Did you read my mind?"

"I don't know how I knew. Information I have no normal way of knowing just shows up in my mind, whether I ask to know it or not. Once upon a time, I thought I was God's creature, but now I guess I have to conclude that I'm the Anaz-voohri's creature." He massaged his forehead for a long moment then gave her the same questioning glance. "How spiritual is that? I'll tell you the answer. Not very."

"I've never thought much about God." Maya had a great deal to sort through regarding her parents, her beliefs, and the change in her mental abilities. "My parents didn't attend church, and now I guess I know why. Their allegiance was to the Anaz-voohri."

How bad could it all be if she had Dylan willing to protect her? Maya felt very glad to have him to talk to. He seemed to understand her. She could fall in love with him with little provocation. Maybe she already had.

Chapter Fourteen

Outside the cave, Dylan scanned the overcast sky, gloomy at noon. When he exhaled, he could see his breath. The temperature had dropped overnight. Light snow fell on the bare-limbed oaks and undergrowth. He would take Maya and head down to the Dial-a-Bike soon. Maybe they could stay warm in the store while they waited for the battery to arrive.

Professionally, Dylan wished he hadn't kissed her because he still might have to follow his directive. He believed Maya when she said she didn't want to do the bidding of the Anaz-voohri. Clearly, she could use her mind to interface with both computer and electrical systems, to send her thoughts through them and to shut them down. He needed to find out right away whether she controlled her powers or the Anaz-voohri did.

Personally, he felt glad he'd kissed Maya. He'd wanted to kiss her again for real ever since pretending to be her husband to fool the police. For a moment back there in the cave, he'd thought she would throw herself into his arms and beg him to take her. Probably overactive imagination on his part. She became more appealing by the moment. He'd give a lot to take her to bed as soon as he could find a warm one for her. He doubted he'd sacrifice his job to do so but hoped he'd not have to make such a choice. He knew one thing; he couldn't make love to her and then kill her. That was way too cold-blooded, dishonorable in his eyes. If he did that, he'd be no better than the Anaz-voohri, using and abusing her.

Only a week had passed since he had met Maya, and already he thought of her as someone he knew and understood. He could love her if he let himself, far more easily than he could have loved Sybil or Cassie. He believed from the bottom of his heart in his responsibility to Mythos and their mission to protect humanity. It took precedence over his feelings toward Maya. Still, he would feel sad if she had to die, sadder still if circumstances conspired to make him the instrument of her death.

A helicopter chugged toward him from the southeast. Despite spitting snow, he recognized the ORION emblem. No doubt others were on the way. He expected the ground search to begin soon and hoped they'd have a couple hours tolerance.

Frozen branches cracked as he squeezed passed them and ducked inside the cave, so dimly lit by the cloud-covered sun that the heater's red light glowed. Dylan worried that it might reveal their presence.

Sitting on a blanket, Maya looked drawn, but a smile brought her beauty back into focus. "Wish I had some peppermint tea." She tossed an empty soda can into a plastic sack. "There's only one Coke left. You want it?"

"No, thanks. Better turn off the heater. ORION's back."

Maya glanced at the appliance with a look of alarm. "You do it."

When Dylan flipped off the heater, he wondered just how unmanageable her abilities were. She must feel truly out of control if she feared touching an appliance.

"Should we get out of here?" Her voice edgy, Maya got up on her knees and reached for her ski jacket.

"Where would we go?" Dylan tried to sound more light-hearted than he felt. "We'll stay here for a while. When the helicopters leave the area, we will, too."

Sighing, she sat back against the trunk. "How long will it take for them to give up?"

Positive they wouldn't, Dylan shrugged. If he could think of a place where they would be safer, he'd take them there. "I don't know." He knelt before her and took her chilly hands, rubbing them between his. "Right now, I know you've got some theories about the abilities the Anaz-voohri implanted in you. I wish you'd tell me."

Shadows from the bushes outside played across Maya's face casting her eyes in darkness. She gazed at him for a long time. Try as he would, Dylan couldn't read her expression.

Maya spoke softly. "I do have some ideas, but..."

"But what?" He needed her transparency. Much more than their lives alone depended on it. The safety of the whole human race remained in jeopardy.

"Don't take this personally, but I've been betrayed by so many people, I don't know who to trust." She sounded tired and older than her years.

"How about me?" Dylan grinned at her, hoping he looked sincere.

Helicopter engines purred in the distance. "I don't really have a choice, do I?"

"Not really." Dylan caressed her fingers. For a long moment, he watched her face while she stared at their intertwined hands. He wanted to give her the time she needed to feel confident she could trust him.

Maya expelled a ragged sigh. "I've mulled over those moments before the blackout many times. After I engaged the software, I lost track of my mental processes. I was a pitiful mess, sobbing and crying over Lola. And then, it seemed a voice spoke to me and said it was time, but it didn't seem like a voice outside myself. I think my grief triggered the program into blacking out the electricity."

"Did you know that when it happened? Did you try to stop the power interruption?"

"Actually I didn't even begin to analyze what happened until I tried to contact you from here in the cave. Schwartz was watching the cabin and I thought he wanted to kill me. I couldn't get hold of my folks. I was terrified." Maya's voice grew stronger. She sounded more confident.

"I engaged the software while giving in to my fear, but then it occurred to me to calm my mind. Once I'd done so, I was able to successfully create a personality, sort of an alter ego. That alter ego got a message to you, and you found me."

"So what you're saying is your thoughts created the software, but your emotions drove the program?" What an intriguing idea. Dylan imagined there could be all kinds of possible applications to espionage. He'd consider the details later.

"That's the conclusion I've come to, yes. When I returned from the spaceship, I was fuming, and I broke my phone and my laptop as soon as I touched them. At some level I'd already started to fight back, or at least had the desire to do so, and my abilities became more chaotic."

"At least you protected the heater." Dylan smiled but she didn't seem to notice.

Maya gripped Dylan's hand, and her fervent voice held him spellbound. "I know what the Anaz-voohri intend. They want me to shut down the communication systems and power grids all over the world." Her brow furrowed with the desperation in her words. "Once I've done that, there can be no organized resistance. They'll pound all the countries of Earth with plagues, fires, assassinations, devastation and diabolical diseases you can't even imagine!"

"Caused by the other six women." Dylan knew she had it figured out right, and she understood all too well the scope of the threat. He shuddered at the turmoil she described. "Seven prongs of attack. Seven sisters of the Pleiades programmed to wipe out humankind."

"Why do you call them that?"

"Because the Anaz-voohri came from the Pleiades."

Eyes wide, Maya said, "They took me there? That far away?"

"I'm afraid so. What do you think their goal is?" Dylan knew the answer but felt curious about her thoughts. "Why do the Anaz-voohri want to kill us all?"

Maya freed her hands and slid them into her sweatshirt sleeves. She restlessly rubbed her own arms. "They want the planet to themselves. I don't know why, to use as a base or to live on. Their ancestors came from here...the Anasazi Indians who disappeared hundreds of years ago."

"Maybe they consider this their rightful home. You know what Mark Twain said?" When she didn't respond, Dylan answered his own question. "'There's not one square inch on the face of the earth in the hands of its rightful owners.'"

"I don't see the humor in that. Earth can't be their home."

"You know it, and I know it, but do the Anaz-voohri know it?"

Finally, Maya gave a wry titter, one he liked to think his prompting had invoked. Such a serious-minded girl. He'd doubt she could ever be fanciful if he hadn't seen the fairy tattoo. He wondered about her other moods. Could she be sensual? Risqué?

His attempts at lighten the mood did little to deter Dylan from the unmistakable conclusions he must draw. The mission of Mythos seemed clearer than ever. Archer had been right to order the executions of the sisters. These seven women had to die if Mythos couldn't neutralize their dangerous capabilities or help them to switch sides. Such formidable abilities eliminated any middle ground.

Dylan knew a lot was riding on his question. "So, if your emotions can break things, it makes sense that, assuming you could focus your emotion, you could fix things. Can you?"

"I haven't tried." Maya sounded grim. "But I think it's time that I do." She crawled to the stack of clothes, searched through them, and picked up the laptop. After opening it, she placed her fingertips on the screen. "Okay, here goes." With a sigh, she closed her eyes and sat still for a long time.

The sounds of helicopters announced ORION had arrived.

Twisting his shoulders from side to side, Dylan cracked his back, settled against the trunk opposite her, and watched. The technique failed to relax his muscles. He wondered what was going on in Maya's mind. In the faint light, he couldn't tell whether or not her eyes fluttered beneath her lids, but she took slow, deep breaths, so he knew she'd entered some kind of altered state of consciousness. To sit idly, watching and waiting, took an agonizing toll, not a situation he could tolerate for long.

A tiny blip issued from the laptop and faint light glowed on the screen, then the program booted up.

"It's on," Maya said, her voice pitched high. She threw her arms in the air and laughed, a welcome sound despite the danger it might bring if anyone outside the cave heard.

"Better keep your voice down." Dylan turned the laptop around and saw the opening message scroll across, *Hello, Maya, how's it going?* He gave her shoulders an affectionate squeeze. "That's terrific," he whispered.

"Where did I put the phone?" Maya had lowered the volume of her voice but not the excitement in it. She scurried several feet across the cave floor near the opening and retrieved the phone from where she probably threw it when she broke it. Holding the phone in both her hands, she closed her eyes and concentrated her power on it.

Dylan hoped for her success as much as she did because that would mean she had control, not the Anaz-voohri. Heat was escaping from the cave fast. He picked up two blankets and moved toward her. Sitting beside her on the cold dirt, he threw one blanket over her shoulders and the other over his.

After a few moments, Maya held the phone out and said, "Oh, Dylan, look!" The digital display glowed. "Do you know what this means?"

"You can call people up?"

His efforts to tease seemed once again lost on Maya, who continued as if he had not responded to her question. "Before the abduction, I lived in some kind of a cocoon. Little Millie Milquetoast! I ran from the sniper and left Lola to die alone. I felt guilty about it, but I was too afraid to do anything else. I was even afraid to take a strong stand against my parents. Now I am free to fight for myself, and I want to."

"I'm proud of you, Maya." Dylan appreciated how she had struggled and spoke sincerely. "I doubt the Anazvoohri have any notion of what they've allowed to happen, otherwise they wouldn't have abducted you last night and given you information."

Maya leaned forward. "I'm ready to fight them." Faint daylight from the opening played across her face, displaying her transfixed expression. "Tell me what to do. I know I can help defeat them. Isn't that why Mythos sent you after me?"

"We knew you had the power. What we didn't know was which side you were on. And who controlled your power, you or them."

The last thing Dylan wanted to admit was the kill order. He'd have to get it rescinded now. Surely, he had the proof, except for the nagging possibility that the Anazvoohri would override her intentions and assert control. He really didn't know whether they could or not, and neither did

Maya in spite of her good intentions. He looked away from her.

"So, why did…" Maya touched his chin to bring his head around. "Dylan?"

As he reached for her to reassure her, she held up her hands, blocking him. Dylan hoped his voice carried more conviction than he had. "Now we know, so everything's going to be all right."

A long silence fell between them.

"They sent you to kill me, didn't they?" Maya's whispered words were snowflakes falling on his heart. "And the other sisters, too?"

When he nodded, Maya backed away from him. Her face a picture of agonized betrayal, she scrambled across the cave and flailed through her possessions. She picked up the ski jacket.

"Wait, Maya, don't go outside."

"I have to…go…" Her voice broke as if she struggled to keep back tears. "To the bathroom."

Dylan heartily wanted to console her, but he couldn't think of any way. "Be careful. There might be soldiers on the ground."

Her face hardened, and so did her voice. "I'll come right back, although I don't know whether I'm in more danger from ORION or from you."

"At least let me check outside." Worried, Dylan threw on his parka and crawled out of the cave. He could see helicopters coming toward him in the distance but nothing appeared to be moving among the trees. The snowfall had covered the ground with a light coating. Anyone would be easy to track. Returning, he said, "Stay close to the cave and be as quick as possible. Try not to make tracks in the snow."

"Thanks." Maya hurried past him, hugging her coat to her.

Dylan chafed his hands. Without the heater, the interior of the cave seemed far colder, a match for her demeanor. Damn, he wished he hadn't admitted the kill order. She'd have figured it out sometime, no matter what he said. How could he expect a person untrained in espionage to understand, especially when she herself was the mark?

How hard he would have to work to regain her trust in him! Maya seemed to actually enjoy his company as much as he enjoyed hers. What might they have been able to share, how might they have responded to each other in a different time and place, without this war thrust on both of them?

The sound of helicopter engines grew louder.

Glancing around the floor of the cave, Dylan knew something had changed, but what?

Maya had taken the laptop and the cell phone! She didn't need both of those to pee, for God's sake!

Dylan tore out the cave opening, brambles catching at his coat and skin.

A dozen helicopters dropped ORION soldiers among the trees. The sky looked like it rained flak suits and parachutes.

Far from the cave, Maya ran away from the soldiers at top speed, chocolate brown hair blowing out behind her. The yellow jacket bobbed along, marking her as a canary on the snow, a bird completely out of her habitat.

Soldiers shouted "there she is" and "get her" over the roar of the engines.

Maya's scream careened through the air. It quivered and died away then rose again, filling the woods with the sound of her terror.

In anguish, Dylan flattened himself against a tree, hoping to escape detection. He had no chance to rescue her if they took him as well. He waited with a heaviness inside that felt like a hammer hitting his heart.

After moments that seemed hours long, a chopper rose into the air, bearing Maya on a stretcher that inched into the bowels of the vehicle and disappeared. The nose lowered, then the lone helicopter took off in a burst of speed. Soldiers stomped toward the cave, shouting to each other.

Crawling inside, Dylan pulled the blankets over him. Aware of what his next move would be were he an ORION soldier, Dylan shielded his head to make a cupped space for breathing and concentrated on not moving the blankets up and down with his breath.

A moment later, a male soldier said, "Well, this is where she was hiding out."

"Anything important in there?" A female soldier called from outside.

"Naw, just clothes and stuff."

Dylan heard the sound of a soda can popping open and held his breath.

The female said, "I'll come in then and see if there's anything that will fit me."

"The hell you will," the male soldier said with a snigger. After a moment, he said, "ouch," then "damn."

The bushes must have clobbered him when he crawled out. Dylan wished to hell he could have wiped the two soldiers out, but someone would miss them. Then others would have come looking for their lost comrades. Better just to delay the game until Dylan had better cards.

The sounds of the soldiers' voices died away in the clatter of the helicopters.

When he felt certain they had gone, Dylan, cautious nonetheless, peeked out of the blankets. He could have done without such a close call.

Damn Maya for running away. She could have remained here safe with him. No doubt the soldiers followed her tracks in the wet snow, otherwise they wouldn't have found the cave so easily. The soldiers had departed as soon as they found her, evidently their sole target. They might not have known to search for Dylan.

Carrick himself must know about Dylan's involvement because the night of the blackout the police officer who arrested Maya had taken Dylan's info. Archer always said that the power of Mythos was greater than the political clout of ORION and GSS combined because Mythos men owed allegiance to no bureaucracy, only to their own integrity. Because they operated secretly, Mythos men had some immunity from arrest. Archer also said never to count on it. Dylan didn't.

Now, that bastard Carrick would have Maya on a platter. If the asshole hurt her before Mythos could rescue her, Dylan would never forgive himself. He finally had to admit he had a conflict of interest of humongous proportions.

There had to be some way to reinvent the directive, to have an alternative to killing Maya. He didn't want her dead at all. He wanted her safely back in his arms. He intended to convince Archer that Maya's abilities could come in handy at Mythos. It was high time they had a female operative, anyway. Maya wanted to join and she would be perfect.

Scrambling around, he found some cheese in a Nitrogen-Pac and some chips. The damned soldier had taken the last Coke. Dylan ate the remaining food and waited until he could no longer hear any sounds outside.

Under a sunless gray sky, Dylan hiked toward the country store, heedless of the snow wetting his face. It seemed inconceivable that less than twenty-four hours had passed since he'd flown up here to Markle Falls. It felt like he'd lost his mind along with his heart.

Without willing it, he'd begun to think of Maya as his own personal agenda, as if her life were his to command, to protect, or to end. Whatever had come over him, he felt more uncertain of his motives and direction than he wished.

The delusion that he would go ahead with the kill order no longer held up. It had died the moment Maya understood why he had come after her. She'd believed he wanted to help her, and she'd been right. His own motives had changed in the past few hours without his conscious knowledge. Now she needed his help far more than she had before.

Dylan must return to Mythos, convince Archer that they should protect Maya, and get her out of ORION's grip. He reached beneath his parka to tap the medallion and realized he no longer wore it. What in hell?

The memory came to him. He had removed it to hypnotize Maya. How irresponsible was that? He'd left it in the cave. Some hero he'd turned out to be, unable even to hang onto his communicator.

The possibility also existed that Maya had taken it when she ran from the cave. If so, ORION would soon be in possession of a vital piece of Mythos equipment that could very well blow the secrecy element of their work.

Dylan turned and ran back toward the cave, colder and angrier with every second of delay. If Carrick killed Maya, all the blame would land on Dylan for being the greatest idiot of the twenty-first century.

Chapter Fifteen

When Dylan neared the cave, he heard the high-pitched whine of his medallion's emergency broadcast signal. At least Mythos technology had not fallen into ORION's hands. Relieved of one worry, he scurried inside and found the medallion under the blanket spread over the dirt.

Once he grasped the crystal shape, it read the DNA in his palm and ceased the whine. Dylan hung the medallion around his neck and tapped the center. "Apollo here. Reporting."

Through the imbedded chip, Dylan heard a young male voice shouting back at headquarters. "Hey, Zeus, Apollo's found." He feared he'd worried his comrades at Mythos unnecessarily.

Archer's voice came on the line. Following the protective convention of code names, he said, "State your condition, Apollo. Are you in trouble? Do you need backup?"

"Thank you, Zeus, I'm fine, cold, but fine."

"Why didn't you answer your beep?"

"I took the medallion off…in the line of duty."

Archer's voice relaxed. He evidently assumed nothing big had happened. "Explain in your report after this operation is over. I've been thinking of having the device completely imbedded. I'll consider your experience to help me make a decision."

Dylan didn't relish the task of owning up to his lapse in memory. He'd deal with that later. Right now, he needed to bring Archer up to speed. "The target has been captured by the Friday the Thirteenth Gang," the code name for Jason Carrick and ORION.

"Do you have any idea where they've taken her?"

"Negative."

"We'll get on it right away." Archer's tone indicated he believed the conversation had ended and was about to click off.

"Wait, Zeus, why were you trying to contact me in the first place?"

"Oh, didn't anyone tell you? Your package is waiting at the linkup point."

"Already?" Dylan glanced at his watch. It was barely past one, and the linkup previously scheduled for two. "I'm on my way." He pressed against the wall of the cave in an unsuccessful effort to avoid scratching himself on the brambles, glad to finally leave such an uncomfortable hideout. "I'll be there as soon as possible. We need to meet right away."

When the line clicked off, Dylan broke into a run through the trees. Snow spit in his face as he concentrated to avoid slipping on the slick ground. He veered out of the trees and onto the country road past cabins, a few with smoke curling out the chimneys, most dark with drawn blinds. It didn't matter who saw him now. He felt pissed all over again at the delay and inconvenience the dead battery had caused.

Damn the right-wing fanatic in charge of the manufacturing company that wouldn't acknowledge the spaceship's impact on the Dial-a-Bike. Damn him for requiring that the new battery that shipped from South Africa. Damn the Anaz-voohri for frying the Dial-a-Bike's battery in the first place. And damn ORION for interfering in Mythos business! Where did they get off kidnapping this woman?

Winded and anxious, Dylan arrived at the country market to find the parcel service boy waiting inside. If the boy thought it strange to be required to await delivery, he didn't mention it and smiled his thanks when Dylan gave him a twenty credit tip.

Dylan installed the new battery in record time. The Dial-a-Bike started right up, and he took off for NYC. He pressed the accelerator gauge to maximum for flight, anxious to get there. His cold clothes clung to him, so he turned on the heater. Soon the interior of the Dial-a-Bike felt cozy despite the sour smell of damp wool.

He tried not to visualize what Carrick or his inquisitors might be doing to Maya at the moment. The more Dylan dwelt on emotional conjecture, the less capable he would be of doing a successful remote viewing when he got back to Mythos. He might not have to take the time for that if Archer could trace Maya's location in some other way.

The fact that he had to have quiet and calm to practice remote viewing annoyed Dylan. One of these days, when he got a break from assignments, he would find a teacher who could help him develop his gift into on-the-spot clairvoyance. He imagined that kind of proficiency required more spiritual development than Dylan had had the inclination to pursue previously. Now, with Maya's life at risk he wished he'd worked on it long ago.

No doubt the soldiers would deliver her directly to Carrick, in any of the headquarters around the world or onboard the Headquarters Flotilla, wherever that now anchored. Or, he might take her to some secret location, depending on how dangerous Carrick considered her to the stability of Earth.

Snow pelted the windshield, and Dylan turned on the wipers. This damn weather might present even more problems with finding her.

Maya's state of mind worried Dylan. She probably felt horribly afraid and abandoned into the bargain. She'd been through so much during the past week. He wished he could have spared her this jeopardy. He'd do whatever it took to rescue her from ORION's clutches, and not just because her loyalty lay with humans. He might as well be honest with himself.

The thing Dylan had most feared had happened to him. Maya occupied his thoughts far more so than Cassie or Sybil. He had wanted to take each of them to bed, but he could imagine an afterwards with Maya. She had such a gentle and open nature, he felt good in her presence, at home with her.

There might be some past-life connection between them to account for that feeling. Even without direct proof, he believed reincarnation was the likely explanation of the afterlife. It would please him to learn he and Maya had been together before.

How had his thoughts become so romantic? This was unlike him. If he didn't know himself better, he'd think he'd fallen in love.

When Dylan arrived at Mythos, he found Archer, in a battered suede jacket, sprawled in his chair, giving directions to a young recruit who took notes on an epad.

Kin Raidon, a Chinese national in a silk mandarin cloak, stood before the map. Dylan had worked with Kin on a previous mission and found him highly competent and quiet, but seriously lacking a sense of humor. The hybrid doctors funded by the Anaz-voohri had tampered with Kin's DNA, like they had so many Mythos operatives. As a result, he resembled a competitive weightlifter with the ability to blend into the shadows like a ninja. Dylan felt glad that the ominous Kin was on their side.

After greeting the men, Dylan checked the map and noticed lights on at the ORION Headquarters Flotilla in Nova Scotia and in their New York HQ.

"We know," Archer said, waving the recruit away, "that Carrick's been at the Flotilla for the past day or so. Before that, he was here." He indicated NY HQ on the map. "We don't know yet where Carrick took Maya Rembrandt."

Stressed from both physical and mental exertion, Dylan took a deep breath and modulated his tone of voice. He wanted his words to sound measured and reasonable. "You can damn well bet the Anaz-voohri are watching. They'll interfere if they can. They can't take the chance that Maya's powers will fall into the hands of humans."

Kin asked, "How powerful is she?"

"She can stop and start machinery by the force of her mind, and she doesn't need a computer to do it." Dylan remembered Maya's excitement over the laptop and felt certain she had grown into her abilities.

Climbing out of the chair, Archer leaned against the desk. He never seemed to have any interest in supporting his weight physically, the exact opposite of his intellect, which was independent and sharp. "Have you seen a demonstration?"

"More than one," Dylan said, "and she's got control. The Anaz-voohri must have feared the possibility that Maya could become an independent agent. The programming they did on her originally created chaos when she started changing her intentions, or maybe I should say having intentions of her own. Everything went wrong probably because Maya refused to obey her program. Could be true for the other sisters, too."

Archer folded his arms and tapped his fingers for a moment, apparently lost in thought. "How much can she control and how much is controlled by the Anaz-voohri?"

"I think she's in charge, now." Dylan felt encouraged at Archer's willingness to discuss the subject. "She wasn't at first. She wants to fight on our side. She hates the Anaz-voohri for the same reasons we all do."

Kin squared his shoulders, even more so, if that were possible. "You take her word for that?"

Dylan realized the weakness in his argument. Might as well admit it. "There's always a possibility that she's their dupe or that she's duped me, but I don't think so." He doubted she had pretended her loyalty to him at the cabin. She had believed he came to help her then.

"Dealing with females requires caution." Kin sounded enigmatic.

Despite an impulse to defend her, Dylan strove for truthfulness. It was essential that he not let his feelings for Maya interfere with his duty to Mythos. "Maya helped me subdue Schwartz and get the confession out of him. He admitted killing her friend, at the request of her hybrid foster parents. Now Carrick's got him."

"I read your report." Archer smiled. "You're positive Schwartz is a hybrid because of cosmetic scars. Good observation."

"Thanks, but he did admit it to us." Dylan tried to return the smile. "If Schwartz went undetected even for a short time, it's highly possible that other hybrids have infiltrated ORION."

Archer nodded. "This is the first proof of collusion we've found, but we can't launch a formal probe. It won't stand up in world court because of patient/client privilege. With Dr. Rembrandt dead, it's a moot point. Carrick himself would never bring Schwartz to trial because the public would find out about the infiltration. He wants to keep his organization squeaky clean, at least on the surface."

"If I know Carrick, Schwartz is as good as dead." Kin looked grim.

"The woman will be, too." Archer frowned at Dylan. "How'd you mange to let her get away from you? It's not like you to screw up like this."

Here it was, the moment Dylan had dreaded. Hating to confess, he drew on his inner courage. "I've got to admit she surprised me. I didn't think she'd bolt. I was at fault there. It won't happen again."

"Mythos has a very low tolerance for failure." Archer's voice was firm.

"Yes, I know." Dylan believed persuading Archer to rescind the kill order took precedence over any career considerations. Dylan spoke in as casual a voice as he could manage. "Maya's proved she's on our side. If she goes to work for us in the future, she could disrupt a lot of hostile activities...at ORION, GSS, and maybe even on the spaceships themselves, if she gets a crack at them."

"There's no question," Archer said, "that we could use someone with abilities like hers."

In his gut, Dylan knew she could be a great help to Mythos. He hoped he'd done right by her with his argument. "Would you rescind the kill order?"

Kin gave Dylan a wilting glance.

"I'll think about it." Offering a handshake, Archer leaned toward Dylan then grinned and crossed his arms behind his back. "You smell gamey, Dylan. Don't you ever change clothes?"

"No reason to smell good for you guys." With a harrumph, Dylan headed for his room. "I'll see if I can get a fix on Maya my way."

"We'll let you know if we discover anything while you're in there," Archer called after him.

Once inside his private room, Dylan ran hot water in the shower, peeled off the stinky clothes, and stepped in. The knotted muscles in the back of his neck ached, so he massaged them and let the steamy warmth flow over him.

While he lathered his hair and body, he worked to empty his mind of worry about Maya and of the anger at his own ineffectiveness. He'd made some mistakes he regretted – misplacing his medallion, telling her about Mythos, and most of all allowing her to leave the cave without him. That moment of confusion should never have occurred and wouldn't have happened if his agenda had remained pure.

This keeping a soldier's mentality had become a life's work. Dylan wondered whether the satisfaction he gained from his missions made up for the emotional isolation they required. Had he devoted his life to Mythos's cause or had Mythos pre-empted his life?

At the moment, staying on task held highest priority. In order to accomplish a successful remote viewing, Dylan had to create as calm a mental state as possible. Serenity would be wonderful, but not likely in his current emotional turmoil. Short of that, he could perhaps conjure openness and relaxation. He prodded himself to let go of the fear of failure that kept cropping up.

Yes, a lot rode on his ability to succeed, maybe Maya's life, maybe the lives of many, maybe his reputation, but stressing himself only made things worse. As he rinsed off, he watched sudsy water swirl around his feet and disappear down the drain, hopefully along with his angst.

After toweling dry, he pulled on white acetate shorts, the ones he wore to work out in and the only clean clothing left in the place. A quick glance in the mirror showed heavy black stubble, but he didn't want to take time to shave.

Rumpling his hair, he lay on the bed, placed his crossed hands over his solar plexus, and gave himself the command to relax, release, and let go. He noticed his breath going in and out and watched it raise his chest in a slower and easier rhythm. Dylan closed his eyes and waited for the lids to flutter, signaling a meditative state.

Where had Maya gone? The need to know where the soldiers had taken her was paramount. He hoped to hell they hadn't hurt her. If they tortured her, he would kill every bastard in ORION. If they killed her, what would he do then? He'd create his own personal vendetta.

Rage filled Dylan, the old rage he'd known since his parents' deaths, unrelieved by any war-like act. Nothing he did in the service of Mythos, from blowing up Anaz-voohri ships to shooting hostile hybrids, would ever bring his parents back. If he failed to rescue Maya, nothing would ever bring her back.

With a ragged sigh, he sat up and took deep breaths. Too much depended on this remote viewing session. When he'd felt emotional stress in the past, his abilities had deserted him. *Damn. That couldn't happen this time.*

Dylan jumped off the bed and opened the fridge. Grabbing a fudgesicle, he unwrapped it so roughly the tip broke off. He popped it in his mouth and bit down, expecting to enjoy the pleasure of chocolate sweetness. Instead, his stomach did a flip flop. He couldn't eat a bite without vomiting.

Bleakly, he admitted to himself he couldn't accomplish the remote viewing in his present state of mind. Archer hadn't heard anything worth reporting or he would have been knocking on the door. Dylan felt sorrow that he couldn't rise to the task. He needed to do something for Maya, something that would honor her.

After tossing the ice cream in the wastebasket, Dylan picked up the epad and keyed in a search for Maya's birth parents to find out whether either of them still lived and, if so, where. No matter what happened, he would need their contact information.

If Maya survived this encounter with ORION, he would reunite her with her birth parents as an effort to make amends. If she didn't survive, he would go to them and personally tell them as much as he knew about their daughter's life and talents and wonderful, gentle character. He'd make certain they knew she had acted heroically. In this way, he would honor Maya. She deserved it.

Dylan felt, if not better, at least more settled. Lying back down, he pulled his mother's quilt over his legs and crossed his hands behind his head.

Perhaps he should talk with God. He had not prayed since the night he'd discovered his medical records. He had felt so much anger toward the Anaz-voohri for callously pre-empting his life and killing his parents that he had blamed God. To be honest, he knew this whole business was not God's fault. It was the Anaz-voohri's fault.

Dylan prayed for renewal of his faith. He prayed for an end to any block to finding Maya. He prayed for her well-being. He prayed for enlightenment about whatever would help him find peace.

The calm state that had so far eluded him wafted over Dylan. His breathing evened out, his muscles relaxed, and his eyelids fluttered. He lost awareness of his body and entered a mental state of great clarity and alertness, he became one with the divine spirit.

Thoughts tumbled onto his mind like rose petals falling on glass.

My anger toward the enemy has been my block. My motive for fighting has been revenge for the deaths of my parents. That has caused negative personal karma. I release all negativity and draw positive karma to myself. Any violent act I must commit will be done with integrity, to protect innocent life or to help bring peace to the planet. I am a warrior and proudly follow my code: justice, kindness, courage, benevolence, veracity, honor, and loyalty. God is with me.

In the quiet that followed, Dylan's consciousness slipped away and flew out over the city. He saw the spires of St. Thomas and the Brooklyn Bridge beneath him. In the midst of nearby skyscrapers, he floated over a windowless concrete building, a dwarf barely ten stories high, ORION Headquarters. Although he couldn't see her, he knew with absolute certainty that Maya was inside. He wanted to discern her exact location, but the clairvoyant moment ended with unusual abruptness.

Dylan catapulted back into his body. Leaping off the bed, he threw open the door and shouted, "She's right here in town!"

From the main office, he could hear the bustle of firearms picked up and drawers closing while he threw on his dirty clothes. Dylan didn't care, he felt so happy to be going into action, knowing he was doing the right thing.

He shouted through the doorway, "Hey, I'm going right now. I could use any help I can get." He strapped on his gun and stuck his knife in his boot then went into the main room, throwing on his leather jacket. "She's at NY HQ. I'm not exactly sure where but in the building."

"Great news." Archer yelled. "Kin's gonna help you out on this gig."

"Great!" Dylan said. "We can make a plan on the way."

Hurrying down the corridor beside him, Archer clapped Dylan on the back. "I've rescinded the kill order with the proviso that the woman can and will fight with us. If that turns out not to be true, you'll have to make sure she dies."

"I understand." Dylan felt a confidence he had never experienced before. "Thank you, sir."

When they arrived at the elevator, Archer leaned against the wall and said, "Kin will assist you in making that decision, should things turn negative."

Having worked as a hired assassin, Kin might not care about Maya as a person and be too eager to get rid of her. Dylan would make certain he alone made the decision, but he had no doubt that Maya would come through. He followed Kin into the elevator and pressed the ascend button. "Not to worry. Everything's going to go right."

Chapter Sixteen

Lost in a nightmare, Maya lay strapped down on a razor-thin board that teetered high above the ground. Great fear of falling consumed her, and she refused to look down. Above her, the mouth of a huge beast opened. It laughed and said it would eat her up, and she could do nothing to stop it. Her arms and legs felt leaden. Trapped by a force she couldn't understand, she wanted to escape more than anything and struggled to consciousness.

Maya awakened with a start, disoriented. Her whole body ached, and she had a migraine that made her head feel like it would explode. Through closed lids, she couldn't tell whether bright lights burned overhead or she lay outdoors in the sunshine.

Unwilling to face the pain of opening her eyes, she tried to get a grip on her location. The bed felt too hard for the one she slept in at home or the one in the cabin. Remembrance of awakening in Dylan's arms on the hard cave floor came to her. Oh, to regain the reassurance of that moment, but she knew she was not with him nor could she be. He had broken faith with her.

Her last conscious memory, of running from ORION soldiers, returned. They must have taken her somewhere. Where on earth?

Shielding her eyes, Maya squinted and took in the picture-less, windowless walls and white ceiling of the small room in which they confined her long ago. She sat up on a cot not much different from the one in the jail the other night. Her bare legs poked out of a white hospital gown or similar garb of a coarse texture. As sick as she felt, she knew this was not a hospital room.

Horrified, she realized she didn't see her clothes in this space with no closet or bathroom. That meant someone had undressed her without her permission or her knowledge. Why would anyone do such a degrading, despicable thing?

Maya ignored the throbbing in her eyes and staggered out of bed. There was nothing to see, not a chair or any of her possessions. Where were the laptop and phone she'd carried with her when she ran away from Dylan? How she regretted having to do that, but he left her without a choice. She couldn't stay and let him kill her. Would he really have gone through with it?

The door had no knob. She tried passing her hand over its electronic eye, but nothing happened. They'd definitely locked her in.

A small lens perched on a ledge in a corner near the ceiling, a remote camera. She didn't know whether it recorded her movements or someone in another place watched her, probably both. Unwilling for her captors to know she'd become aware of the camera, she resisted the urge to stick out her tongue.

What impact might she have on the camera? She had made the laptop and phone work, but she'd held them in her hands. She'd been able to break machinery with her mind all along but didn't know whether she could have any effect without physical contact.

Could she shut the camera down with her mind? Should she bring attention to herself by trying? Did her captors know about her abilities? They must have some idea, or they'd not have locked her in this damned cell.

As Maya sat on the cot to consider her situation, the door swung outward and two medics walked in. The Hispanic male and the Anglo female both wore white lab coats over ORION trousers.

Maya jumped up and gathered the back of the gown together over her bare behind.

"Let's go." The male medic towered over Maya and held up a syringe. "Behave yourself or I'll use this."

The female medic stepped behind Maya, grabbed her hands, and clamped handcuffs on.

Aghast, Maya calmed herself. She could never let them witness her fear. She would find a way to elude these people yet. She had to trust in her own abilities because no one would come to help her. Dylan's betrayal hurt her more than any because there had been such promise in his eyes.

Clutching the edges of her gown to hold them together, she walked between the medics down a long corridor that looked exactly like the room, plain walls and camera lenses everywhere. The ceramic tiles felt cold on her bare feet. She and the medics entered an elevator in silence.

The elevator rose to the tenth floor, and the doors opened onto a reception area. She made a mental note of the location of the computer console. It could become an ally, should Maya get the chance to get close to it.

A swarthy, buxom lieutenant sat at the desk. She leered at Maya with an expression of dark pleasure more reminiscent of eighteenth-century guillotine watchers than twenty-first-century government workers. Sympathizing with what poor Marie Antoinette must have experienced in her final hours, Maya shuddered with the thought that these could be hers.

The lieutenant leaned back, passed her hand over an intercom without breaking eye contact with Maya, and said, "Rembrandt's on her way in, General Carrick."

The female medic held the door to the inner office open but didn't enter when the male medic guided Maya through. She hated his rough touch and snide look, but they were nothing compared to the menacing aura surrounding the man she saw at the desk inside.

Harsh black hair framed Carrick's broad face that looked so filled with hostility that she doubted he'd ever had a kindly thought toward anyone. On his crisp uniform, thin metal bars indicated much valor and much promotion. The thing Maya found most sinister was his eyes, an unnaturally shiny light gray color. His glasses magnified the left eye, which looked watery as if quicksilver ran through it.

Behind him video screens displayed a synchronized screensaver of ocean waves. They allowed her to conclude that a CPU probably stood in the desk drawer, the normal location for it. The CPU surely connected to a mainframe somewhere in the building. She noticed a phone on his wrist and one on the desk. A sound system console stood next to it, a price tag still visible on its carton standing nearby. There appeared to be no other electronic equipment, but that was plenty, should she get an opportunity.

Breaking into a smile that looked ludicrous on such a face, Carrick rose and moved around the desk then leaned against it. "Well, if it isn't the fucking Anaz-voohri mole herself!" With a wide gesture he said, "How do you like our hospitality?"

Maya realized this building could be anywhere. At least people spoke English, but that could be true of ORION offices throughout the world. She had no idea how long she'd been unconscious. She felt very hungry so it had probably been a day or more. When she did free herself, she needed to know her location. Maybe Carrick would give her a clue, so she said, "You mean in New York?"

"I'm asking the questions here, and you'd better answer up smartly." Carrick walked around behind her. "Hmmm. Very nice tattoo. Bet you can make the wings flutter when you get humping."

Maya tried to cover her behind. What a loathsome man. She turned around and glared at him.

With a ghastly leer, Carrick said to Maya, "Face the desk!" He said to the medic, "Take a break, I can handle this."

"Yes, sir."

Afraid to disobey, Maya turned toward the desk and heard the medic go through the door. It banged shut behind him. She hated being alone in the room with this man, but maybe that would work to her good.

"Where are the other moles the Anaz-voohri abducted? Do they all have tattoos like yours? Is that how I'll recognize them?"

"I don't know where they are." Maya could feel his breath on her shoulders as he stood behind her. She didn't want him to touch her. As long as she could slide by with the truth, she would. She didn't doubt he would use truth serum if her answers didn't satisfy him. "I barely remember being in the Pleiades at all. I was very young. I know there were some other little girls with me, but I don't remember them."

Striding back to the desk, Carrick waved a slip of paper at her. "You don't seriously expect me to believe that, do you?" He consulted the paper. "Where is Astoria Blair?"

Maya didn't want to make eye contact with him and stared at her feet. She wanted to focus on being as innocuous as possible while she did a mental scan of the email Nanobot in her brain. "I don't know."

"Ally Curran?"

"I don't know."

"Celene Dupres?"

"Don't know."

"Tierney Grant."

Maya's head shot up. "The President's daughter?" That must have been why Maya had felt such a familiarity. They had spent time together as children. She wondered how much Tierney remembered of the abduction. Or the others, whoever they were, did they remember?

"The very same. You know that scrumptious bitch, don't you? What is she rigged to do?"

"I've seen her on TV, that's all. I don't know her personally." Maya felt very glad she didn't know any of these women and couldn't betray them now.

"You're lying, mole. Tell me about Electra Monroe."

"I don't know who she is." Maya's mind registered a fault in the programming of the email Nanobot in her brain, probably caused by a virus. Of course, that had to be the reason it hadn't worked. Maybe that's what caused her headache.

"Maeve Shivaun?"

"I don't know."

"You want to make me believe you don't know any of these fucking moles, you little hybrid bitch?"

Maya shook her head and spoke softly but firmly. "I'm not a hybrid. I'm a human being, just like you." She'd never known anyone so awful.

"Okay, here's the deal, miss 'I'm a human being, just like you'." Carrick mocked. He appeared to enjoy brutality. "You will be executed as soon as this interview ends. There's no dickering on the outcome. But I am a reasonable man, and I could be persuaded to order a swift end where you just go to sleep and don't wake up. Or your death could last for days and be ugly and painful. If you want examples, I can give you some. But you're supposed to be so smart. You can probably imagine the details yourself."

Sickened, Maya refused to give in to fear. As long as she was alive there was hope. She would find a way to free herself yet. She mentally directed the Nanobot to do a virus scrub of its program.

Carrick folded his arms. "The Anaz-voohri don't make mistakes. They put you here in New York, rigged to blow up communications, didn't they?"

"Yes." *Might as well own up to what they both knew.*

"The Anaz-voohri don't do anything without a plan. Tell me what they want you and the others to do."

"They want us to destroy humanity. You should be helping me stop them, not persecuting me." Maya wondered if the man was too stupid to recognize the truth when he heard it.

That grotesque smile crossed his face again. "Tell me how you blacked out the eastern seaboard."

"It was an accident." Maya remembered the little voice speaking to her then and wondered why she'd not heard it since.

"Where's your software?"

"I don't know."

Reaching across the desk, Carrick grabbed the software disk from her laptop and waved it in her face. "Our experts have tried to simulate what you did. There's a trick to it we don't know, and you will tell us."

"The software requires a mental fusion." Maya didn't want to tell him she'd begun to teach others at NexTech. That would jeopardize their lives, too. Terrible as Carrick was, at least she didn't have to mask her thoughts like she did with the Anaz-voohri captain. Maya doubted Carrick would be a match for Captain Kavak, but how delightful to think of them battling each other.

Leaning forward, Carrick opened the front of the desk, exposing the CPU. "Show me how to do the mental fusion."

Maya shrugged but didn't respond aloud. She reserved all her energy for the virus scrubbing. Only a few seconds to go and the Nanobot in her brain would be ready to perform. It had grown far beyond its original programming into a powerful tool she alone commanded. If the device ever was going to work again, it had to be now.

"You have fifteen seconds to start talking."

"All right, I give up." Maya shed real tears of frustration despite the fact that a part of her mind remained calm and aware that crying would make her seem more convincing to this Neanderthal. "I need to use my hands to interact with the computer. I can't show you without using my hands. Would you take these handcuffs off?"

Carrick's leer returned. "I don't know if I should or not. You're awfully sexy wearing them."

Maya didn't know whether she could control the power building within her. If the Anaz-voohri voice tried to reassert control, she might blow herself up into the bargain.

The vulgar man watched her thoughtfully for a moment, as if considering whether or not to take off the handcuffs. "All right." Carrick walked behind her.

Either the nub of his coat sleeve or his fingers rubbed against the skin on her behind, she couldn't tell which. It was all Maya could do to keep from flinching, but she managed. He snapped open the handcuffs.

Maya activated the Nanobot with an inner destruct sequence. Ten, nine, eight...

She took the few steps necessary to reach the desk and picked up the software program disk. Seven, six, five...

She inserted the disk into the laptop. Four, three, two...

"Well?" Carrick gave her a condescending look.

"Here's the way you do it!" Maya lunged forward and grabbed the CPU with both hands.

Sparks flew out of the CPU, and Maya fell back as it exploded. Shards shot everywhere with the crunch of splintering plastic.

"What the fuck?" A look of dismay crossed Carrick's ugly features.

The screensavers went black, and the wall of monitors crackled momentarily like lightning across an autumn sky, then blew apart. Fried bits of monitor shielding floated down like leaves.

"What the fuck have you done?" Carrick lunged toward Maya. She kicked him in the groin, and he grunted as she headed for the door.

Fire sizzled through the electrical wiring of the sound system, and it blew up. Flames shot all over the console.

Smoke billowed around Carrick as he struggled to grasp the desk edge. The lights blinked then went out.

The office door fell open, its lock a cinder. Screams came from the reception area.

Maya dashed through the door. ORION officers ran in all directions.

Coughing and sputtering, Carrick screamed from the office. "Stop her! Stop that mole!"

The lieutenant held her hands over her mouth, transfixed by her burning monitor. That told Maya the mainframe had blown, too.

The lights went out in the reception area as Maya dashed to the concrete stairwell. Yellow painted arrows showed the evacuation route in case of disaster. She took the steps two at a time on her way down. The stone treads scuffed her bare feet, but she didn't care. All she wanted was to get out of the building before someone figured out how to lock the doors.

At the bottom of the ten stories, two doors with singed locks stood open. A cold wind blew snow onto the floor through the one with the now dark exit sign over it. Gloomy daylight let Maya know it was day and not night, small comfort considering she had no clothes.

Going out that door could be deadly without knowing what city she was in. Maya might freeze from the cold before she found anyone to help her. The better choice would be to go onto the main floor and steal an overcoat from a rack. Surely there were many in the building. Then she could head outside.

Maya peeked through the door to discern the layout before entering. Filtered light from a lobby window illuminated an ORION officer lying on the floor nearby. He appeared to be unconscious because his chest went up and down with breaths. He wore a shirt and slacks but unfortunately no coat.

Holding her gown together in back, Maya moved on across the marble lobby floor, around a corner with restroom signs beside the elevators. She heard a sizzling sound, similar to a phase gun but more substantial. As she was about to hide in the restroom, she saw the most amazing thing.

Dylan, his hands in the air, walked down the hall toward two surprised-looking ORION officers. Dylan called out, "I'm unarmed. Make way."

Maya swore she saw a shadow beside Dylan. It fired some kind of pellets. One ORION officer dropped to the floor like an overripe apple. The other ran away.

Alarms began to shriek, a sign that some control appeared exerted over the electrical system. The floor lights cane on above the elevators, and fluorescent lights sputtered in the ceiling.

Damn! She'd not been able to knock out the emergency power this time. Maya needed to work on that.

"There she is!" Dylan shouted to the empty space beside him then ran toward Maya. "Thank God, you're alive."

Maya wondered why he was here. Had he come to rescue her or finish her off, if ORION didn't? Should she try to escape him? If she did, what would his disembodied companion do?

With a hearty laugh, Dylan swooped her up into his arms and crushed her to him. He smelled of shampoo and leather. Angry as she'd felt toward him, Maya was glad to see him. She hoped his appearance here meant he had come to rescue her, after all.

The shadow hovered behind Dylan. A voice from within it said, "Let's get out of here."

Maya glanced fearfully at the shadow. *What in the hell was that?*

"Don't worry," Dylan said to Maya. "He's on our side." Dylan let Maya down, whisked off his jacket, and draped it around her, its tail mercifully long enough to cover her bottom.

Maya dashed into the stairwell and out the exit door. Dylan and the shadow caught up with her. Together the three, icy breath blowing out, ran down the alley with gigantic buildings on both sides.

Her feet freezing on cold snow, Maya imagined herself once again in a dream, but this time reality was more bizarre than any dream. The shadow materialized beside her in the form of a Chinese man, tall, muscular, and handsome. He nodded a salutation.

Hoping she could trust him, Maya nodded back.

Dylan, running on the other side, smiled like the Cheshire Cat. "Here we go." He indicated a taxi parked across the end of the alley. After he opened the door, all three piled inside, Dylan beside Maya and the materialized shadow on the facing seat.

A gush of warm, tobacco-filled air engulfed them. The driver said, "Good job, guys. I was afraid you wouldn't be able to get her out." He threw his cigarette in the street as the taxi took off. "Shoulda known better."

"Maya," Dylan said as he squeezed her shoulders like an old friend, "That's Bill, our driver, and this is Kin. They're Mythos, too. Kin, Maya Rembrandt."

Maya nodded a greeting to the two men and said, "Thanks, I think."

"That was you, wasn't it?" Dylan said to Maya as he waved toward the receding building. "You shut down the ORION electrical system?"

"Yes." Maya acknowledged to herself that she could be in more danger from these two. "What are you going to do to me?"

"Take care of you," Dylan said, his voice serious, "as we should have all along, right, Kin?"

Kin's nod seemed to bear more meaning than Maya could interpret.

Dylan took her hand and looked into her eyes. Relief shone on his face and joy warmed his voice as he said, "The kill order has been rescinded."

Maya felt relieved even though she doubted Dylan could have done it, anyway. Who was he kidding? Exasperated at the casualness with which everyone seemed to regard her life these days, Maya spat at him, "Am I supposed to be grateful?"

Kin relaxed back, closed his eyes, and folded his arms.

Someone should remind him that he is still visible, Maya thought. Maybe then he'd really disappear. In fact, she felt rage at all three of these Mythos whatevers!

The windshield wipers clicked, and cars in the street honked. Looking through the dirty window, Maya wondered where they now headed. Snow poured down so that she could barely distinguish forms.

Pulling her toward him, Dylan tried to put his arm around her, but Maya resisted. "Leave me alone."

They rode in silence for a time then the taxi pulled off the street and stopped.

"Thanks," Dylan said to Kin.

With a brief nod, Kin opened the door and stepped out. Beyond him airport shuttles passed. It occurred to Maya to get out too, but Kin slammed the door and the taxi took off.

Dylan pulled the collar of his jacket closer around her neck and gazed at her with the same tender look he had in the moment before he kissed her in the cave. "My sweet Maya, I am profoundly sorry for putting you in harm's way. Can you find it in your heart to forgive me?"

The strength that had preserved her so far began to crumble and break inside her. Maya began to tremble, and she wasn't even cold. She whispered, "Could you have killed me?"

"Not since I started to love you."

"You love me?"

His breath felt warm on her face, and he pressed his lips to hers in the sweetest of kisses, tender and possessive. "How can I make it up to you?"

It was as she had hoped all along. Dylan would never have actually killed her, no matter what he'd said. She could let herself love him. She couldn't stop herself, actually, but she refused to say so now with this other man in the car, maybe never. "You could get me some clothes and something to eat."

Chapter Seventeen

Grateful that Maya had consented to come home with him, Dylan bade farewell to the Mythos taxi driver and ushered his cold, weary, barely dressed, wonder love into his loft. If she had refused, he hadn't any idea where he could have taken her. With ORION onto her house, the cabin, and her worksite, the only hope left to protect her was that they'd not linked him to her or that Archer's pull in high places would cover them for a while.

Once inside Dylan convinced Maya to take a relaxing bath while he ordered some food. Even though she readily agreed, he heard the lock click on the bathroom door behind her, conclusive proof that she didn't trust him. Not that he blamed her. He'd told her the truth when he said he would make it up to her. Exactly what that might entail, he had yet to figure out. He hoped she would give him the chance.

The sound of gushing water filling the tub issued from the bathroom, so Maya must have decided to take some of his advice. Since he didn't know what she wanted to eat and didn't want to disturb her to ask, Dylan phoned the deli and ordered salad, wine, beer, hot tea, pastrami sandwiches, linguine and clam sauce, cheese sticks, jalapeno poppers, chocolate cake, and ice cream sundaes. He felt like splurging to celebrate finding Maya alive. His worst fear had been that ORION would kill her, and he had no doubt they had intended to before she thwarted them. Saucy little chick.

Dylan fished around in his footlocker and found the ORION uniform folded beneath baseballs, bats, and gloves. Archer had provided him ORION, GSS, and NYC disguises over a year ago, only for use when absolutely necessary. He dowsed the rumpled uniform in wrinkle release spray. That improved the look, not much, but enough to slide by in damp weather. ORION was known as the most persnickety branch when it came to grooming.

With the window blinds open, Dylan could see that the storm had intensified. Snow blew against the pane, turning mid-day dark. No one with a telescope could see in, so he shed his jeans and shirt and donned the uniform. Very uncomfortable with its high collar and tie. Why anyone willingly put on such a monkey suit every day to go to work he'd never understand. He appreciated the casualness of his own attire anew. He'd definitely have to shave before he left, if Maya ever came out of the bathroom.

The food arrived and he set out the items, still wrapped and labeled, on the table of the booth, so she would know what she was eating. There was so much food he almost set the jukebox on the floor but decided against it. It made the place look festive. He called, "Maya, lunch is here. Are you finished yet?"

The tumbler clicked in the lock, and Maya came out of the bathroom. A surprised look crossed her face when she saw him.

Dylan held out his arms to indicate his clothing. "Think I can pass for ORION?"

She nodded but didn't question him. With no makeup and wet hair looking black, she was ravishing in one of his Yankees t-shirts, so big it fell down one shoulder. Her bare legs showed, and he wondered if she wore anything underneath.

When they ran from the ORION soldiers earlier Dylan had taken notice of her gorgeous behind, fairy and all. It had been impossible not to. That had not been the appropriate moment to mention that he found her body attractive. A moment would surely come soon when he felt free to let her know how much he wanted her.

"Hope you don't mind." Maya pulled up the t-shirt to reveal a pair of his running shorts.

"No, of course not.   Come and eat."   A bit disappointed, Dylan sat in the booth and indicated the table he'd spread. "You've got lots of choices."

"Breakfast, lunch, or dinner?   What time is it, anyway?"

"About two in the afternoon.   You can't really tell from this weather."

Maya stared out the window for a moment then looked rather helpless. "Maybe you'd better tell me what day this is."   She sat opposite him.

"Saturday, the seventeenth."

"I was only in there for a day?   It seemed like a week."   She brushed back her hair with a trembling hand.

"Close to twenty-four hours."   Dylan reached across the table and took her hands in his. "I'm sorry they were so rough on you.   Do you want to talk about it?   I'm a pretty good listener."

"I know you are."   Maya gave him a warm smile, but her wistfulness was unnerving.

Dylan decided to act as casual as possible.   She might be suffering from shock or something. "You said you were hungry."

"Very."   Maya read the labels and opened the linguine.

"How about some wine or hot tea?"

"Tea, please."

While he poured two steaming cups, Dylan watched her taste the first bite of pasta.   She held it in her mouth, closed her eyes, and sighed before she swallowed it. Immediately, she took another bite and did the same, tasting it even longer.   When she swallowed, her face suffused with delight.   He loved watching her take pleasure in the flavor. He remembered how sexy she'd been, eating cookies in the cave, and couldn't decide whether he enjoyed linguine or cookies more. "Is it good?"

"Oh, yes." Her warm smile held a new familiarity, no wistfulness now. She held up her plastic bowl. "Try some."

Dylan sampled a forkful of linguine. "Excellent. I love clam sauce."

"Me, too." Maya held the bowl before her and took several bites, chewing greedily.

It was so much fun to watch her Dylan neglected to eat.

"Here, you want any more?" Maya held up the almost-empty bowl.

"I'd rather have this." Chuckling, Dylan unwrapped one of the pastrami sandwiches and bit into it while she tore into the salad. The sandwich had a hearty taste he particularly enjoyed, but it was no match for the entertainment value of watching Maya devour lettuce and tomatoes with extra salad dressing.

Fork in hand, she pointed at the jukebox. "Does that work?'

"Sure, if you put dimes in it."

"Dimes? I've not seen a dime since I was a kid."

Dylan reached under the table and produced a mason jar full. "My dad's. He never turned his collection in when the government stopped making change, so I inherited it." Dylan dropped a dime into the slot and punched a button. Johnny Mathis's voice came through the tinny speaker, singing *Chances Are.*

"That's wonderful," Maya cried. "I've seen these in museums, but never a real one."

"This one is only thirty years old. It's a facsimile, but it sounds authentic, doesn't it?"

Maya listened for a moment. "That's a very pretty song, poignant almost." Her face took on a melancholy expression. "What should I do about my parents' funerals?"

So that was what bothered her, still sad over the death of her hybrid foster parents. Dylan hoped soon he would have a way to salve that wound if he managed to contact her real parents, but not yet. "I'll help you handle those details. In fact, Mythos can take care of it for you. That would probably be better. Don't worry now. You need to get your strength back."

Maya laid down her fork, picked up a piece of chocolate cake, and set it down, sounding torn. "I forgot for a little bit, you know."

Rubbing her hand, Dylan said, "I know how you feel." He didn't look forward to talking about her parents. She must have a lot of unsorted feelings about them. "I was really proud of you for shutting down ORION. There's hardly a person alive who could do that. You have an astounding ability."

Her nut-brown eyes, huge and soulful, lit her face. "The way that Neanderthal Carrick treated me was unforgivable. I want to get even with him and with the Anaz-voohri. I was serious when I said I would help you and Mythos."

"I'm glad you still feel that way." Dylan grasped her hand more firmly. If she lied or misled him, he would sense any withdrawal on this important question. "You're positive now that you control your power? No voice going off in your head, making you do something you don't want to do?"

"No more. In fact, I've grown with the ability." Maya pointed toward her forehead. "The Nanobot and I have become friends. He's more than another alter ego now, more powerful than Hermie or the Fairy Godmother." Her hand lay still in his.

"Fairy Godmother?"

"My computer at NexTech." Maya looked pensive. "Do you think I'll ever get to go back there?"

"Maybe someday. Now, you need to go away. It's just a matter of time before the ORION computers are up and running. Who knows what Carrick will do then! He doesn't like being one-upped, and you did a real number on him."

"What are you suggesting? Where should I go?"

"Mythos will take care of the details, if you're willing to go undercover for a while."

"Alone?"

"If you want to be alone, that's fine. I was hoping to go with you."

"How safe will I be?" The question sounded coy but the expression on her face showed genuine distress.

"I wasn't kidding about loving you, but we've got plenty of time to talk about that later. Right now, make a list for me of things you need from the house, and I'll go get them. You can't go near that brownstone for quite some time. ORION will have a guard posted for months."

"So that's why you're dressed up in those hateful togs?"

Dylan couldn't agree more. He patted her hand and rose from the booth. Rummaging in the drawer of the school desk, he found a scrap of paper and pencil then laid them before her. He went into the bathroom and shaved.

When he returned, Maya placed her list in his hand. Concern in her voice, she said, "Don't be gone long."

"No worries about that." When Dylan drew her to him, she didn't resist. She opened her mouth to him and kissed him with as much gusto as she had attacked the salad. Soon he hoped to be the linguini and broke the kiss unwillingly. "I'll be right back. Don't answer the door or the phone."

When he dashed down the stairs, she called after him, "You be careful, too. I don't want to have to come and break you out of ORION."

Dylan's departing laughter elated Maya. Running from him and leaving the cave had been a foolish reaction, which she regretted. Only in the first moments after Dylan announced his charge to kill her did she really believe he would ever have gone through with it. Now he had gone so far as to say that he loved her, and she wanted to believe him.

She knew unquestionably that she loved him although she felt far too shy to say so. She needed him, too, to get through the dangers created by her new-found abilities and to deal with the adjustment it would take to think of herself as a freedom fighter and an orphan. Any sorrow regarding her foster parents she struggled to postpone.

The snowstorm had ceased, and fragile sunlight through the large window made her spirits brighter. She gathered up the remaining food and stored it in Dylan's tiny refrigerator. Because his wastebasket already overflowed, she decided she would be safe to set the trash outside.

ORION's people didn't know where she'd fled, and even if they did they'd hardly had time to reorganize. Her success with the Nanobot and its growth in her brain convinced her that the Anaz-voohri knew her location at all times. They'd programmed her with a tracking system she'd recently found in her mental software. Hiding from them seemed pointless. She needed to find another way to resist their control over her.

Donning Dylan's leather jacket completed her ensemble entirely from his wardrobe. Wearing his clothes made her yearn for him, the rough t-shirt cloth and his musky scent constant reminders of his allure. She almost wished he hadn't gone to collect her things.

If Maya had been born male, she could only have hoped to become as handsome, courageous, sexy, and truly original as Dylan with his clairvoyance and seemingly endless variety of talents. He had an odd brand of integrity she didn't understand. Regardless, it made him special.

Trash bags in hand, she started down the stairs, pausing for a moment to admire the lithograph he'd bought the night they met. That she had not noticed it at all when she entered earlier said a lot about her state of mind. She'd felt more confused, troubled, and overwhelmed than she'd allowed herself to admit. Dylan's loving kindness had lightened her mood, along with the gargantuan meal.

The Triple Elvis set off the landing perfectly. In fact, the whole loft rang with the sense of derring-do that pervaded Dylan's personality, down to the gun collection, the 1950s reproductions, and baseball memorabilia. His love for those things hadn't surprised her at all. Maybe she was developing some psychic abilities of her own. She hadn't noticed a bed and wondered where Dylan slept. How lovely it would be to sleep with him in a real bed. She hoped that experience lay in her future.

Maya opened the front door and found herself standing in a pool of light far brighter than the winter sun. She dropped the trash bags when paralysis seized her. Helpless to command her arms and legs, Maya drifted on the beam of light. She needn't strain to see from whence it came. The spaceship hovered several hundred feet above the adjacent apartment walls. With no protest, she allowed them to pull her along the semaphore's path over the walls and up the other side.

It was about time she and Captain Kavak confronted each other. Shutting down Carrick's operation gave Maya the confidence to seek a way to disable the spaceship. She prepared herself mentally for whatever lay ahead. She was capable of far more than a normal human being, thanks to the unwelcome tinkering done by the Anaz-voohri. She would throw that in their faces if she got a chance.

Maya wanted revenge for all the wrongs they had done to her. They deserved whatever fate she could mete out. Although nervous because her efforts could turn sour and she'd die, Maya felt willing to die if she had to. She only regretted not having the chance to make love to Dylan.

The spaceship hovered above a baseball diamond in a small park. Near the wire dugout a NYC police officer had his hand on a dog's collar. Two men with briefcases stood beside a car. All appeared to be paralyzed. Fortunately, few people were about because it had stopped snowing only a few moments before. Otherwise, many more might have to suffer this unpleasant experience of paralysis.

The grand doors of the spaceship opened, and Maya floated inside. The pull of the beam dissolved, and she walked under her own power onto the bridge.

No one came for her and none of the crew acknowledged her presence. Why had they abducted her again?

Maya strolled around and noted the placement of the computer consoles. They had decorative navigation keys, featuring eagles and coyotes with a holographic interface, which made it appear as though live animals actually perched on the console or flew above it.

About the configuration of their interior components Maya knew nothing, but the exterior appeared much like human computer technology. She reasoned that the similarities probably outweighed the differences, otherwise the Anaz-voohri would have no use for her abilities, steeped as she was in human university technology.

The slate floor hummed, and Maya could sense motion, but the ride was so smooth she could hardly discern the spaceship's movements. She must remember to tell Dylan all the details because he had such an interest in flying one. It troubled Maya that she didn't know their destination. If the Anaz-voohri didn't return her to a location she recognized, how would she find him again? On the other hand, they probably wouldn't fly her far from New York, if they wished her to continue their abysmal work.

Maya walked up behind a crew member to get a closer look at the interface. He ignored her when she smiled at him, so she figured he didn't care what she did. She knelt down and saw a mainframe beneath the console. A small switch, shielded by a metal casing, bore a black skull and crossbones. *Aha! A self-destruct mechanism.*

The female who had guided Maya out of the cave entered from another room. She spoke in a stern voice, "Come."

Unwilling to cause trouble at this juncture, Maya followed the guide into the operating room.

A tall male Anaz-voohri in a white robe hovered beside the table, arranging surgical implements on a silver tray. Maya recognized him as the man in her dream, the doctor who had strapped her head down and operated on her. It was all she could do to keep from running away from his appalling presence.

This bastard had hurt her as a helpless child. Now, getting revenge held even more significance.

The doctor pointed a long finger at Maya's forehead. Her first reaction was to follow the compulsion to go limp with paralysis, what she knew he intended and the way she had previously reacted. But she realized she could resist and did. In a passionless way, the guide and the doctor grabbed Maya and tried to force her onto the table. Again? It seemed these Anaz-voohri repeated behaviors. She pushed against them, but they overpowered her, so she lay back and acted resigned.

Quelling her fear, Maya gazed up at the tall man and said, "There's no need for force. Just tell me what you want me to do, and maybe I can cooperate."

"We need to adjust your programming." The doctor picked up a needle. "Nothing for you to be concerned about."

The roll of surgical tape on the tray jolted Maya's memory of her former helplessness. Terrified of anyone tying her down, she jumped up and shoved the tray away. She must have surprised the doctor because he moved back and stumbled when his feet hit the floor. He had seemingly lost his ability to hover, and the machinery in his head lit up. The guide gripped Maya by the shoulders and held her still.

Hovering, Captain Kavak entered from her office and said to the doctor, "You called?"

Although he did not speak, the doctor's machinery twinkled.

Captain Kavak's voice sounded shrill. "Ridiculous! You can't handle a simple assignment any more? Imbecile!"

"Forgive me, exalted leader," the doctor said.

Maya thought her chances might be better with the captain and asked, "Why have you brought me here?" She remembered the command to use the repulsive salutation. "Exalted leader?"

"Ah, my pet." Captain Kavak patted Maya on the head with something bordering on the affection one might have for an animal. "There is something wrong with your programming."

"How can you tell?"

"Your trigger keeps going off ahead of schedule. We are going to fix you." With her deformed hand, Captain Kavak indicated the doctor and the surgical implements.

Maya doubted her ability to suppress any thoughts, but she had to try. She instructed the Nanobot to help keep anything from reading her mind. "I don't think I need to be fixed. My trigger has been going off because I didn't understand how to use the program, but now I do. It was just a matter of growing into the abilities you so graciously gave me."

The captain turned to the doctor with a questioning expression. He shrugged and held up his arms in a helpless gesture.

Maya didn't need telepathy to know she had confused the doctor. *The imbecile, indeed.*

Captain Kavak wagged a finger at Maya. "Naughty, naughty." She turned to the guide. "Search her."

The guide stuck her big hands in all of Maya's pockets, or rather Dylan's, but found nothing, not even a handkerchief.

Wishing Dylan were there to help her, Maya realized she'd better monitor her thoughts more carefully. She instructed the Nanobot to monitor her thoughts and keep them free of emotion.

"Where is the toy?" the captain asked. "You've lost the toy I gave you?"

"Toy?" Maya remembered leaving the purple eagle in the cave. "Oh, no, exalted leader. I don't have it with me. I put it away for safekeeping."

"For a moment I thought you were as incompetent as your parents. Their charge was to keep you contented until we needed you." Captain Kavak warmed to her subject. "They had the audacity to expose you to high stress, along with that worthless Schwartz. Then your trigger went off before I was ready. I even gave them an extra copy of the software. Still, they made a mess of it." Captain Kavak leaned against the table. Perhaps the display of emotion caused her to lose her ability to hover, the same thing that had happened last time. She glared at Maya. "You saw what happened to your parents for disobeying orders? They got exactly what they deserved."

"Yes, exalted leader, I know better. I won't let you down." Maya realized Schwartz had told the truth. He and her foster parents had murdered Lola. Yet another reason to best these…The Nanobot interrupted her thought. Thankfully, Maya calmed herself.

The captain shouted in Maya's face. Her breath smelled of sewing machine oil. With halitosis like that, of course these Anaz-voohri liked to drink. "You've been going around blowing things up without my direction. We are the superior species. Do not forget that."

"Yes, exalted leader. Just tell me what to do, and I will do it."

Captain Kavak sounded mollified. "It's important that you only institute your programming when you receive word from us."

Maya realized that the captain and perhaps all the Anaz-voohri had less control over her than they let on. Doubtless they didn't want Maya to know, so she pretended. "You see that's part of what I didn't understand before. I'll be happy to do what you wish now that you've explained to me. I will wait for your signal at all times. How will I know it?"

"You will recognize my voice in your head, not your own voice."

"I understand, exalted leader."

"That's wonderful." Captain Kavak walked to the glass panel in the wall, probably to make a toast.

The captain must have felt the encounter had been successful and that she had Maya under control. Otherwise, why make a toast? Again, the predictability of the captain's behavior struck Maya. She wondered if all Anaz-voohri behaved equally predictably, perhaps to a mechanical point, like their leader.

That sounded just gauche enough to be an Anaz-voohri joke, but Maya didn't think she'd share the humor with this group. They didn't seem like people who could laugh at their foibles.

"Thank you for being so patient with me and explaining things." Maya looked up at the captain hopefully with a big-eyed, soulful expression. *If she thinks of me as a dog, maybe this is the time to lick her face.* She almost thought *yuck*, but the Nanobot interceded.

Captain Kavak had obviously not read Maya's thoughts, or had not tried. Maya had succeeded in duping her captors!

Four champagne flutes filled with blue liquid issued from the glass panel. Captain Kavak turned a beaming look on all she unquestionably saw as her minions.

Maya shook free of the guide, hurried to the cabinet, and picked up a glass. She held it in the air while the three Anaz-voohri took theirs in hand. "To Anaz-voohri rule!" Maya shouted with enthusiasm.

They clinked glasses and drank. Maya ignored the taste, so intent was she on getting out safely and quickly.

With one more revolting promise to Captain Kavak to await orders, Maya left the surgery. She tried not to run but walked with a brisk stride across the bridge to the doors. Those mechanical monsters at the controls might act nonchalant, but they paid attention.

Maya paused at the doors, as if she'd forgotten something. If her plan worked, she would take a lot of Anaz-voohri out of action. If it didn't, at least she would have given her life for a worthwhile cause. She would die comforted to know she had protected Dylan and much of humanity.

Nanobot, rip open the casing and trip the self-destruct lever.

At the sound of crackling metal, an alarm beeped all over the ship.

"Land this ship right now!" Maya shouted.

The crew members on the bridge scurried around, their craniums winking wildly. Their lips clicked in the words of their odd-sounding native language.

Captain Kavak dashed in from the operating room. "What have you done?"

"You're on self-destruct, you imbecile," Maya shouted. "Land this ship."

With the captain beside them giving mental directions, the crew pushed buttons and read gauges. Maya let them try to undo the sequence only for a moment.

Nanobot, land this ship!

"Do as she says," Captain Kavak yelled, and the bridge crew worked to maneuver the ship into a landing course.

In seconds, the ship bumped down. Maya's guess had been right. They hadn't traveled far from the earth's surface.

Nanobot, open the doors.

The self-destruct beep warned with a steady rhythm as the doors opened and the semaphore turned on.

The Nanobot had performed superbly, learning and growing with her, a part of her mind that observed situations and adapted in a compatible way. She melded with the Nanobot in a profound privacy and willed her energy into the spaceship's mainframe.

Nanobot, destroy the mainframe.

Maya leaped outside and jumped off the domed rim of the spaceship, clearing the weather shields over the perimeter lights. She dashed through the snow-covered countryside and into the woods. She hid behind an oak tree and pulled the jacket close around her nose so her breath couldn't show.

For a moment, nothing happened.

Then, popping sounds issued from the interior, followed by a most satisfying boom. With it the tractor beam dissolved, and the semaphore that projected it went dark. The white lights around the base winked out. The spaceship looked like an abandoned clamshell on the murky ocean bottom.

The beep continued to sound, oddly hollow in the bleak afternoon sun.

"Gotcha!" Maya shouted.

A reddish glow grew from inside. Captain Kavak's long, scrawny silhouette stumbled onto the skin of the doorway. She'd had no choice but to abandon ship. It was that or die.

Out came the doctor, the guide, the bridge crew, and several other Anaz-voohri, who made clicking noises or screamed. Several carried phase guns and other large weapons Maya had never seen before.

The guide leaped off the side, brandishing a phase gun. "Where are you, worthless earthling? I'll rip your head off."

Captain Kavak yelled, "Leave her alone. Who knows what else she can blow up."

The Anaz-voohri ran into the woods in a line, following their vicious leader.

A great explosion from within rocked the spaceship. Bright light preceded flames that roared up and turned the spaceship into a molten ball.

The heat from it warmed Maya, who stayed as close as she dared. When she buttoned Dylan's jacket, his musky scent reassured her. He would be proud of her.

Maya loved the sense of completion the blazing spaceship gave her. Something of a payback for her abduction, for the grief her birth parents must have felt, for the price her foster parents had paid, and most of all for the setback the Anaz-voohri had received in their assault on the human spirit.

Maya could get used to being a freedom fighter. It felt great!

Nanobot, tell Dylan where I am.

Chapter Eighteen

At Mythos, Dylan and Archer studied the map. Yellow lights for NYC police officers and blue for ORION indicated their activity in the section of the city where Dylan lived.

Leather crinkled when Archer folded his arms across his chest. "How in hell did you manage to lose her again?"

More pissed at himself than Archer could ever be, Dylan said, "I left her in my apartment and went to get her stuff. I couldn't let her go into her own house. Then Carrick would have gotten her again."

"Now the Anaz-voohri have her." Archer's mood was none too pleasant. "It's hard to say which is worse."

Dylan thought Mythos might be the greatest danger to her but said, "When I got back with her suitcases, there were police swarming all over, taking affidavits. Several people witnessed this sighting. It's probably all over the news services by now." I found my trash on the sidewalk in front of my place. They must have taken her from there. While she was carrying out my trash!"

"Damn."

Forcing calm on himself, Dylan scanned the map. A purple light blinked. "There's a spaceship."

Archer climbed out of his chair. "Two in eastern Pennsylvania. Not far from here. Think that's them?"

"It's got to be." Dylan prayed that Maya would remain safe despite this convergence of spaceships. That would take some doing on God's part, but nothing was impossible.

"This is the first time I've ever heard of two spaceships in the same area."

"What do you think is going on?"

"Beat's the hell out of me, but you'd better get up there fast." Archer called to have the chopper fired up. "I'll send backup right away."

There was no time for a remote viewing session. Dylan packed his Maglight, night vision goggles, and phase gun. He ran out of the office and into the elevator. Even though it took only a few seconds, what seemed a slow rate of ascent agitated him, past the street floor and up the tower to the landing pad.

A cold wind blew when he stepped into the waiting helicopter. Damn, he was sick of this weather. A Rocket Propelled Grenade rested between the seats as Dylan sat down next to the pilot and nodded. He was glad for company on the assignment.

Dylan's heart ached to know where Maya was. He dreaded to find her in danger or worse. He brushed his emotions aside and focused on doing the job, whatever that turned out to be. He'd faced spaceships before and come up the victor. He remembered with satisfaction the one he'd eradicated over a week ago. If his luck held, he would help rid the earth of two this time. There had to be a finite number of those damned ships. It just seemed like an endless supply.

The snow that had fallen much of the day had ended. Dylan believed a break in the weather portended good fortune. Pulling the epad out of a pocket, he checked his email, just in case. Words scrolled across the screen. *Get Maya,* followed by the same coordinates that had shown on the map back at Mythos. Thank God, she was alive. Thank God, Dylan had taken the time to change out of the ORION uniform into his own clothes. Otherwise, he'd not have had the epad with him.

Although the chopper felt cold, they had a calm flight and made good time. The pilot kept his eyes on the flight path. Dylan didn't feel like making conversation, even if they could, above the noisy engine and propellers.

The helicopter arrived at the destination in eastern Pennsylvania after the sun sank in the western sky. Against its faint orange hue a black-domed Anaz-voohri spaceship hung in the sky momentarily then tore away. Another spaceship burned beneath the chopper, lighting the snow-covered expanse of clearing and trees.

Dylan prayed Maya had not been inside either ship. He tapped his medallion. "One just took off. We didn't get a shot at it."

Overhead the Mythos fleet of F-21s shot across the sky in pursuit of the spaceship.

"To the south? Right." Archer's voice boomed in Dylan's ear. "We're tracking it! For once this damned equipment is working."

"We're over the other one. It's on fire." Dylan felt relieved to know one more previously eliminated. *Where was Maya?* "We're going to set down and reconnoiter."

The pilot called local firefighters just as the chopper touched down.

In case Dylan had to go into the woods, he set the night vision goggles on his head and leaped out. When he headed toward the glowing ship, his ears rang from the roar of the fighter planes.

Had he heard Maya call his name? For a moment he imagined he had manufactured a fantasy out of fear for her, but then he heard running feet behind him.

"Dylan!" Maya hurtled herself toward him. She crashed against him with a squeal of delight. She'd feared, after all the victories of this day, she would die of cold. Now, he had come to rescue her.

"What the hell is going on out here?" Dylan cried.

Maya grinned at him and gave an exaggerated shrug. "How should I know?

"You did that?" He pointed at the flaming spaceship.

Maya rolled her eyes in feigned pretense but could contain herself no longer. "There are some very unhappy Anaz-voohri up there." She pointed to the sky. "They had to call their buddies to come and get them. They couldn't get their computers to function. Wonder why!" She tried not to jump up and down, but she couldn't help it, she felt so excited at the broad smile on Dylan's face.

Dylan threw his arms around Maya. They both laughed out loud as he picked her up and twirled around and around.

Dylan's arms felt strong and exciting and most of all warm. Maya longed to stay in them forever. Nothing could be better than sharing joy with him. She looked down at his shining face, thrilled that she could bring him happiness.

On an impulse, she kissed his lips. He smelled like damp wool, but she didn't care.

Returning the kiss, he set her down and enfolded her. For a moment they pressed together, one in elation. His happy kiss turned passionate and he searched inside her mouth. His exploring tongue riveted her attention and sent heat all over her body. She felt joined with him in a most delicious way, at the same time comforting, nerve-wracking, and frustrating. She ached to be closer to him still.

So this was what it felt like to want someone!

"What's up, Apollo? Come in." An unfamiliar, masculine voice spoke, it seemed, in Dylan's ear.

With a look of great reluctance, Dylan released her. He mouthed the words "I'm sorry" and tapped his medallion. "We've got her. She's alive, and now we know something more about her. She can cook crispy critters."

When he walked away, out of hearing and out of reach, Maya felt deserted. She wanted his arms around her. He made her feel protected and loved and desired.

The pilot jumped down from the helicopter and held out his arm. "Come on, ma'am. I'll help you up."

Climbing inside, Maya sat in the co-pilot's seat. The pilot settled into his.

It wasn't long before Dylan squeezed into the seat beside her and pulled her against him. "Destination Happy Days," he said to the pilot.

Maya wondered what that meant, but she felt so thrilled to be in Dylan's arms she'd go anywhere with him. The helicopter felt toasty, and Maya thought the fire might very well be inside her.

After a short flight, the pilot landed the plane at the Reading, Pennsylvania airport. When he finished refueling he would fly back to New York City.

Maya and Dylan thanked him and set off, walking inside the terminal to the car rental office. She wondered how he would manage to rent a car without giving away their location. All her worries returned about the police and their ability to track credits.

Dylan whispered in her ear, "I had thought we'd have the Dial-a-Bike and our suitcases before I had to tell you this."

His secretive tone startled Maya. "Tell me what?"

"Our new identities. Jane and John O'Hara." He handed her a money credit card with her picture and the name Jane Ellen O'Hara stamped on it.

"Can we get away with this?"

Dylan grinned. "Traveling under assumed names, or traveling together?"

"You know what I mean." Maya's stomach turned over. They were still in danger. When would this ever end? "Where are we going?"

With a mysterious shrug, Dylan said, "No particular place. We're just hiding out until a terrorist strike somewhere or another world calamity takes ORION and Anaz-voohri attention off of us. Then, who knows?"

When they rented a Ford Explorer, the credit card cleared the computer with no problem, so they went to a mall. Santa Claus sat in a golden chair before poinsettias massed in the shape of a Christmas tree. A little girl climbed on Santa's lap. The normalcy of the event brought tears to Maya's eyes. She'd never had the good fortune to experience such a childhood. It was, after all, that sweetness of life they were fighting to protect.

In a department store she and Dylan bought toiletries, new clothes, suitcases, and a turquoise coat for Maya.

"I've always wanted one." Maya turned around and modeled the coat for Dylan.

"It's great, and the best part is I get my jacket back."

Maya hadn't realized he could be a tease, but then every minute since she'd known him felt packed with urgency and uncertainty. She liked him relaxed, or at least not running for his life.

"You hungry?"

"Always." Maya smiled at the memory of their sumptuous meal earlier in the day.

While they ate dinner in a mall restaurant, Maya described her abduction from Dylan's loft, the way the ship felt in flight, and the conclusions she had drawn about the aliens. "The Anaz-voohri can manipulate others with technical power, but they aren't as adept at controlling human intentions as they think. Their pride and belief in their own superiority get in their way. Even their telepathy diminishes when they get too full of themselves. And, fortunately for me, they get low on energy and lose the ability to hover when they get excited or angry."

"This is valuable information Mythos can use." Dylan squeezed her hand. "We hope you'll come to work for us."

"I'm glad I could help. Yes, I want to work for Mythos." Maya blushed at the thought of working with Dylan all the time. She didn't know whether she could bear so much pleasure and excitement.

"I suggest we start a cross-country drive tomorrow morning," Dylan said, "with no particular destination in mind."

Even though Maya agreed, she said, "Maybe we could end up in San Diego."

"It's better to wander with assumed identities and stay out of sight for a while when you're trying to dodge the bad guys. We don't want to go any place they might think to look for you."

"No one would connect me with that place just because I went on a vacation there once, would they?"

"Not likely." Dylan indicated her empty plate. "If you're finished, let's get out of here."

They drove to a hotel and rented a room for the night. Maya felt so excited at the prospect of actually sleeping in the same bed with Dylan that she doubted she'd get any real sleep at all. She wondered if he would make a pass at her this time. But then, the way she felt about him, it couldn't legitimately come across as a pass. It would be called making love.

That miserable night with Mark flashed through her mind. Would Dylan think she was a rape victim? She had little idea of how she should behave during the sexual act except for romance books. If the situation arose, she would take Lola's advice to go with the feeling.

Carrying their shopping bags, they rode the elevator in silence. After so many hours together, Maya hadn't run out of things to talk to him about, but she felt awkward. No matter what happened, she sensed something about their relationship would soon change.

Hiding out for the long term had a different texture to it, at least for Maya. She wondered what Dylan was thinking about and glanced up to see an easy grin on his face. Whatever he had on his mind probably didn't go too deep. She acknowledged with relief that things had gotten better. At least no one had tried to kill them in the past few hours. Maya relaxed and smiled back.

The elevator doors opened, and Dylan held out an arm. "After you, Mrs. O'Hara."

The dim hallway, carpeted with dirty red and orange swirls, smelled of stale cigarette smoke. The depressing space probably hadn't been redone in years.

When they reached their room, Dylan set his shopping bag on the floor. "I've got the key card in my pocket."

"Hold on. Let me see if I can do this." Maya thought *open* and the door swung free. Delighted, she laughed. "For the most part, I've considered this ability of mine a curse, but it's sure got a handy side to it."

"You've impressed the hell out of me." Dylan picked up the bag and followed her inside. The table lamp turned on automatically. He chuckled. "My pal, Maya, the human movement sensor."

Two double beds with pretty spreads and new paint made the room passable. Maya set her bag down beside the dresser and inhaled the glorious citrus smell of real fruit in a bowl. "If we do go to California, I may never want to leave."

Dylan plopped on one of the beds. "Does that mean you're okay with having me along posing as your husband?"

"Guess I should be used to it." Maya hedged as a sudden apprehension came over her. When the door had closed on this room, she felt more alone with him than in the cave. There, they'd had to deal with the cold and potential discovery. She doubted anyone would try to break into the hotel.

Even though Dylan didn't act one bit threatening, all at once Maya felt trapped and afraid. She would excuse herself so she could have some private time to think.

Dylan said, "You returned my kiss in front of the police officer." He reached for her hand, but she avoided him and walked past the beds. "That's how I knew you trusted me. That and when you gave me Schwartz's gun." He had picked up on her mood right away.

"I did trust you." Maya smiled to mask the fact that he had touched a nerve. "It turned out that I trusted you more than you deserved." She grabbed the bathroom door handle.

"Wait a minute." Dylan bounded to her and blocked the doorway. He looked impish despite his serious tone. "The last time you said you had to go to the bathroom, there was hell to pay."

Maya found Dylan lovable, and she wanted to say she loved him, but she hated the fact that he had intended to kill her. It was the same conflict she felt about her foster parents. She cared for them for raising her all those years, but they had lied to her and ultimately turned against her, killing her friend. Was there no such thing as a constant friend, one who would remain true?

Caught in her anger, Maya avoided Dylan's gaze, not an easy thing to do because he stood so close. He touched her chin and tipped her head up.

His face, a picture of anxiety, mirrored her feelings. "Maya, talk to me."

"You were going to kill me. I'm not sure I can get past that." The words escaped her mouth before Maya thought about it. Maybe a good thing. This life of considered speech and logical analysis had brought her disappointment and loneliness. What did she care, anyway? If she ended up cooped up for days, weeks, who knew how long, with this man, she might as well be honest with him.

Dylan heaved a ragged sigh. "This is the hardest part." He let go of her, wandered to the overstuffed chair, and sat, looking forlorn as he leaned back. "Knowing in advance that you might have to kill people, it's very hard to take them seriously, to consider the enemy sentient beings. The old hideous Hun propaganda our government did against the Germans, the Japanese, the terrorists. Dehumanize the enemy. Forget that he's the same as you. Otherwise, you won't be able to shoot his brains out. Every government teaches that. Every agency. Mythos, even."

"Did you do that to me? Dehumanize me?"

Raising his hands in supplication, Dylan asked, "When you were running from ORION and from the spaceship, suppose you had been required to take someone's life?"

"But I didn't!"

"I know, but if you had to kill to survive, how would you feel afterward? You'd know it had to be done to preserve your life, or the lives of others. How would you feel?"

Her heart went out to Dylan. He looked so distraught. Maya regretted her anger but couldn't repress it. "I would feel awful."

"But would you do it?"

Maya remembered her monumental desire for revenge against Carrick, and even more so against the doctor and the captain on the spaceship. "I would have to, wouldn't I?" She might even have enjoyed it. All the repercussions had escaped her until now.

Covering his brow with one hand, Dylan gripped the chair arm with the other. She could tell from his pained expression that he'd struggled with these issues for a long time. "Yes, you would have to do it." His voice quivered. "And that's what happened with you. Archer and I agreed that, if the Anaz-voohri controlled you, we'd have to kill you." He laughed in a cock-eyed way. "You shouldn't take it personally. Strange as that sounds. Killing you was what we might have had to do to keep the world safe. Can you understand?"

Maya realized that, given the same situation, she would have come to the same conclusion. She knelt before Dylan, reached up to the chair arm, and laid her hand on his. "I do understand. You were doing what you had to do."

Peeking out from beneath his cupped hand, Dylan asked, "Can you forgive me?"

"Yes, I can forgive you and I do, at least intellectually. Emotionally, I guess I still feel self-protective. Perhaps the anger will eventually go away. Can you understand that?"

"Unquestionably." Dylan looked like he'd had a shot of adrenaline. He sat up and grabbed her hand in both of his. His voice became rich with commitment. "The life of a warrior is not easy, but it is rewarding…and necessary. These are things you need to know. That was your first lesson."

"Are you to be my teacher, too, along with all the other roles you've played?" Maya knew the answer already. He would teach her many things, and she would relax with that knowledge. She could trust him now. Her heart told her so.

When Dylan nodded, his voice took on a loving tone. "Forgiveness is the second lesson. Like the old philosopher said, forgive your enemy in advance so you go into battle with a clear conscience. Is there anyone else you need to forgive?"

"My parents. My foster parents, that is. They were just doing what they had to do to protect themselves. Like everyone does. They never intended to harm me. The opposite, really. They tried to protect me."

"Can you forgive your mother?"

"That's the toughest one." Maya hoped in time memories of her mother's eagerness to please and genuine concern would overshadow the domineering ways and betrayal. "She was just human enough to care what happened to me and just Anaz-voohri enough to insist I follow my programming. That's where everything broke down. Poor Carolyn. How awful it must have been for her never to belong. She had an unhappy life, not appreciated by anybody. Even her husband didn't like her very much."

Rising, Dylan pulled Maya up with him. "I know one good thing we can say about her. She had a terrific daughter." He grasped Maya's waist and lifted her into the air. He looked up at her, black eyes radiant, an adoring expression on his face. "You turned out great, despite whatever your foster parents did. At the risk of repeating myself, I'll just say that I love you." He carried her airborne to the bed and tenderly laid her on the nubby spread. "If you don't love me yet, maybe I can figure out a way to make that happen."

When Dylan covered her mouth with a kiss, he eliminated any thought of verbal response from Maya's mind. His lips were full and demanding. She smelled his musky scent and tasted the salty heft of his tongue as she curled hers around it. She willed the kiss to convey her love in a way she couldn't express with words.

His arms felt strong and protective around her, his skin warm through their clothing. She felt certain he was going to make love to her. How would he do it? What would he do? She feared she didn't know how to respond. Would he hurt her?

Sliding his hand beneath her t-shirt, he caressed her breasts. His touch felt surprisingly soft and hesitant despite his chapped skin. Maya's nipples hardened. She wanted him to linger over her breasts to ease the tingling there, but his fingers traveled down her hips. She lay still, captivated by his light touch as it skipped along her legs and explored her womanhood through the thin cloth of the gym shorts.

"You feel so good. I want to make love to you." His deep voice trembled. "Do you want me to?"

Maya nodded, disregarding an irrational fear that rose within her.

Dylan stood and removed his shirt, tossing it on the chair. For a delightful moment she gazed at the line of bare skin from his broad shoulders to his chin to his disheveled hair. The medallion hung against his smooth chest. He was even more handsome than she'd guessed. He deserved his code name, Apollo.

After sitting in the chair, he pulled off his boots and socks, then unzipped his jeans. Maya watched transfixed by the natural way in which he revealed himself. When he slid the jeans down his legs, he freed his swollen member. With a sweet smile that made him look vulnerable, he stood naked before her. "This is the real me."

Did he fear she would reject him? Maya had never considered that possibility. She wanted to reach out and touch him. Did he want her to? Should she ask? What would it feel like to take him into her hand? She couldn't, she felt too inhibited.

Maya needed to shut off her analytical side and enjoy. It seemed like cheating to ask the Nanobot for help in this most basic of human encounters. She had to do something positive on her own. "I want you to be my teacher. Teach me how to love."

"There's nothing I'd rather do," Dylan murmured with a wide smile.

When he went to the window and closed the blind, the sight of his perfect butt made her moist. He turned off

the room lights.   Only the bathroom light remained on.
Maya felt grateful for the semi-darkness.

Dylan returned to the bed and gazed down at her.
"May I take your clothes off?"

Maya wanted to reciprocate his open manner, to
offer herself. She stood by the bed and held up her arms.
He pulled the t-shirt over her head, bent to kiss her breasts,
then tugged down the gym shorts. He stepped back and
looked at her. "You are beautiful."

Instead of feeling self-conscious, Maya felt glad to
let him see her. The desire on his face sent delicious chills
all over her.

Dylan pulled down the bedspread, and Maya lay on
the cool sheets, anticipating the pleasure of his touch. He
joined her on the bed and lay with his head propped on one
hand, surveying the length of her as if she were French
pastry. His hand, firmer now, caressed her breasts, and she
felt good, relaxing and enjoying the moment. She wanted
him to touch her and know her. She reassured herself that
there was nothing to fear from him.

While his tongue probed her mouth with long, slow
thrusts, his warm and supple fingers brought her to climax,
the first she'd ever experienced without the assistance of a
battery. For a person who could shut down computers all
over the world, she considered that a major event.

"Oh, Dylan." She clasped her arms around his neck,
laughed, and gave him a fervent kiss.

"I want to be inside you." His voice cracked, as if
he choked back emotion.

Maya wanted him to take her, but she felt afraid. He
hadn't asked this time, and she didn't answer.

He lay on top of her, and his weight came down on
her chest and on her legs. He took her face between his
hands. Although his lips were gentle, a ripple of terror tore

through Maya. She couldn't move. She felt trapped! A small cry escaped her lips. She struggled to get away.

Jumping off her, Dylan cried, "What's wrong?"

"I'm afraid."

Dylan cuddled her, and his voice sounded kind and firm. "Maya, I will never hurt you. You are free to act any way you please with me. I want you to be yourself."

Uncertain what that meant, Maya longed to trust him. Tears slid down her cheeks. He wiped them with a gentle hand. She wanted to explain that he'd done nothing, that her old fears had arisen, but she felt too fragile to speak.

"It doesn't matter what anyone ever did to you." Dylan kissed her cheeks, her lips, her throat. "I love you as you are." He kissed her arms and trailed his tongue across her stomach. "You are safe with me."

His mouth lingered further down. Slowly, gently he kissed her womanhood, bringing her to an intense focus. Ecstasy washed over her, and Maya discovered that release was not a mechanical reaction in her body but a flowing stream of joy.

Dylan lay beside her, and she could feel his erection against her leg. His presence filled her mind and heart. She wanted, not just to make love, but to make love to Dylan. She wanted to give him all the desire she had stored up. Her lips brushed his as she spoke. "I want you...inside me now."

When he entered her, the fear dissolved, and Maya responded with all the passion she had built up unexpressed. With easy rhythm and loving kisses, he came to climax, brought her again, and himself again.

After so much self-doubt and lack, Maya learned that lovemaking was one of the easiest things she'd ever done. She blended into Dylan and he blended into her in such a familiar way that Maya couldn't tell where either of them ended or began. She should have expected him to turn making love into an astonishing act.

Later, as Maya lay in Dylan's arm beneath the cool sheets, she thought about thanking him for trying to rescue her. He deserved such praise. She thought about telling him he was a fine man. He was. She thought about telling him that she loved him. She did, more than she'd ever realized it was possible to love another human being. "Dylan," she murmured, "would you do that again?"

"Can't do anything again." His chuckle sounded rich and throaty. "But we can do something similar."

"More words from the old philosopher?"

"Yep."

"Who is he, anyway?"

"Me." Dylan enfolded her in a kiss. Their bodies in sync touched at every point. "Lesson number four coming up."

Chapter Nineteen

Sickened by the disorder at New York Headquarters, Carrick didn't intend to stay around and wait for painters to redo the scorched walls or technicians to install new computer systems. It would take weeks for things to get back to normal. He could not stand the chaos the disaster caused even though he wanted to stay near where the mole had escaped. It galled him to think of how she'd tricked him. Dumb fuck that he was when it came to a piece of ass. Never again would he let his guard down.

The bitch would not have escaped at all if Mythos hadn't gotten involved. Carrick knew damned well they were in this mess up to their eyeballs. He had a healthy enough respect for President Grant to know that killing his friend Archer was out of the question. The best Carrick could hope for would be to take out a Mythos operative or two, if he could make it look like an accident. It didn't stop that bastard, Dylan Brady, with his cocky ways, from making a prime target.

In the meantime, hybrids and aliens all over the world required snuffing out. Carrick appointed an interim commander to replace Hillenbrand in New York and ordered his personal cadre to return the Flotilla with him.

Before Carrick left the building, he picked up the plastic tarp he had requisitioned for this explicit purpose and went to the prison ward. When he walked into the cell, the dumbass hybrid, Schwartz, lay on the cot, rheumy eyes staring up at the ceiling. Blood matted the stubble on his chin. "Attention!" Carrick shouted.

Somewhere inside the addled brain, Schwartz must have heard because he raised one shoulder then collapsed back on the cot. His loose white gown flopped around his bruised groin.

Carrick called for the Hispanic medic, who administered a shot of medication designed to bring Schwartz's consciousness into focus. After a few moments, Schwartz swallowed and sighed.

"He's as ready as he'll ever be, sir," the medic said.

"Schwartz," Carrick yelled. "We're looking for Maya Rembrandt. We need you to tell us where to look for her."

Schwartz lay like stone and stared at the ceiling.

The medic cried, "Get a grip here, man, your commanding officer is addressing you."

Still, Schwartz did not respond.

"Fuck." Carrick unpinned one of the medals on his uniform and sunk the needle into Schwartz arm.

The slob didn't even realize the puncture.

The medic bent over Schwartz and peered into his eyes. "He's in a coma."

The world weighed down on Carrick with too many burdens. He spread the plastic tarp on the floor. "Help me."

Carrick and the medic slid Schwartz onto the tarp. Slobber ran down Schwartz's chin.

Drawing the phase gun out of his holster, Carrick fired into Schwartz's head. Blood gushed onto the tarp. At least Carrick got to snuff out one hybrid over that fucking mole. He folded the edges of the tarp together. "Get somebody in here to empty this trash."

As Carrick strode down the hall, he vowed to do better next time. He'd get that Rembrandt bitch once and for all. And he would destroy all her worthless hybrid sisters.

In his haste to make love last night, Dylan hadn't managed to completely close the curtains. Through a sliver of exposed window, early morning light shone. A storm brewed. The first flakes floated onto the neighboring hotel's roof, already loaded with several inches of old snow. He had to get Maya out of town fast and drive straight south, away from snow and ORION's prying eyes. The threat that the Anaz-voohri would return in a different ship remained constant, too. He'd have to make their assumed identities work.

Beautiful Maya lay asleep on her stomach beside Dylan. Her shiny hair, the color of coffee with a bit of cream, just the way he liked it, splayed across the pillow. Her skin against white sheets gave her the look of a rose blooming in the snow.

He had not wanted to love her, but it was far too late now. How did she feel about him? She behaved like a woman in love, but she hadn't said a word. If he had to make a choice, he'd rather have her acting as if she were in love with him than saying so in words, but he really wanted both.

That fear of hers hadn't surprised him. She'd been abused by the damned Anaz-voohri. Whatever it took Dylan would help her overcome it.

"It's time to wake up, Maya." Dylan hated to awaken her, but they needed to get out of the area soon. He hoped their wonderful night of lovemaking hadn't tired her. He wanted her rested for more.

When he pulled down the covers to get a closer look, she moved restlessly. Although she did not awaken, the fairy did, at least in Dylan's fancy.

With his fingertips, he traced the outline of the fairy's tiny body. It quivered as his suntanned fingers feathered out, following the lines of the pretty aqua wings and yellow hair. Maya's gorgeous pink butt trembled with anticipation.

Maya was awake now. That pleased him, but she had to wait.

Dylan had wondered what in Maya's nature provoked her to get the tattoo in the first place. He had seen something of wildness in her last night, and he wanted her to unleash it on him.

He withdrew his hand until she relaxed back into sleep. It contented him to look at his own leg, darker and more sinewy beside her lightness. Their bodies blended beautifully in color and in movement. Looking at her and remembering the pleasure he'd felt inside her last night made him feel hard again.

That pleased him, but he also had to wait.

Like the touch of a feather, Dylan bent and traced with his tongue the outline of the fairy, slowly, tortuously. Maya gasped and lay so still he knew she held her breath.

When he caressed her bottom, Maya moaned. She turned over with a look of pleading and offered herself to him. He entered her gladly and held still to allow her to give him her wildness.

It was merely one in a thousand lessons in love that lay ahead of them. Dylan had a feeling they would learn much from each other.

An hour later, Dylan and Maya had showered, packed, and retrieved the Explorer from the parking garage. They agreed that Dylan would drive first.

As he pulled onto the freeway, the snow grew heavier, and the automatic wipers came on. Dylan asked, "You sure you're not hungry? What happened? I thought you always were."

Looking terrific in her turquoise coat and black sweater, Maya gave him a happy smile. "I found something I enjoy more than tasting food. Tasting you." She leaned across the space between the bucket seats and gave him a quick kiss.

"I appreciate the compliment, but I'm starving."

"Okay, let me take a look." With a gloved finger, Maya punched the buttons to bring up a map of the area.

"I'll find us a good place to have breakfast." She began poring over the map as if she'd never seen one before.

Dylan paid attention to his driving, relieved at the light Sunday morning traffic. Snow blew about the windshield, causing slick pavement. He'd opted to get snow tires, thinking they'd probably not need them for long, but the last thing he wanted was to get stuck and call attention to their vehicle in any way.

Maya pointed at the map on the screen. "There's a little town called Willow Branch off to the west about twenty miles. Why don't you stop there?"

"Anyone who might want to find us would probably expect us to head west so I thought we'd go south. After we get out of snow country, we may decide to go west."

"You mentioned that before. Why would anyone expect us to go west or to California?"

Dylan gave a noncommittal shrug. He didn't want to tell her that her birth parents had moved to San Diego. He had easily confirmed that fact and that they still lived, but he had to wait for a Mythos operative out west to find time to approach the people in person. Archer hadn't wanted such a piece of news delivered on the phone.

"It's nothing, really," Dylan said. "I just want us to avoid fixing on a direction. We'll be less detectable without a pattern. For example, no half-way intelligent operative in ORION is going to expect us to hang out in cold, windy southern Pennsylvania."

"Would they expect us to eat in sizable towns with restaurants?"

"Probably."

"All right, then, let's go to Willow Branch. Population eight hundred and twelve. I doubt they'll even have a McDonald's."

"Damn, artificial intelligence experts and their logic. Okay, what exit do we get off?"

"Forty-two."

When they pulled off the freeway at exit forty-two and stopped for the cross street, Dylan saw a McDonald's banner to the left and turned on his blinker. The little town lay in the opposite direction.

"Turn right here." Maya gazed through the snow-covered side window as if entranced.

Surprised, Dylan glanced at her. "Fast food is this way."

"Turn right." Maya's words sounded more like a command than a request.

Curious about her motives and to humor her, Dylan turned right. "Where are we going?"

Maya didn't answer but peered ahead as if looking for something she couldn't quite remember. After they passed a baseball diamond with about four rows of bleachers, she said, "Turn left at the stoplight."

"Yes, ma'am." Dylan would have laughed, but something about her intensity stopped him. He knew the Anaz-voohri had abducted her from somewhere in Pennsylvania, so she might be having a *déjà vu* experience. She'd never mentioned that kind of thing, but there was a lot about her he didn't know.

They rode along a narrow two-way street, barely more than an alley. Quaint one-story clapboard bungalows sat back beyond giant, bare trees. The old neighborhood sported new paint, no doubt a restoration project only outlying towns could afford. Cities spent all their extra funds on bomb repair after terrorist attacks.

"There it is." Maya pointed to one of the bungalows, no different from the rest. "Stop here."

Pulling into the driveway in need of shoveling, Dylan felt relieved to hear the snow tires' sturdy crunch. He set the gears in park and left the engine running. "What is this place, Maya? Do you recognize it?" With no cars parked in the drive and no smoke coming out the chimney, the house appeared empty.

"I don't know." Her voice carried a tone of wonder, and she stared at the house, lost in thought.

"Have you been here before?"

"Maybe. I can't remember." Maya turned to him, and a distraught expression spread across her face. "I'm trying to remember, but..."

Reaching out, Dylan squeezed her hand. "It's all right. It will come to you."

Tears stood in her eyes. "Something very important happened in that house."

Dylan slid over to her seat and drew Maya against him. She laid her head on his shoulder, and he held her while she wept. He had an intuition that he could bring the information out of her subconscious mind. If this were her original home, he considered her strong enough to encounter any memories she might uncover.

After she stopped crying, he moved back to the other side of the car, tapped his medallion, and asked the young recruit at Mythos to run a check on past owners. Dylan read the address off the mailbox and ended the call.

Maya seemed comforted by his request, and they headed back to McDonald's for breakfast. Over a triple order of bacon, eggs, pancakes, and hash browns, two orders for Dylan and one for Maya, the Mythos youth called back. The rundown of owners included no Porters. He confirmed that, although Maya ended up abducted from this town, she had lived at another address.

Dylan dipped his hash browns in catsup. "Do you want to see the house you used to live in? We can drive by there."

"Yes, of course. I'm amazed that I picked this town out. How on earth could I do that?"

"It's a form of clairvoyance, knowing your way around places without having actually being there. Or seeming to recognize people you've never met. You have been here in this town, so I'm not sure it counts, but as déjà vu experiences go, you've done very well. You were only two, after all, when you...uh...left."

"I wonder if I'll recognize the house when I see it." Maya played with her food.

"I don't know." Dylan pointed at the bacon on her plate. "Are you going to eat that?"

"No." Maya shoved the plastic plate toward him. "This is quite a mystery. If I lived in one house for the first two years of my life, why did I remember the other house so poignantly?"

Dylan speared her bacon and crunched it between his teeth. "Why don't we try to do another hypnotic regression? We know you're a good subject. Maybe there's more we can uncover."

"Yes, I want to do that right away." Maya leaned back in her chair.

Amber highlights flickered in her eyes as she gazed off in space. She looked distant, but lovely, when she was thinking. Dylan didn't want to interrupt her. She thought so long he'd finished every bite of her food before she spoke.

"I've got an idea." Maya sounded excited. "You brought your epad, didn't you?"

"Sure." Dylan tapped his coat pocket.

"I think I can use the Nanobot in the trance. If all goes like I think it will, you'll be able to see what I see. Give it to me."

"Great idea." Dylan handed her the epad then stacked papers and cups on the tray. "When we get some miles under our belt, into Maryland or Virginia, we'll stop at a motel and do it first, okay?"

A wry grin lit Maya's face for the first time since they'd left Reading. "What's second on our agenda?"

"You know." Dylan reached under the table and rubbed her jeans-clad thigh. He rose and stashed the tray.

They left the restaurant and drove back to Willow Branch. The snow stopped, and the sun came out. So did some of the inhabitants of the little town. Dylan asked directions to the house where Maya once lived and drove there. They found not the residence since it had been torn down with a library built in its place.

"I'm disappointed." Maya gazed at the library. "I don't want to leave this town. Not yet. So much emotion I can't really identify is floating around near the surface of my mind. I feel compelled to bring it out."

Dylan drove up and down all the streets but couldn't find a hotel, inn, or even a seedy motel. Nowhere with the privacy that a regression required. "Tell you what. Let's go out on the highway and stop at the first place we find."

Maya agreed and they took off, traveling only a few miles before they found a roadside motel. She gestured toward it. "Think this will help to throw off anybody tracking us? Stopping at eleven in the morning, for the night, I mean."

"If it's a guy, I'd say one look at you and he'd guess I'd be stopping as early as possible. So, no."

"Why, thank you, Dylan." Maya gave him a sweet kiss. "I think you've paid me my very first compliment."

"You can bet it won't be the last." He gave her his best boyish grin, the one that had gotten him a lot of dates, and steered into the motel parking lot.

Climbing out of the Explorer, Dylan rented a room and carried their suitcases inside, glad to be away from the vehicle and the snow.

Following him, Maya made no comments about the décor. She didn't seem to notice much. It looked fine to Dylan, clean and neat. That's all that mattered.

The dreaminess Maya had displayed while they drove around Willow Branch had returned. Dylan propped up some pillows on the bed and asked her to recline there. She removed her coat and sat back against the pillows, the epad in her hands. She looked so inviting that he would have liked to kiss her, really more than just kiss her, to be honest, but he didn't want to ruin the chances for a psychic connection.

They would have plenty of chances to make love while they crisscrossed the country. He prayed he would keep his darling love safe from ORION and the Anazvoohri. He counted himself incredibly lucky to get this detail. If Archer had assigned anyone else, well, there was no point in considering that. Thank God, he hadn't.

While Dylan stood beside the bed, he removed his belt.

Maya's eyes grew large. "Are we going to make love now?"

Laughing, Dylan sat beside her. "Later, maybe, if you want to." He swung the end of the belt back and forth slowly before her eyes. "Let your eyes follow the belt and completely..."

"Why aren't you using the medallion?" Maya whispered.

"I'm afraid to take it off. I might miss a message."

"But you used it last time."

"Yes, and I almost missed a very important message." Dylan didn't want to add that he had almost lost his job into the bargain.

"Oh." Seeming satisfied, Maya settled back and took a deep breath.

Dylan spoke in a modulated voice, low and slow. "Don't think about anything except the belt and how completely and totally relaxed you are. Nothing can interfere with your willingness to fall into a quiet, peaceful trance. This is a place with answers. You can trust this place in your mind. It will uncover truths that you need to know."

Maya closed her eyes without a suggestion to do so. She looked very peaceful and more relaxed than he had ever seen her.

"You will go to the same place in your mind where you went before. It will be very easy for you to find that place and drop down into a trance. Once you are there, you will hear nothing except the sound of my voice, and you will always respond to it, no matter how deep you go."

When Maya began to exhibit rapid eye movement, Dylan decided to abandon his set patter and skip ahead. She flushed and breathed unevenly, all sure signs of trance. What a terrific subject. Was there anything this woman couldn't do?

"Imagine that you are going back in time. The years of your life are fading away. You are twenty, fifteen, five, four, three, and two. Remember an event, an important event that takes place in your home here in Willow Branch. It will be a day when you were very happy here."

Maya appeared comatose. Beautiful and still as death.

When Dylan squeezed her finger, she did not respond. He had a great deal of faith in the procedure and knew that many people had good experiences under these conditions. He trusted Maya.

Although she had little familiarity with navigating alternate brain wave states in trance, she knew her mind and its capabilities better than the average person did. In fact, her brain far exceeded the capabilities of most humans. She was genius range in intelligence, and she had improved on the Anaz-voohri's alterations of her brain. In the bargain, she had developed the Nanobot's capabilities in excess of anything he'd heard or read.

This woman, his sweet love with a fairy on her butt and a weakness for a certain Mythos warrior, had perhaps the most adroit mental aptitude of any human being on the planet. He would worry if an ordinary person failed to respond to his suggestions. But not Maya. She was on an adventure he couldn't wait to hear about, or see, if the Nanobot worked correctly.

Dylan stretched out on the bed beside Maya. She didn't react. He lifted her and held her in one arm. Her affect remained unchanged.

"Bon voyage, my love," he whispered, tipped the epad so he could see its screen, and settled back to wait it out.

Chapter Twenty

Maya stopped listening to Dylan's droning voice and relaxed into the emptiness of a deep trance. Although one part of her mind remained aware that he lay beside her and held her, she felt as if her essence, or her greater self, drifted in time and space. She no longer considered her body a vessel for her mind and freed her consciousness.

Nanobot, take me into the past.

Out of the spacious silence, her imagination moved. She stood before the same bungalow they had driven to earlier, but a miracle had happened. The house looked much newer.

In the yard young trees stood low to the ground. Their branches brimmed with red and gold leaves. She felt the warmth of the autumn sun on her bare arms as she stood on the steps of the bungalow and gazed at it with rapture. She held the hands of two little girls with burnished hair. They smiled shyly, pretty in skirts, rolled down socks, and shoes with laces.

In a baseball uniform, Dylan stood on the porch and held the door open. He didn't look like himself, blond and shorter, but she recognized him as Dylan. He beckoned to her and the girls to come inside.

When she glanced down, she saw that over her own belly she wore a maternity dress. The girls tugged at her, and all three walked inside. Their footfalls rang hollow on the hardwood floors.

Dylan excitedly showed them around the tiny house with only four rooms. The sepia-toned walls faded at the edges into nothing.

She wanted to believe this could be their home. It looked so lovely and they'd lived with her parents much too long. "Are you sure we can afford this?"

"My darling." Dylan's face shone with the same youthful grin. "The school board's promised a one hundred dollar raise. That makes my salary thirty-two hundred, enough to qualify for a mortgage."

"I'm so happy. This is a dream come true." She threw her arms around him, and the girls jumped up and down.

The scene changed in a flash. She lay in a bed in one of the bedrooms, exhausted. She, Dylan, and the girls stared in astonishment at the baby boy in her arms. The baby had a mop of wavy brown hair just like hers.

Once again the scene changed. She stood in the small kitchen, lighting candles on a cake decorated with baseballs and bats. It read "Congratulations Team". She carried the cake into the living room where more than a dozen young men stood around with Dylan. He patted their backs and everybody sang and laughed. Finally, they had won the championship, after much work and sacrifice.

More scenes flitted by – of the girls grown and wearing wedding gowns, of the boy blowing out birthday candles, of herself painting water colors and stashing them in a closet, of Dylan dancing her around the living room.

Nostalgia swept over her for the poignancy of their lives.

And then she lay on the bed once more. She tried to hang on. But she didn't have the strength. Her spirit wanted to leave her body.

Dylan dug her watercolors out and hung them from tacks across the waning walls. He had wanted to cheer her, but she didn't feel cheered. She felt sorrow for the brevity of their joy.

Sitting beside her, Dylan held her hand, a distraught expression on his face. With tremendous effort, she raised one hand and touched tiny crow's feet at the corner of his eye. Too early, she thought. Too soon to leave my family. Too soon to leave my beloved.

The daughters and son stood around the bed, crying.

With a sigh, she relaxed and liberated her soul from the wasted, skinny body. She floated up to the ceiling and gazed down at her adored husband and children. She watched them sob and hold each other.

"My darling, don't go." Dylan fell across her lifeless body, his shoulders shaking.

She wanted to comfort them and thought, "Please don't cry. I'm still here."

*But they couldn't see her or hear
her, and all the gladness left the house.*

Years went by.

*Dylan sat in the living room,
drinking beer. He faced the TV but didn't
watch it, so lost was he in grief. His
children visited him, brought grandchildren
to see him, but he ignored them all. They
went away.*

*Maya whispered in his ear many
times but couldn't make herself known to
him. She gave up and floated away, adrift in
the peaceful emptiness.*

When Maya awakened from the trance, she gazed
into Dylan's eyes and saw the soul of the other Dylan whose
name she didn't know. His name didn't matter. He
belonged to her.

Under the spell of the dream, or whatever it was, she
touched his cheek. "My dearest one, I love you. From the
bottom of my soul, I love you. I always have, and I always
will." Her former reluctance to profess her love had
disappeared.

Laying her hand on his neck, she pulled his awed
face toward her. She poured her soul into the kiss and sealed
their bond. She could feel his muscles relax as he returned
the kiss, and she felt the promise he made from his heart.

"I love you, too. Now and always." Voice husky,
Dylan spoke, his lips against hers. "You went back in time,
didn't you? I saw it all on the epad." He murmured the
words as though speaking aloud might break the spell. "We
were married to each other in a former life. We had
children. No wonder we fell in love so fast!"

"Oh, Dylan, we were so much in love. Our marriage
was the centerpiece of our lives. We lived for each other,

and that was great while we were both alive, but when I died you lost your will to live. You didn't care what happened to your children and grandchildren, and you hurt them with your selfishness."

Dylan cuddled her and whispered in a conspiratorial way. "This explains so much. It helps me understand the meaning of our lifetimes. We came here to learn the true meaning of ourselves."

The aura of the trance with its acceptance of the images at face value remained with Maya. "I loved you and my life so much that I was reborn in the same place. The abduction by the Anaz-voohri forced me into reevaluating myself. In this lifetime, I couldn't stay home and be the helpmate, even though I've had the impulse to. I've had to make my own place in the world."

"That sounds right. I've only known you for a week but you've changed enormously. You're strong, confident."

Touched that he noticed, Maya acknowledged to herself that recent events, despite their traumatic elements, had helped her grow psychologically. She was a woman, now. "I'm done with Little Millie Milquetoast, but I needed you to help me get through it."

"No more than I've needed you. Now it makes sense that I was born blind. I failed to see the value in my family then. Get it? Failed to see, so born blind. Classic karma. My parents were taken from me because I didn't value family before. Payback with the chance to make things better in this life."

"Maybe our children are still alive. They'd probably be in their seventies by now. How bizarre to think of having children at all, let alone that they are fifty years older! Do you think we could find them?"

"Wouldn't that be something?" Dylan gave her an enthusiastic squeeze. "You know what? I'll bet we can figure out what our names were then." Dylan tapped the medallion and waited until the young man answered. "Remember that address I gave you a couple of hours ago? Get me a list of all the owners in the twentieth century."

Maya lay so close to Dylan's ear that she could hear the young man when he said, "Don't have to. Already got it from the last search."

"Okay, who owned it in the 1950s?"

"Let's see. 1942 to 1957 Annabel Williamson. Sold to Jed McCall, high school teacher, who owned it until he died in 1980. Passed to son, Jed Junior."

"That's it! That's all I need. Send me a report on email. Thanks." Dylan was so wound up he could barely speak. "Darling, do you know what you've done? You've told me my past life. My name, for God's sake! I was Jed McCall. Your husband. I've always thought reincarnation was the way of things but never expected to move from theory to proof."

"It's possible." Maya's analytical mind finally kicked in. Reincarnation seemed to explain her experience, but she remembered having seen the images of the same man and the woman in her software program before. With this trance, nothing seemed proven except that she'd gained some insight she didn't normally have. Another issue she had to stash to ponder later. "Proof requires more tangible evidence."

"You don't buy it, huh? Well, I do. The God I believe in is that fair, to allow us the chance to atone for wrongs and earn rewards. And to let some of us remember our past lives. Thanks, God."

The time to think about God might come later. Right now, Maya recognized Dylan's love for her, she read it on his face. This moment would never come again. Her body yearned for him. "I'm more interested in living this lifetime with you."

When they made love, it was as lovers who knew each other intimately, a dance of sensations they had offered to each other many times over many years. They knew how to please each other without asking. It felt kindly and comforting, familiarity its own exotic elixir.

So this was what it was like to make love with a husband!

Afterwards, as they lay together, Archer's annoying voice came through Dylan's chip. "Hey, Apollo."

With an exasperated sigh, Dylan rose and stepped into the bathroom, his splendid body as perfectly shaped and defined as a Greek god's.

Maya wished she could always feel so happy and contented, but she presumed their delicious little interlude had ended. She gathered up their clothes that had been cast hastily onto the floor, and laid them out on the bed. She smoothed them, as her foster mother had taught her to do, and felt compassionate toward the woman once again.

At least now Maya could remember her foster parents without a surge of anger. They had raised her, provided and cared for her. They had done the best they could, following the directives of the Anaz-voohri, as they had probably been taught. They might even suffered through the procedure to surgically program to do as they had done. Perhaps it was unfair to judge hybrids by human standards. In time, Maya might forgive them completely.

When Dylan returned from the bathroom, he kissed her in a way that suggested he'd rather take her back to bed than do what he had to do. She caressed his firm butt with both her hands. It thrilled her just to touch his skin.

That old boyfriend Mark had been out of his mind. All Maya had needed was a man to care for her and let her blossom as a lover. She felt grateful to Dylan because he had shown her the sensual side of herself.

"We've got to go, darling." He'd never called her that before, except in the dream, or whatever it was that happened in the trance. "That's the bad news." He went on as if he'd always called her darling. "The good news is Archer says you're on the payroll, and we'll talk about salary later."

"I'm glad to hear that. I'm ready to join the fight against the Anaz-voohri, and ORION too if they persist in obstructing us. I told old Neanderthal Carrick he should be fighting with us, not against us."

"I'll bet you did!"

They dressed and left the motel in minutes. The cozy love making and the glow of the trance had left Maya unprepared for the cold wind and blowing snow as they ran to the Explorer and climbed in. Winter seemed to go on forever.

To her surprise, Dylan headed down the road on which they had traveled. "Are we going back to Reading?" she asked.

"Uh, huh. It has the closest airport." Dylan grinned as though he enjoyed keeping a secret from her. "The way to keep the bad guys guessing is to do what they don't expect."

"That's why we were not heading for San Diego earlier, even though I wanted to. The logical conclusion…that's where we're going, after all."

"You guessed it!" Dylan settled casually against the car door and looped his arm over the steering wheel. He looked like a kid at the fair, happily steering a bumper car. He must love driving because he hadn't suggested she help. "I had wanted to keep this piece of info from you until later, but things aren't working out quite as I'd planned. That happens a lot in this business. You'll get used to it."

"One thing I already know about you Mythos men is that I'll never get bored. Abducted maybe, shot at maybe, but bored, never."

Dylan didn't respond to her banter and spoke earnestly. "Prepare yourself."

Tensing, Maya said, "The last time you told me to prepare myself my foster parents were murdered." She hated surprises. She liked to control her time and experience, probably residue from the helplessness she'd felt during her abduction. Telling Dylan of her dislike didn't seem appropriate at the moment. She would take bad news, if need be.

"We're going to meet an operative on detail in California. He has made contact with your birth parents."

"They're alive?"

With a nod, Dylan said, "And living in San Diego."

"You're kidding!"

"You probably knew at an intuitive level, and that's why you wanted to go there."

Maya was stunned. Her birth parents! How would it be to actually meet them? She had no idea whether she would recognize them or they her. After all this time and grief, would they have anything in common? "This is so hard to believe. How long have you known?"

"Just a few hours. Our operative Marcos was supposed to do the leg work, but he's hit a snag. You and I will have to go." His serious tone lightened. A tease was on its way. Dylan always forecast them by a certain lilt in his voice. "I want to meet them too, especially your father. Guess I'm just old-fashioned about some things. I've got a question to ask him."

This guy was just way too much fun. "What question?"

"If I can marry you." Dylan's face darkened as if he doubted what her answer would be. "Think he'll say yes?"

These revelations hitting so fast made Maya reel. To lose her parents, to potentially gain new parents, to possibly remember a past life, to have a husband. How different her life would become, already had, in fact. So much emotion felt overwhelming. She needed quiet time to analyze and interpret events and get her mind around them. She'd hardly had a moment's reflection since Lola's death. Grief for her even seemed old now, as if Maya had gone through it ages ago.

"I'm sorry if I presumed." Dylan's tentative tone let her know he'd misinterpreted her silence.

Maya knocked the disk player out of the way and slid across the space between the seats. She couldn't get to her fantastic man fast enough to reassure him. "Oh, yes, my love. I want to marry you more than anything." When she threw herself in front of him and kissed him, she could feel his body tense as he looked above her to see the road. Giggling, she returned to her seat. "Sorry. I want you to drive safely. You never know, we may want to have children someday."

"You mean more!"

The way he beamed at her suggested Dylan might turn into quite the family man. She'd been so caught up in her own issues she'd not thought much about his needs. She doubted they were much different from hers. In fact, they had much in common. They'd both received ill treatment from the Anaz-voohri. They both had unusual mental powers. They both were orphans. Well, maybe not Maya. Neither had had brothers and sisters. It occurred to Maya that she might have siblings, after all. What an idea! If she did, she would definitely share them with Dylan. She would make certain he never felt lonely again.

In the airport, Dylan and Maya kept an eye out for ORION but saw no indication of its presence. They turned in the rental car and bought airplane tickets. The credits went through without incident. Dylan carefully called Maya *Jane*, and she called him *John*. Everything about their new identities appeared to work well.

Maya dozed in the airport while they waited for the flight. The minute they boarded the plane, she felt glad to put New York and Pennsylvania behind her. She didn't care whether she ever came back. Dylan fell asleep during the flight. She enjoyed watching his adorable face in repose and hoped her presence had contributed to his peaceful and contented expression.

When they landed in San Diego, a huge crush of people filled the tiny airport. Why on earth would a major city have such a dinky airport? Maya found it annoying jostled by so many people. She and Dylan followed signs to get to the exit. As soon as they strode through the glass doors into the open air, her annoyance dissolved.

Warm evening air felt like silk against her skin. No need to wear a coat. Palm trees illuminated by honey-colored lights lined the parking lot across the street. The scent of jasmine floated on the air, probably piped in to mask the stench of gasoline, but still a great touch. She loved the California effort to create ambience.

"There's our man." Dylan pointed across the walkway.

Toward them strode the tallest, classiest Hispanic man Maya had ever seen. He wore a dark silk suit and looked more like an ad for Armani than a Mythos operative. He couldn't have been more opposite to Dylan's jeans, down home talk, and earthy style.

Although obviously pleased to see the man, Dylan nodded a salutation and didn't offer to shake hands. Was the guy an untouchable? Maya intended to keep a close eye on him to see what kind of trick he could do. Could he disappear like Kin? Or do remote viewing like Dylan?

"Maya," Dylan said, "this is Marcos Devante, our man in California, Columbia, and assorted other places."

Marcos bowed as respectfully as if he had just the met a queen. Maya imagined that he had met more than one, but he made her feel just as important. His was an inclusive kind of elegance. "*Señorita*, so good to meet you." The Spanish accent evoked boarding school breeding.

"Nice to meet you, Marcos."

"Please, if you will, *mis amigos*." Marcos guided Dylan and Maya to a stretch limousine where a chauffeur held the door open. She thought only movie stars used such extravagant vehicles.

Dylan sunk back against the black leather seat. "Got any beer?"

"Certainly." Marcos pulled a Dos Equis out of a small fridge. And you, *señorita*?"

"Nothing, thanks."

Dylan tipped up the beer bottle. "Okay, brief us." He took a long draught.

"*Señor* and *Señora* Porter are irate." Marcos poured bourbon over ice cubes in a glass. "They don't believe that Ms. Rembrandt is their daughter. They say their daughter was kidnapped. A few months later, the police said she was murdered, although no body was ever found. They say if we pursue this, they'll sue."

To sue seemed overboard to Maya. These poor people must be distraught. She glanced at Dylan. Sure enough, she could tell he had her welfare in mind because he put his arm around her.

Dylan asked Marcos, "What's Archer's take on this? I doubt he's happy about it."

"Money isn't an issue," Marcos said. "I could pay court costs out of pocket change, but the reputation of Mythos could be sullied in the eyes of those who know of it, and the secrecy element would be eliminated completely.

The Porters will not be pacified. Mythos can't take the negative publicity."

A surreal feeling pervaded Maya. Was she the object of this mad discourse? With it came renewed hatred for the Anaz-voohri. Whatever happened, her sympathy lay with the Porters.

"Do they know we're on our way?" Dylan asked.

"No, but I've got a feeling they'll let us in." Marcos sipped the bourbon.

Maya wondered whether he'd made a guess or a prediction. She glanced out the darkened window of the limousine at freeway traffic silently sliding by. She dared to hope that these actually were her birth parents and by some miracle they would recognize her. She wished she believed in a god to pray to, but she didn't, so she prayed to Dylan's, the god who allowed souls to reincarnate and who listened to warriors' prayers. She might as well. Maya had become a warrior, too.

Night had fallen by the time they reached the Porter home and stepped out of the car. Recessed lights illumined as clearly as if in daytime the one-story stucco house with a red-rile roof. High up Christmas lights twinkled in the shape of Santa Claus and a sleigh. Tall trees, their drooping branches laden with silvery leaves, rustled in the breeze. A wrought iron fence surrounded the grounds, and a camera sat above a security monitor on the gate.

Maya vacillated between happy anticipation and dread. She didn't want to scare these people, but she deserved the chance to meet them. If they really were her parents and they all missed the chance for a life together, how sad would that be? Maya clasped trembling hands together, relieved to feel Dylan close behind her. Marcos rang the buzzer.

In a moment floodlights came on, and the leery face of a middle-aged man appeared in the monitor. Maya felt pity for the great fear the people in the house obviously felt. Not surprising, after what they'd been through. Whether she was their daughter or not, they had suffered a great loss years ago and didn't deserve to go through the grief again.

The man's image peered out of the monitor, then an expression of recognition came over him. "Oh, it's you. I told you not to come back."

Marcos spoke in clipped tones. "We'd appreciate a moment of your time, *señor*."

"Who is it, Rick?" A middle-aged woman's face peeked over his shoulder and gazed through the monitor.

"It's that Mythos guy again." The man glared through the monitor. "We'll see you in court." The monitor went dark.

Disappointed, Maya turned away. She'd not wanted to get her hopes up but had done so in spite of herself.

"It'll be all right." Dylan whispered in her ear and guided her toward the street.

"Don't leave yet." Marcos acted more positive than the situation called for.

All at once, the gate swung open, the monitor came on bearing the man's image, the front door opened, and the woman shouted, "Wait. Don't go."

"Thank you, *señora*." Marcos held the gate open. Maya and Dylan passed through before him.

"Damn, Marcos," Dylan said, admiration in his tone, "you hit that prediction right on the head."

The woman hurried to Maya, walked up close, and examined her. They were the same height. Although the wavy hair had grayed, the brows remained the same brown as Maya's. The woman took Maya's hands and spoke earnestly. "Maya, is it really you?"

Maya's eyes filled with tears as she gazed at the face, etched with premature wrinkles, so like hers. This had to be. "Mother. Yes, it's me. Do you remember me?"

Crying out, the woman clutched Maya to her in a bear hug. Maya gave herself to the natural embrace and pressed her face into the woman's neck, overwhelmed by her scent. It took Maya a moment to realize that the woman's skin smelled familiar, exactly like her own. This was the bond she had missed with her foster parents.

Rick shouted, "Is it her? Are you sure?"

Maya's mother, tears streaming from her brown eyes, pulled back from the embrace enough to place her hand beneath Maya's cheek and hold her face up for Rick to see. "She looks just like me."

Gladness filled Maya. She knew it was true and smiled up at her birth father's anxious expression. She would love him someday soon. "Father?" The image of her foster father flitted across her mind. He would have approved. Had he been here he would have called it a healing moment.

Rick enfolded Maya and her mother in one embrace. "I can't believe it. Oh, my God, I can't believe it."

The three hugged and kissed. Maya felt excruciating happiness and glanced up, longing to include Dylan.

The only one not smiling, Marcos spoke briskly to Dylan, "I'll do the report."

"Thanks." Dylan folded his arms.

"De nada." Marcos strode to the limousine.

"Hey, Merry Christmas, Marcos." Dylan called.

Without looking back, Marcos climbed in and closed the door. The limousine pulled away from the curb.

Releasing Maya and her mother, Rick shook Dylan's hand. "Rick Porter here and my wife Millie."

"Dylan Brady. Good to meet you, sir."

"Mother, Father." Maya spoke words she thought she would never utter and broke free to take Dylan's arm. "Dylan and I are going to be married."

"With your approval, that is." Dylan grinned.

"Looks like we've got a lot of catching up to do here." Rick held the door open.

After they went inside the comfortable living room filled with Early American furniture, Millie called into a side room, "Billy, come out here. I want to introduce you to someone."

A boy of twelve or thirteen entered with a confused expression on his face. Maya didn't need to know who he was. He looked just like Hermie, the boy in her laptop software. A brother, too? Wonders kept adding onto wonders.

Even though Rick introduced Maya as the sister returned, the boy stared at her suspiciously. Maya could sympathize with the unpleasant requirement to give up only-child status. They both had that adjustment to make. She wanted to hug him but shook his hand instead.

Once they had settled down at least outwardly from their respective emotions, Maya, Rick, and Billy sat around the maple dining room table. Millie brought in a tray filled with wine glasses, one 7-Up, and cheesecake.

Dylan couldn't have fit in better had they been his family and helped Millie set the glasses around.

"Billy gets the 7-Up." Millie spoke firmly

When Dylan set the 7-Up in front of the boy, Billy groaned, "Aw, Mom."

"You're too young to drink, and you know it." Millie ignored her pouting son.

"I noticed your name," Dylan said to Millie. "I've been working on a case involving Jed and Millie McCall in Willow Branch. Are you by any chance related to them?"

"Oh, yes, she was my grandmother." Millie set a plate before Maya and smiled a beautiful smile. "Your great-grandmother, dear. I didn't know her, but I was named for her. She died of cancer at a young age."

Sliding onto the nearest chair, Dylan gave Maya a pointed glance as if thinking, *aha, I told you so.*

The full force of the past life memory dawned on Maya. As she lay dying, or fancied herself dying, so many years ago, a circle of love and inevitability had already destined her for this moment.

"Why are you investigating my grandmother?" Millie asked. "I thought you worked for Mythos."

"I do. It's just a real estate dispute." Dylan leaned back with that bad guy stance of his that masked the depth of his understanding of human nature. "I'll tell you about it some other time."

Maya felt glad he dodged the whole reincarnation subject, at least for now. It would take her some time to get accustomed to a career in espionage and learning about her mother, father, and brother. Accepting the idea that she was her own great-grandmother, tantalizing as it was, would have to wait for another day.

Rick held up a flute toward Maya. "To the most wonderful Christmas present ever!" They all took up their drinks.

With a smile like a dancer's, Millie toasted Maya and Dylan. "Here's to your new life together and to sharing it with us."

"Hear, hear." Dylan said, and they all drank.

"Thank you all." Maya remembered the duplicity of her toast onboard the spaceship and said with a full heart, "To us all and to victory over the Anaz-voohri!"

Millie frowned. "Does this mean you'll be joining Mythos, Maya?" Her voice quivered.

"I already have. Dylan and I will be undercover for a while, but later we'll get back into the fight."

Setting down his empty glass, Dylan turned a serious look toward Rick. "Suppose you could drop the law suit? It would sure help."

Rick shook his head. "I never intended to file it. I was just trying to protect Millie from more emotional pain. Your Mr. Archer called and explained the importance of secrecy to your organization. He only told me because of Maya's involvement. Without you good Mythos men, I'd never have seen my precious daughter again."

Millie patted Maya's hand. "What do you intend to do while you're undercover?"

A flush rose along Maya's throat as she looked at her darling man. "We're going to get married and maybe start a family." Her own words touched Maya, words so common and yet so unique.

Love and approval shone on Dylan's face. He drew her to him, kissed her, and whispered, "We'll look for our other children, too."

"I can't think of anything I'd rather be than a grandmother." Millie's eyes filled with tears she didn't try to hide. "Dylan, would you like some cheesecake?" When he nodded, she set a plate in front of him.

Lovable Dylan bit into the cake with his usual savor. He didn't need to say he liked it. Maya read the extent of his delight. She had already experienced it herself. She looked forward to a lifetime of being the object of his love and desire. Many lifetimes, in fact.